Loving
the
Texas
Stranger

Loving
the
Texas
Stranger

Mary Connealy

CHAPTER ONE

Case Garrison tried to suppress his edginess as he strode down the busy Washington D.C. sidewalk. It took him awhile after an assignment ended to relax and stop expecting a sniper around every corner.

He'd just come off the biggest bust of his FBI career. A special assignment that took him in and out of the country undercover.

Now he looked forward to a few weeks to unwind and relax. He'd go see his family, help on the ranch. He'd get some peace and quiet. Triumph surged like adrenaline through his veins. Case wanted plenty of time to savor his victory.

He didn't get it.

Someone slammed him backward against a metal railing at the top of a stairway. Pain radiated from his spine and knifed through his body. The concrete wall behind him exploded and shrapnel peppered Case's arms and neck.

Ducking the spray of concrete, he pitched down a short flight of stairs. He cracked his head every time he made contact with a new step as he plummeted to the bottom. The concrete burned the skin off his hands as he tumbled. He was only vaguely aware of being hauled to his feet.

Stunned, he heard someone bellow, "Move."

It reminded Case of a sadistic drill sergeant he'd had at boot camp so many years ago. Just like then, he obeyed. Staggering to his feet, he let himself be dragged to an escalator and was barely aware he was running down, taking three steps at once. Shoved along. Another explosion burned the railing near his hand.

He was gonna break his neck.

They tumbled over each other at the bottom. He landed flat on his back just a few feet from the drop-off to the Metro rails.

Two viselike hands grabbed the lapels of his blazer and hurled him over the edge of the platform onto the tracks. The unmistakable scream of an oncoming Metro train locking on its brakes cut through the daze caused by those blows to the head.

From flat on his belly, Case glanced up into the coldest eyes he'd ever seen and knew he was going to die. Anyone with eyes like that could kill without remorse. Some instinct made him want to face death head-on so he jerked his head around to face the on-coming train. Sparks sprayed out of the protesting brakes. The terrified eyes of the Metro driver connected with Case's.

Then she yanked Case to his feet—again. "Third rail! Watch out! Move!"

She. It was definitely a woman trying to kill him.

His head cleared enough to avoid the deadly electrified third rail.

The train roared past, so close suction drew him toward the crushing wheels. She towed him like so much dead meat across the second set of tracks, yammering about the third rail again.

She rammed him against the five-foot-high Metro platform and he was ready to pitch in and climb out but she wasn't holding committee meetings to decide her next move. She snatched the front of his white shirt in one hand and sunk her other into his crotch and, with a barely human growl, heaved him to safety. Slapping her hands onto the floor next to him, she leapt up beside him. Then, just when he'd decided she had super powers and might shoot a web out of her wrist and swoop them away, one of her arms slipped and she fell backward.

Case caught her by her hair and, with a wrench of his arm that hurt him more than it should, he plowed her into his own body and they rolled away from the platform ledge.

She stabbed him with her icicle eyes. "Move!"

Her favorite word. It brought him to his feet.

The Metro train finished shaking the earth and disappeared into the tunnel. Case glanced across the double tracks and looked into the eyes of a dead man.

Case had a code of honor that cut black and white through everything he did, no gray areas. His friends hassled him about it, but he saw life that way and refused to change. He put his faith in God mainly because in his line of work, he'd spent too much time cozying up to people who richly deserved to burn in hell. Well, maybe not *mainly*.

But if he'd never believed in God, he'd start right now, because there couldn't be a devil without God and there was no way anyone but the devil inhabited the soul of the man who'd just tried to kill Case.

Case had seen death before, many times—too many times. He knew; the lifeless, gaping eyes, the slack jaw, the awful inhuman color of a corpse.

Everything about this man's expression screamed of death, but this dead man was standing. He was moving. He was raising a nine-millimeter automatic.

Case reached for his own weapon, the weight comforting in his hand as it emerged from his shoulder holster. A gun appeared beside him, sliding into her hand as if from thin air. She handled it like an extension of her body. They aimed, fired. The smell of cordite burned his nose just as four puffs of dust kicked up from the gunman's chest. All four heart shots. All four kills.

The dead man staggered back, but he stayed on his feet. Killing him just made him mad.

Case didn't need to be told to move this time. He grabbed her and she grabbed him and they dove behind a steel girder with such perfect synchronization that it could have been a ballet—except for the crash landing.

And the hail of bullets.

They both rolled as the girder in front of them and the wall behind them flashed sparks and echoed with the high, sharp whine of gunfire and ricocheting bullets.

Case knew now why the wall had exploded behind him when she first crashed into him. He also figured out she'd been trying to save his life even then. He had started a step behind but now he caught up fast. He towed her to her feet, doing his best to make his body thinner than the metal shield between them and their attacker. He locked his eyes on the exit sign right in front of them. A bullet screamed past them at an upward angle and he knew the man had shot from a lower angle, he'd dropped down onto the tracks.

Another train roared through the station and Case wished it would run the gunman over and solve their problem. But nothing in Case Garrison's life had made him an optimist.

They didn't even look at each other, they just snagged a handful of the person beside them, dove between the moving walls of the escalator and barreled up a flight of steps to the street.

Case, his fingers locked into the fabric of her shirt, looked around. They had the length of time it took a high-speed train to pass through a station to get out of the line of fire.

She growled, "Move," again and his instincts, his best friend for a long time, told him to do what she said. She ran full tilt into four lanes of traffic— rush hour traffic that actually rushed for a change. Shoving him ahead of her, they jumped into the burned-out body of a doorless minivan being towed past them at thirty miles an hour. The angle of the stripped-down van made them roll to the back door of the wreck. He smashed against the tail gate, expecting it to give and drop them both onto the street in front of the wheels of an oncoming car. It was that kind of day.

The tail gate held.

He caught his breath, ready to leap, ready to *move* if she said so. He grabbed onto the van wall and opened his mouth.

She snarled, "Don't move," then pinned him by lying full length on top of him.

"Shut up!" She slapped her hand over his mouth.

The sleet that covered her eyes thawed, replaced by a burning intensity that could have ignited what was left of his shirt. She looked all around her. Case turned his head to see what bullet to dodge next but she wedged his head into the corner between the van floor and the tail gate.

She snapped, "Are you going to shut up?" Case took it as a threat not a question.

He nodded and she lifted her hand—her hand slick with blood. Her hand so slick she'd almost fallen into the path of a train.

They looked at her hand, then they looked at each other. He saw surprise in her eyes and he knew he looked the same. They both said at the same instant, "You've been shot."

They were both right.

"I set them up!" Claudia de Nobili clutched at a Faberge egg on her desk as she rose to her feet. Hurling the priceless artifact against the wall, shattering it into twenty thousand pieces.

Prometheus observed indifferently that each piece was now worth a hundred bucks.

"I tell you where!" The pointed toe of Claudia's alligator shoes lashed through the glass front of a display case and made shards of the case. Baccarat crystal dropped through the broken shelves onto the floor of the cabinet. This was her second office, here in Washington D.C. She'd come to town hoping to celebrate the last two deaths. The really fancy stuff was in her headquarters elsewhere.

"I get them together!" A jeweled Romanov dagger sliced through the air and imbedded itself in the wall less than a foot from his head. That was serious because she had no skill as a knife thrower which meant that rather than trying to scare him she was beyond caring if she killed him or not.

Prometheus would have been angry if any emotion remained in his soul.

"Together! Together! Together!" Each time she said it her voice pitched higher. More ear piercing, more violent, more insane. He'd known she was crazy going in.

"I wanted them to die together!" She ripped an elaborately carved ivory-handled Katana sword, relic of a Japanese Samurai, off the wall and swirled it furiously over her head. She was tempted, he could see it, so tempted to vent her rage by drawing his blood. The desire he felt to rip her throat out didn't count as emotion. It was professional disappointment.

Not for failing to kill them.

Although it was rare, he'd missed before on the first try and a couple of times on the second. He'd get them.

His disappointment was for taking this job without getting the whole picture. Sloan had called it personal and offered a fortune. So, Prometheus said yes and now he worked for a mad woman.

But he'd worked for Sloan before and knew the money would come through and the intelligence info would be dependable and on time.

Only after he'd fired the first shot, smugly trying to get a kill shot with one bullet just to amuse himself, had he realized he'd taken on professional warriors. Worse, in his haste to finish them off, Prometheus had let them see him. It was defeat, sharp and burning—and temporary.

He'd taken half her money. She wanted them to die together. He'd do it like she wanted.

Then she'd pay what she owed and he'd sell her organs on the black market.

Her fanatic raging ebbed as she exhausted herself swinging the sword wildly in the air. He waited for an opening. He was still mad from the sting of those bullets hitting his Kevlar vest. All four kill shots. They were stone cold pros and he'd hired on to assassinate them. He needed to take his failure out on someone.

Prometheus waited until Claudia swung all the way to one side, then moved in to catch her arm and relieve her of the priceless sword, twisting her wrist so she cried out with pain. He swung it up to her neck. He pressed a nerve in her elbow that he knew caused excruciating pain. Driving the blade against the back of her neck, he placed the edge precisely at the hair line of her perfect, chin length blonde hair to avoid the carotid artery and hide the cut as he nicked her.

When he held the razor sharp blade up to show her the blood, he saw a little reason clear out the insanity from her eyes. Then she leaned her elbow into the pain to increase it, her eyes fluttered shut and she inhaled sharply as she savored the agony.

"You'll have your bodies, Claudia. You'll have them together." Unexpectedly his dead emotions awakened to enjoy her masochism.

She leaned her arm into the pain a little more. A slashing heat stirred in him.

11

CHAPTER TWO

S he left a hand print of blood across his face.

Natalie assumed he'd been shot until he said those same words to her. The fact that her left shoulder was on fire suddenly made sense. She'd seen that gun come up behind her, reflected in the glass cover of a billboard in the Metro entrance.

She'd seen ruthless, soulless eyes shift very deliberately between her and the stranger strutting down the sidewalk toward her. She'd seen the glint of a gun. Years of living one step ahead of death made her react. She tackled her fellow victim and tossed him down the stairs and onto a Metro track.

Now she looked at her left hand coated with blood. His right shoulder aligned with her wound. She was nose to nose with a total stranger she must have something in common with if someone wanted to kill both of them. She wiped the sleeve of her leather jacket across his face to get rid of the blood. "He got us with the same bullet. He was trying to kill us both. I saw him."

"You're sure? Maybe one of us got caught in the crossfire?"

"I'm sure." She looked into his eyes, saw him assess whether she was a good judge of things like this. When he nodded, the respect that went with his trust got past her rock steady self-control.

"He waited. He lined us up."

The way the man responded to that information only underlined what she figured out when he had produced the Glock in the Metro. He was a Fed.

"With one bullet." His voice sounded like five miles of gravel road. Rough and gritty, it jarred something inside her like she was riding that road too fast.

He added, "Like two shots would be a waste of ammo."

She slid his brown tweed blazer off his broad shoulders then turned to his blood soaked shirt sleeve. She noted the well-used shoulder holster with approval before she ripped his sleeve open, using the convenient hole left by the bullet.

"It's in the muscle, but no bone. It's bleeding a lot. Let me just use this..." she ripped the sleeve the rest of the way off and wrapped it snugly around his bulging biceps. He lay still, dispassionately watching her work.

He was a man who'd bled before.

She looked back at him, straight into his eyes. He wasn't much taller than her, if she could judge while they were laying down. She estimated five eleven, dark hair cut short recently judging from the ring of untanned skin around his ears. Regular features, good looking but no matinee idol, except maybe for his eyes. There was something compelling in his dark blue eyes, like a placid Scottish loch that hid a sea monster in its icy depths.

After his eyes, his body was the most notable thing about him. He was ripped. The entire hard length of him, every muscular contour, every inch of his rippling abs, felt like iron under her. He must be a work out fanatic to be this tightly honed. She knew what that was like.

She dragged her attention back to her doctoring, reassuring herself that her inspection was about picking him out of a lineup later if it became necessary. She hoped it wasn't about identifying his body at a morgue. She tugged on the knotted fabric. "It's not fancy, but it'll hold you until we get something better. Your face is scratched."

She used her fingernail to pry on his cheek. "It's shrapnel from the cement wall behind you." She worked a little longer.

"If the wall behind me took a bullet, then the gunman was in front of me and behind you. How'd you see him?"

Nat loved a suspicious man. She wouldn't respect any other kind. "There was a poster behind you. A road show for a play. The glass front was like a mirror. I saw him."

She went back to work on his face. "It's just a scratch. I've got it."

He growled, "Your turn."

The way he said it made her wish she'd been gentler with his face. She had to ease her leather jacket off and was surprised to see her whole arm bright red. She felt her stomach heave a little at the extent of the blood loss.

He quit being the suspicious, laconic patient and moved swiftly to rip her sleeve away. "He may have nicked an artery. The bullet passed between your arm and your chest." He quit talking, and heaved her off of him. He rolled her onto her back.

"Hold it, hold it." Nat snapped. She reached behind her back and pulled her gun out of her holster. Then lay down without letting the gun out of her hand.

Case knelt beside her, which wasn't easy because the van sloped upward at about a forty-five degree angle. Every few yards the van would bounce over a pot hole or round a corner and he'd fall on top of her, but he tried to keep his balance.

He focused his attention exclusively on her arm, using her left sleeve to create a pressure bandage, then her right sleeve to bind it. It occurred to Nat that they were ripping each other's clothes off. That wasn't as much fun as it sounded.

He pressed hard on the wound and it took all her self-discipline to keep from slugging him. No, not fun at all.

Through tightly clenched teeth he said, "It's soaking through."

She heard anxiety in his rugged voice and she didn't like it. He didn't seem like the hand wringing type.

She decided to snap him out of it. "Look, Cupcake, if you're going to swoon, back off and let me fix it myself."

One side of his mouth quirked into a smile for just a second but no humor reached his eyes. He jerked off his shoulder holster and tore open the top two buttons of his white cotton shirt and pulled it off over his head. A nasty looking knife appeared in his hand. She knew a lot about him just from seeing that knife. She had one just like it in her boot.

He sliced his remaining sleeve off his shirt and added it to the growing bulk on her arm. Then, not satisfied, he cut two strips off the bottom of his shirt, tied them together and used them to bind her left arm tightly against her body, wrapping the cloth over her breasts and under her other arm and knotting it to hold it firm.

"We've got to get you to a hospital. Your arm is still bleeding. The bandages aren't doing the trick."

She exhaled loudly with disgust. "Quit whining and put some muscle into stopping it. We're not going to a hospital."

That's when they really looked at each other for the first time. At each other, not wounds, or guns, or grasping, shoving hands.

He rasped at her. "Yeah, I know it. But I've seen it and you haven't. We avoid officials right up until you start bleeding to death."

She wasn't about to let him get away with kindness. It would ruin their up to now perfect relationship. "Dry your tears, tourniquet the sucker off, and let's get out of here. I can sew with my right hand."

"Sew a severed artery?" He said with angry skepticism that she knew wasn't aimed at her, but was a reaction to the whole mess.

"Severed, or nicked? You said nicked before. I can handle nicked." She'd done it before but not on herself.

He stared at her wound. He didn't take the bandage off to study it which raised her opinion of him. Instead she could see he was remembering what he'd seen before he started stanching blood.

After just a few seconds he said, "Nicked. Yeah, definitely nicked. And I'll do the sewing. Let's get out of here."

He levered himself up to look out the van's glassless back window. She noticed his effort to push against something besides her body. She appreciated it even though he had limited success.

"I know this neighborhood. I know a guy who can get us what we need." He slipped his shoulder holster back on and tied his gun down.

"Forget it. No familiar neighborhood. No 'guy'. The man who shot us was a pro. He'll have eyes everywhere."

She watched him nod, glancing nervously at her arm. He was right. She hadn't seen it. And the fingers on her left hand were going numb.

"Okay. This van must be headed to an impound lot. In this part of town there's one..." He looked out again. "We're almost there. We have to get out before he stops." He hesitated.

She said. "Watch for a corner, reach through the window and open the tail gate."

He looked doubtfully at her arm, then surprised her by grinning. "It'll hurt."

Nat tucked her gun away, snapped the strap that held it in place and said indifferently, "It's been that kind of day."

He grunted and hoisted himself up again. "I had the same thought myself." He studied all directions, as aware of witnesses as he was of hitting the ground. He looked down at her. "It's time. He'll slow down at this corner. We'll drop. He'll turn off and never notice us."

She nodded.

He reached his arm out to find the latch, then before he pulled he looked down at her again. "Name's Case, FBI. You're the most interesting woman I've met in years."

She grinned. Distracted for a minute from her tingling fingers. "Nat. My uh...company...doesn't have initials."

He looked sharply at her. "That deep, huh? What've we stumbled into here, Nat?"

She watched the steel cords of his muscles clench against the battered handle on the tailgate before she said, "I don't know. But I predict we've got a lot more stumbling to do before we're done."

He nodded thoughtfully and wrapped a protective arm around her head and pressed her face against his bare chest. His coarse chest hair scratched her cheek and his powerful arm tucked her close against him. It gave her an unusual sense of being cared for. She shook off the sensation and turned her attention to the very real possibility of brain injuries. That was their biggest risk right now, so she put the arm she had that was working around his head, too. He yanked on the outside handle and sent them both crashing onto the unforgiving pavement.

"He's clear for two weeks. He didn't tell me where he was going and I didn't ask. He's been in the field for eighteen months, he deserved some R and R and I gave it to him." Carlos Lorenz wanted to slug the man standing in front of him but it would be killing the messenger. Still, it would relieve some stress. And for once the messenger had it coming.

"He's been an agent for eighteen years. Six years under you. Don't tell me you can't reach him," Jerry Sloan snapped.

"It's the way Case likes it. He blows the place off when he's between jobs. It keeps him sane. It helps him remember what he's fighting for," Lorenz replied evenly.

Sloan grabbed the phone off its base and shook it in Lorenz' face like a fist. "Get..him...in...here...now!"

Lorenz watched that florid, belligerent face for a long second. He clenched his fist and mentally relished how the impact would feel. When he was sure Sloan got the message, Lorenz relaxed enough to jerk the phone out of Sloan's chubby fingers. He lifted the phone and turned his back on Sloan, and dialed a number no one could trace to anything, which didn't mean Case might not check and see there'd been a call.

He let the phone ring twice, broke the connection then hit re-dial and let it ring once. He called again and let it ring for a full minute.

He slapped the phone back down and turned to smile at the overweight, pig-eyed man in front of him who had been getting kicked upstairs because of some connection to the governor in his home state for his entire career while Lorenz lagged right behind him, always one step down the ladder. Lorenz always cleaning up the mess Sloan left behind while doing his own job and most of Sloan's, too.

Public service, you had to love it.

"Not in," Lorenz said with deceptive mildness. "I'll keep checking."

The unhealthy shade of Sloan's face deepened to something close to maroon. Lorenz noted abstractly that his wife had just bought a couch that color.

"If you don't track him down in the next twenty-four hours, his leave is going to be permanent." Sloan slammed his fist on the desk.

"You're going to fire Case for taking a vacation after a year and a half of not even having a Sunday off?" Lorenz asked mildly. "Or, will you say he's fired for bringing in fifteen potential Oklahoma City bombers?"

Lorenz snapped his fingers as if he'd had a sudden inspiration. "Maybe you can cut him loose 'cuz he tracked down the psycho who sent the president all those threatening letters, then confiscated his warehouse full of guns and explosives. Yeah, let's say he ruined the underground arms business in this country, and fire him for that. We can call it a terrorist recession. Or maybe we can give him a pink slip for saving your life a decade ago? He might even have it coming for that."

Sloan's fists tightened furiously and for a second Lorenz thought he might come across the desk. Lorenz watched, hoping. He knew Sloan was too spineless to take on a cranky nun let alone a former Navy SEAL. But it would be so sweet. Several things flickered through Lorenz' mind to say that might push Sloan over the edge and bring on the attack. He didn't say any of them.

Lorenz had been of the opinion up until now that Sloan was being his usual pain-in-the-butt self. But there was more going on than that. There was an edge of desperation to his demand to see Case Garrison. Lorenz didn't trust desperate people in general. And he didn't trust Sloan in particular. A desperate Sloan set off all Lorenz' alarms. He made some gruff assuring noises to get Sloan out of his office, making sure to be nasty or Sloan would be suspicious.

Sloan left and Lorenz pulled out his secure cell-phone and dialed in the private code of three phone numbers that he and Case had used for years. Then he called a beeper number. He waited for Case to reach through the phone lines and grab him by the neck for disturbing his vacation. Fear prickled up and down Lorenz' spine when his phone didn't ring.

Finally, Lorenz called a number he'd only used once before, the time Case's wife and daughter had been killed by a drunken driver. If he didn't hear from Case within twenty-four hours, it would mean Sloan wouldn't have to bother to fire Case.

It would mean Case was already dead.

CHAPTER THREE

Case hit the pavement doing his best to shield her from the impact of the landing. He bounced twice then rolled to his feet and half carried, half dragged her to the side of the nearest alley between two decrepit brownstone apartments and flattened his back against the brick wall, with her still wrapped in his arms.

A quick glance told him the bandage on her arm was soaked again. She'd ripped both knees out of her jeans, probably when they made their exit from the van because he hadn't noticed it before. Her forehead was bleeding, that was definitely new. He saw a slight bulge that he identified as a knife tucked into her ankle high boots.

She was ignoring all of that as she surveyed the area for anyone who might have seen them. Case didn't like anyone, but he was having a hard time not liking Nat.

He didn't take time to plan their next move, he just started walking. Right now moving was an end in itself. A moving target was always harder to hit.

"Start second guessing yourself, Case. When you're pushed, a person tends to react in character. Are we being predictable? Are we following a pattern?" Her voice faded a little at the end, although she walked steadily beside him, not allowing him to bear any of her weight.

21

Case knew she was right. He crossed the street at the far end of the alley and reentered the alley directly in front of them. She came along. They didn't talk, didn't discuss where to go. She was thinking just like him. That sounded like predictable to him. Right now, they had a more pressing problem. "How about we start being unpredictable after you quit bleeding?"

She said ruefully, "That's soon enough, I guess."

He was shirtless. She was wearing a blood-soaked white cotton shirt with the sleeves torn off and a crude bandage roughly the size of the Pentagon wrapped around her arm. But this was a seedy section of Washington D.C. People didn't hang around on the streets and if they passed by they minded their own business.

He looked at her and, except for the blood, the only words to describe her were nondescript. Her hair was a medium brown he could tell was dyed. It was blunt cut with no bangs and she wore it pulled back into a ponytail. Straggling ends escaped the rubber band and reminded him he'd used that ponytail as a handle when she started to fall onto the Metro tracks—painful but effective. She hadn't complained, he liked that.

He noticed her eyes were the same color as her hair, but he detected tinted contacts so he wasn't sure about that. Her nose was perfectly straight, not long and not short. Her mouth was more notable for the rapid-fire orders that came out of it than for the shape of the lips. She was fairly tall for a woman, maybe five nine and he wasn't overly tall. She looked up only an inch or two into his eyes. She'd done absolutely nothing to enhance her looks.

He was an expert, but he didn't think the average person would recognize her the second time they saw her, especially if her eye color and hair color changed. But she was special. In fact, she was extraordinary. The common appearance was all disguise. He saw through it and knew he'd recognize her anywhere.

The neighborhood seemed to be mainly crowded with abandoned buildings. It took them three blocks to find a store that was open, then it was a pawn shop that, judging by the front window, seemed to specialize in watches and other slightly used, slightly stolen merchandise. Behind the window they saw a mish mash of clothes and furniture. It was about one step up from a dumpster.

Nat's bandage was bright red by now and the blood from her blouse had smeared most of the left side of her blue jeans. Even so, the bleeding seemed to be slowing a little. Case hoped that wasn't because she was running out of blood. They'd walked fast the whole way, a pace set by Nat. She didn't look pale or unsteady. Case got a picture of the forged steel she was made of.

"Stay out here," Case said, thinking about the blood.

"No, this place looks like its run by someone who knows how to make a deal. He'll keep his mouth shut."

"Yeah, with the cops. But if anyone else asks about us, while waving cash under his nose, he'll sell us out in a heartbeat. I can get what we need from the guy."

Nat hesitated, then nodded and dropped back into the nearest alley.

Case was struck by a sense of urgency by the very act of her agreeing with him. So far, they'd been following her orders.

He made short work of getting a change of clothes for them both, a needle and thread and a few other necessities that caught his eye.

He hurried back to the alley and couldn't find her. As his footsteps sounded, she emerged from a shadowed spot that didn't seem to be a hiding place.

"This way," she waved him toward her. She had kicked a door in on a condemned building. Sitting on the stairs one flight up was almost as civilized as sitting in a living room compared to the hour they'd just lived through.

He pulled a bottle of whiskey out of his brown paper bag of goodies.

"The pawn shop sells whiskey?" she asked.

He looked at the bottle and arched one eyebrow at her to let her know he was disappointed in her for asking the obvious.

"Is it used?" she asked dryly.

"Does it matter?" he retorted with a grin.

She shook her head and took off her blouse without comment. She wore a no-nonsense, non-sexy sports bra. It was bloody, so Case wasn't sure about the non-sexy. Since she might be bleeding to death he couldn't concentrate on sexy. He unwrapped her arm. He didn't like the look of the mean, oozing bullet wound. It didn't have an entry and exit, it was just a deep graze, but the dark rivulet of blood was stubbornly flowing. He unscrewed the lid on the whiskey bottle and said, "It's gonna hurt."

"Compared to getting shot?" she asked sarcastically, tugging the bottle out of his hands.

He waited patiently while she had a few swallows.

"I'd be a cheap drunk tonight, with so much blood loss."

"I love a cheap drunk, Nat."

She laughed a deep husky laugh that sounded rusty, like she was out of practice using it and handed him back the bottle. He poured it on generously and she didn't flinch. Not even when the needle bit into her flesh.

An overly pleasant man's voice said, "I'm calling for Miss Natalie Brewster. I have unclaimed property for her in the state of Maryland. An insurance reimbursement from Blue Cross and Blue Shield."

"Oh, Natalie's got money coming," Peg squealed gaily. "Oh, dear, she doesn't live here anymore. I'm afraid we've lost touch. I haven't seen her in years, you know kids these days. They think their parents are trying to ruin their lives. But I do hear of her from time to time. From mutual acquaintances she's stayed in touch with. Now let me think..." Peg Brewster replied with her sweet vapid voice. Meanwhile she was waving her hand frantically at her husband. She finally threw a book at him to get him to look up from the football game. He was on his feet instantly. He came quickly to his wife's side and read the note she was scribbling.

He nodded his head with a quick jerk, moved across the room and punched the code into the keypad hidden in the kneehole of their antique, roll top desk. The desk opened, he picked up the phone concealed there and started dialing. When the phone was answered he didn't wait for anyone to speak because no one ever would. He whispered tersely, "Get a trace on our house line. Someone's looking for Natalie Brewster."

"Are they still on the line?" the mechanically altered metallic sounding voice asked.

"Yeah, Peg's got them talking," Steve Brewster said.

"Try to keep them on," Metal Voice said unnecessarily, then he hung up.

Peg's simpering concern echoed across the room. The worried little mother voice always turned Steve on.

"Has she been in the hospital? Why would she need insurance? Oh, she's not sick, is she?" Peg winked at Steve and he came across the room to wrap his arms around her from behind.

He kissed her neck while he listened in on Peg's visit with the solicitous stranger.

While the caller tried to milk Nat's mother for information, Peg was tracking him down. Using the Brewsters for parents was pretty insulting because according to rumors they were only about five years older than Nat, but they were the third layer of Nat's cover. If someone called them, then Nat was being hunted.

The other line lit up. Peg glanced over her shoulder and gave her sassiest grin to her husband. "They've got him," she mouthed. Steve pulled her shirt out of the slim waist band of her jeans and slid one hand up and the other down. Peg's head dropped back on his shoulder when she ended the call.

"You are such a bad boy." She turned in his arms and kissed him until they both had about one functioning brain cell left. But that one was working perfectly.

Metal-Voice would warn Nat and deal with whoever was hunting her. It wasn't part of the Brewsters' job to help further and they didn't want to help. Why should they? They'd never met Natalie Brewster. They weren't even sure if she existed. In a shadowy line of work, Nat was the deepest shadow there was.

CHAPTER FOUR

I can't believe you had the nerve to sneak into a hospital. I'm more of a Kick-The-Door-In-Serve-Them-A-Warrant kind of guy."

Without looking at him she said loftily, "We need those kinds, too."

She picked the lock on the cabinet of fresh blood then sorted through types like she was picking out a flavor of fruit juice.

He was tempted to swat her for being so sassy. He probably would have if she didn't need a transfusion.

She found a sink and gulped down four glasses of water, then she dragged an uncomfortable chair into a supply closet, relaxed into it, jabbed a needle into the back of her hand, rigged herself to an IV and gave herself a shot of penicillin.

Case studied her through the open doorway for a second. She had pulled the chair against the back wall so her head could rest in the corner. The closet was lined with shelves holding clearly labeled bottles of obscure chemicals as well as standard medical supplies. There were no narcotics so nothing was locked up once they got past the lab door. Finally, thinking of the effective but crude job he'd done sewing up her bullet wound, he said, "Why didn't we come to the hospital for what we needed to begin with, Nat?"

She shifted around in the chair then pulled her gun out of the holster and rested it in her lap, her hand wrapped around the butt. "I wasn't sure I'd live long enough to get here."

She said it lightly, but it chilled Case to hear her so casually weigh her survival. They'd walked thirty blocks before they'd come to the hospital. She'd never shown a second of weakness in those blocks, but she'd bled steadily the whole time.

"She's immortal, except she needs blood to live. Wait, isn't that the description of a vampire?" Case asked dryly.

She curled one corner of her lips in a smile, then she started ordering him around again. "If you feel yourself nodding off wake me. You don't have to stay in this closet. You can stay out there," she nodded at the slightly ajar closet door, "...unless you hear someone coming. I don't think we'll be bothered, they do lab tests in here and that's mainly a nine to five job. But one of us should keep watch. Now shut up and let me get a few minutes' sleep."

"Should you sleep with your contacts in?" he asked casually.

Her eyes popped open and she looked at him sharply, "You made the contacts, huh?"

"Gimme a break." He rolled his eyes like she'd insulted him.

She quirked the corner of her mouth into another smile then shrugged. "I shouldn't sleep with them but I'd decided I would rather than uncover my eyes. I guess since you already know and we're hiding from everyone else in the world..." with a minimum of fuss she removed her contacts and dropped them into her jeans pocket.

"Won't you need them later?"

"They're only for color, there's no correction in them. My eyes are a distinctive shade."

He looked. She was right. Her eyes had an odd, almost yellow cast.

There were flecks of dark and light gold in them and they seemed to glitter even in the dim light of the closet.

"Hazel," he said out loud without really meaning to. But hazel was too tame a word for Nat's eyes. They were feline, the eyes of the patient predator. They had the mystic color of a witch's familiar. Eyes the color of magic.

"You can see why I keep them covered. They're different."

"No one would ever forget them. They're beautiful." He hadn't meant to say that either. She didn't respond, just watched him steadily, then she let her eyes go closed like he hadn't said a thing. She seemed to fall instantly asleep.

Case passed the next two hours re-bandaging his minor gunshot wound and sorting through lockers, stocking up on supplies they'd need while they were on the move. He was careful to leave no fingerprints and take what he needed from the backs of the cupboards so it wouldn't be easily noticed. With luck no one would ever know they'd been here.

Case checked his wallet and found seventy-five dollars in cash. Nat had salvaged forty bucks from her jeans pocket before she tossed them into a dumpster and put on the used pair he'd gotten her at the pawn shop.

He pulled on a lab coat abandoned on a coat rack in the lab, went down to the hospital restaurant and bought sandwiches and two bottles of juice. Then he went into the large closet with Nat and closed the door. He sat on the floor and leaned against a cardboard box full of tongue depressors. He ate his crummy little meal. He reminded himself that he'd been shot today too and he should rest. But he couldn't relax. His muscles were protesting the prolonged inactivity. He was used to working out two hours in the morning and another hour at night in addition to his physically active life. He got the duffel bag he'd picked up at the pawn shop and pulled out his only impulse buy, a pair of hand weights. He started curling the weights, feeling the endorphins rush into his brain and lift him to the high he craved.

He gave his wounded right arm a light work out, only two sets of twenty reps, then pushed his left arm through his usual hundred reps.

His heart sped up at first, but after he'd gotten into the zone, it slowed and he felt his muscles pump up and his cells flood with oxygen. After the weights, he did a hundred sit-ups pushing himself to do them quick since he was shorting himself on so many other parts of his routine.

He started slowing down at around fifty push ups because his arm started bleeding again. A logical part of his brain told him not to keep going but his body demanded the activity. He kept going to a hundred hoping it would help him sleep.

Finally, he cooled down with martial arts stretching exercises, packed the weights in the duffel bag, cleaned the blood off his shoulder, put on a clean bandage and eased himself against the wall to consider where they went from here.

They had almost no money. They had no friends they could trust. They were being hunted. He wasn't worried about surviving, he was good at that. He'd learned to do without almost everything in his two decades in the military and the FBI. He'd gone hungry, he'd gone thirsty, he'd gone without sleep, he'd endured cold and heat and pain. He'd learned to focus on the moment and not care about discomfort.

He looked at his fellow traveler. He was obsessed with working out, so he was particularly conscious of muscle tone. Hers was phenomenal. She had shoulders that were pure, striated sinew. Her arms, even relaxed in sleep, looked hard enough to be carved out of stone. When she'd flexed them to toss him off the Metro tracks or into the van, biceps and triceps rippled to life under her sleek tanned skin. He'd seen her rock-hard abdomen when she'd so nonchalantly stripped off her shirt in front of him. No doubt about it. The woman was shredded, just like him. The gun she never let go of, even in sleep, only added to the impression.

He'd thought she was nondescript until he'd seen her eyes. Their sparkling hazel color brought vitality to every other feature on her face. They deepened her tan to a burnished gold and enhanced her hair color, though it was a dye job and deliberately plain. The real change was in the way they revealed her character. He looked at her relaxed in sleep and knew she could spring instantly awake, gun drawn, moving, running, fighting, if trouble caught up with them. All she knew, all she'd seen, glowed out of those magic eyes.

He knew she'd gone beyond all the limits of human strength today. Ignoring personal comfort was something that no one could really teach you. She'd learned it the same way he had, in the same unforgiving school. You learned to survive by surviving and the ones who didn't learn it weren't around anymore.

Her deep sleep didn't fit with what he'd learned about her character. He wondered if technically she was unconscious. He closed his eyes and let himself sink into the twilight world between awake and asleep. He knew he wouldn't miss a sound. He flickered his eyes open occasionally to watch as the pint of blood emptied slowly into the back of Nat's hand.

He knew the second she woke up. She didn't move, didn't open her eyes. But he could sense that she was instantly alert and searching the room for danger.

After she had satisfied herself it was safe, her eyes flickered open. Their eyes met and they studied each other for a prolonged minute. Finally, she shook her head as if to rid herself of the last of the sleep and pulled the needle out of her hand. He offered her some of his captured booty. She swabbed the needle prick with an alcohol-soaked gauze pad, then slapped on a ball of cotton and a bandage. She swallowed the sandwich in about five bites without commenting on how awful it was, acting as if she were refueling a car. Then she looked up at him and smiled.

Case had the sudden impression that the unstoppable Natalie he'd been dealing with was only a dim echo of the real thing.

"Put some blood in the woman and watch out, huh?" he asked.

She laughed, then stopped like the sound of her own laughter had surprised her. "There is nothing funny about our lives right now, Case. Let's get out of here."

He agreed.

She listened at the door for a second.

"No one's been out there."

She went out, checked the supplies he'd taken, then added a few of her own. She made a quick once over of the room to make sure they left no trace of themselves, then wadded up the evidence of her transfusion and took it with her. They walked boldly out of the hospital, past dozens of scurrying people. No one looked at them twice.

They moved along the sidewalk until the bustle of the hospital was behind them, then Nat said, "I think it's time we had a talk."

Case nodded. "Past time."

Millie Hastings lifted her hand from the steering wheel and noticed the faint tremor. Not bad today she thought proudly. The monster that had eaten up her family from the inside out was now gnawing away at her. But she was still strong. She still walked everyday. She still carried her own groceries and took the photographs that she loved.

She didn't mind dying. She was sixty-two years old. She'd lived too long.

She and her husband, Leland, had moved across the country to care for their only son, Matthew, and ended up with front row seats to his death. She and Lee had suffered as they watched him struggle for every breath he took and they blamed the evil habit of smoking for cutting his life span to only thirty-five years.

Matthew was newly buried and they were considering whether to go back to the city they'd lived in all their lives, New Orleans, when Lee started coughing.

The doctors shook their heads when Lee protested that he'd never smoked a cigarette in his life. They dismissed his disbelief by saying, "It can run in families."

They subjected her husband to the same chemotherapy torture they'd visited upon her son. The few extra months of life it had bought Lee came at a terrible cost.

Now, after two months alone, trying to find a center for her shattered life, Millie felt the deep pain in her chest and knew without asking what was wrong.

She'd gone to the doctor because she wasn't a fool and didn't want to die because she was too stubborn to take an antibiotic. But she'd called it right.

She'd walked out on the doctor's litany of treatments, to be started without a moment's delay. She made the terse announcement that she'd be in touch when and if it suited her. And she'd never looked back.

The death that lived quietly inside her and Lee had combined to attack and kill their son at a young age. They were both carrying the predisposition for lung cancer. And the two of them together had created a child who was doomed from birth.

There was no one left. Her younger brother had married a woman who hadn't wanted to share him. Her older sister had Alzheimer's, she was widowed and living half way across the country in a nursing home. Lee came from England and they'd never been close with his three sisters. She had a few nieces and nephews but none who were interested enough in her to stay in touch beyond a Christmas card.

That suited Millie just fine. Family would be a burden to her now, just more people to weigh down with grief at her death. She stayed in the house her son had built on the remote desert road. The house where she'd lost her son and husband. She photographed the Arizona sunsets she'd come to love. She walked down to the spring and kept her coughing muffled so she could hunt nature with a lens.

She'd die like she was living. Alone. She was resigned to it. In truth she welcomed it. She knew lung cancer wasn't a fast way to die. It had seemed fast when she'd watched her loved ones slipping away, but when it was happening to you two months was a long time to linger. She'd probably go faster than they had, since she was accepting no treatment at all.

It wasn't dying that worried her. Not even if it came slow and hard. In fact, despite her oncoming death, she felt a vitality inside her that surprised her. She'd never been a fitness buff, preferring bending over a keyboard manipulating pictures, to going out to snap them.

But since she'd come to Arizona, she'd discovered a new side of herself. The dry desert heat and the harsh beauty of nature had beckoned her almost from the first. Her son had adopted a vigorous lifestyle, jogging, lifting weights and rock climbing. He continued most of it as long as his health permitted.

Millie had found herself jogging along with him. Taking five mile hikes just to burn off her newfound energy. In contrast to Matthew's waning strength, she and Lee had embraced thriving health and she still had a lot of energy, even with each breath becoming more painful. She was determined to enjoy it as long as it lasted. She was a Christian woman so death just seemed like another step. Another birth canal to pass through. She was ready.

If she became too weak to feed herself, then she'd starve. Three to five days she could live if she fell and couldn't get up. The book she'd read said she'd die of thirst in that time. The thought didn't phase her. What bothered her was thinking of someone finding her dying but not dead. She didn't want interference. She still shuddered when she thought of the endless tubes and monitors they had attached to Matthew and Lee in the end. The IV nutrition to prolong life. The morphine to make the agony bearable.

She'd hated it, but once the hospital and doctors got hold of someone, they just took over.

They might as well have thrown Matthew and Lee into a dungeon and hooked them to Medieval torture devices instead of respirators and beeping heart machines. They held a horror for her that she knew bordered on the irrational.

She'd made a Living Will. She'd spread her considerable estate between her nieces and nephews. They weren't bad kids, just busy. She'd done everything to die as she wished. But she still didn't trust the doctors. She had decided to begin the process of cutting herself off from everyone. She'd told her few friends she was moving back to New Orleans. She'd already quit her church groups.

Today she'd stocked up on groceries so she would be seen in town but this would be the last time. From now on she'd bypass the sleepy little town of Canyon Diablo on the edge of the Navajo Indian Reservation and make the slightly longer drive into Flagstaff. She had arranged automatic payments from her bank for her phone, electricity, and credit cards so no busybody bill collector would happen by and save her.

She'd had her mail forwarded to an extra-large post office box in Flagstaff so if she didn't pick it up for a month no one would notice.

She pulled her Jeep Cherokee up to the beige adobe brick house her son had built with his own hands. She looked at her home and remembered those brilliant hands of her beloved son. He had loved to build. He'd been earning a solid reputation in Flagstaff as a contractor. In his minimal spare time, he'd dug into the muddy earth near the spring that supplied the house with water. Out of this land so many people would think was wasteland, Matthew had made adobe bricks.

The arid heat had baked them into stone and created a home that was so perfectly in harmony with nature that Millie's heart surged every time she looked at Matthew's creation.

Tears burned her eyes and a slash of anger cut through her. He had been so gifted! Why had he only been given 35 years? Why hadn't God seen fit to take a few years from her and Lee and give them to Matthew? He would have left the world a more beautiful place if he'd had time.

She studied the house for a few moments longer. She didn't have time to waste on such foolishness as anger anymore. Because of this house, the world was more beautiful. Matthew could have done more, but he'd done enough. He was a believer and he was free of pain in heaven now.

She was anxious to join him.

She got out of the car and hefted a case of tomato juice cans onto one shoulder and a fifty pound bag of potatoes onto the other. She estimated she had six, maybe as many as twelve weeks to live, and she marveled at the extraordinary strength of a small, lonely, dying woman.

CHAPTER FIVE

Nat didn't bother with a preamble, she cut right to the chase. "I was told to show up at that Metro terminal at that precise time to receive a package."

"Not UPS, I'm guessing?" Case asked dryly.

Nat blew a short hard breath through her nose that was almost a laugh. It was what passed for amusement in her life most of the time. She thought about how she'd laughed out loud at Case's lame attempt at humor a few minutes ago and wondered where that had come from.

She sat on the cement steps in the back stairway of the mostly deserted tenement building. "I haven't had a second to think about it until now, but the way the call was handled didn't arouse any suspicion and, thinking back on it, it still doesn't. That means it came through the right channels. That means..."

"An inside job," Case interrupted brusquely as he sat two steps above her and leaned forward to rest his forearms on his splayed knees.

"Yeah," Nat agreed with quiet thoughtfulness. "And my channels are way inside. Getting to me that way..." She dropped into silence as she ran her thumb over her lips and mentally tallied the short list of people who could have contacted her. She tried to decide which one of her most trusted associates wanted her dead.

In the silence Case made an impatient move and reached for his duffel bag. He pulled two hand weights out and started curling them.

"Where did those come from?" Nat was startled by their sudden appearance. The tension of the last few hours made her long to grab them and work off some of her built up energy.

"The pawn shop. Lifting, jogging, working the heavy bag, I need it to stay sane." Case's arms pumped the iron rhythmically.

Nat watched his biceps tense and relax smoothly like a hydraulic machine. He was in fantastic shape. She eyed the weights. Her longing to have a turn was almost like hunger.

Case turned the conversation back to the topic at the forefront of Nat's mind, "With me, it's not that hard to get through security. But it was still a pretty slick deal. I'm just in from an undercover assignment and I'm supposed to be out of the loop for a few weeks. Only one man knows how to get in touch with me. I trust this guy. He would never sell me out."

Nat knew she must have looked cynical because Case said, "I know even the best friend you have in the world could turn if someone was holding a gun to his daughter's head. Not Carlos. I don't believe it. He didn't betray me. That means someone has access to something he has that gave me away. So, I can't go to him even if he is clean, because he's being monitored."

Nat caught the grim look on Case's face when he said, 'only one man knows.' She knew it was a man he trusted implicitly. If that one man turned out to be the source of their trouble, Case was going to be deeply disillusioned. She knew how cynical people got in this line of work, especially undercover. You were always wading through the dregs of humanity. She hated to watch one more piece of Case's faith in humanity get ripped away.

"Okay, without ruling anything else out, lets start from the angle that this is connected to work. That's where I make enemies. You've been undercover. Can you say where?"

Case hesitated, working the weights, thinking. Nat moved suddenly. "Give me those. My turn."

Case gave her one but stopped her from lifting the left one. "Not the injured arm. You'll ruin the pretty needlepoint I did."

Nat nodded her head. Case took the single weight back and they both worked. Case switched arms occasionally. Nat's wounded arm protested the neglect.

Finally, he laid his aside, tucking it into his bag again. He circled his shoulders like he had kinks to work out of his muscles. It made Nat aware of how long it had been since she'd last jogged. She was used to ten miles a day. She was exhausted, but she still longed for the release. She worked the single weight harder.

"I've been cruising an underground network of terrorists for the last year and a half," Case said. "I've been in and out of the country. I took a lot of names and faded out of the picture while other people arrested about fifteen wannabees out of about ten cells of extremists scattered all over the Western Hemisphere, mostly in Central and South America."

"Do you think your cover was broken? That could explain the hit on you." Nat gave up the weight when she felt her heart rate slow and her arm muscles hum with contentment. She handed it back to him and he put it away.

She eased back on the stairs, pulled her Glock out and ejected the clip. She checked the chamber. There was a round loaded. Two shots gone from the clip, right into a hitman's heart. She muttered, "Should have gone for a head shot." Then louder she said, "I need to reload." She snapped the clip back into place with one efficient slap with the palm of her hand.

Case pulled his own gun out to do the same quick but thorough inspection. "As far as I know, no one made me for a Fed. I cruised in and out of the different groups, using what I knew from one cell as credentials to infiltrate the next. When I'd finally tracked it to a wacko named Reardon who was funding most of it, I brought the whole thing down, but not directly. I don't think they knew I was the leak. Anything is possible though."

"Okay, what do we have in common?" Nat said, as she jacked a shell out of the chamber then back in. She flicked the safety off, then back on and tucked the gun away. She made sure the cotton shirt Case had bought her hung loose down her back so her gun was covered. She wore the shirt unbuttoned and had a plain white T-shirt under it.

Case holstered his gun and pulled the razor sharp five-inch knife out of his boot. He used the inside of his blue plaid shirt to wipe traces of blood off the handle. His shirt and white T-shirt matched Nat's except her over shirt was solid blue denim with long sleeves to cover her wound. He narrowed his eyes while he examined the knife. Then he pinned her with a hard gaze. "What have you been working on?"

Nat didn't pull out her own knife because she wasn't sure he knew she had it. He'd spotted the contacts, he'd probably spotted the knife, but self-preservation was an old habit. She met his eyes coolly. "I can't say what I'm working on. That's just how it is. You tell me about your recent life, and I'll tell you what fits."

He looked back at his knife and nodded. "That's what I figured you'd say." He tugged his jeans up at the ankle and put his knife away with a soft brush of steel on leather.

He pulled one knee up close to his chest and rested his forearm on top of it. He extended his other leg out straight and leaned back with one elbow on the stair above the one he sat on.

"That's not how it's going to be. We aren't going to play this by the book. 'Need to know' is a phrase I hate above all others."

"It's not about what you need to know." She said shortly. "It's about national security. I know things that could get people killed if..."

"Yeah...like me." Case stood up impatiently. "Good luck surviving the next forty-eight hours. We might be better off splitting up anyway." He grabbed his heavy duffel bag, slung it over his shoulder and headed straight down the steps.

She jumped to her feet. "We're not going to get to the bottom of this separately. Whatever caused that attack this afternoon was aimed at both of us. It's only by comparing notes that we can stop this guy."

She clamped the vise-like grip she was so proud of around his wrist. He whirled fast enough to throw her off balance on the higher stair. He grabbed her hand off his wrist and twisted it painfully before she could react.

She stood there and took the pain like it didn't matter, because it didn't. She controlled the urge to counter attack but the effort made her break her words off harshly. "No one likes having a partner less than I do. My last partner got himself killed and almost took me with him."

"Well, there's something we have in common," he sneered. "Only I'd say, I got my last partner killed. Maybe that's the way it happened to you too, but you're too arrogant to admit it."

That made her mad because it sliced right down to the truth, so she broke his pathetic excuse for a hold on her hand and jerked him forward hard enough to lay him out flat, face down on the stairs. She twisted his arm and shoved her knee into his spine for about a tenth of a second before she found herself flat on her back on the landing with him straddling her stomach. She arched her back to throw him off but he just leaned all his weight on top of her, grabbed her hands and held them crossed against her chest.

He settled in like a ton of bricks only dumber.

She had several lethal blows she wanted to demonstrate about now but she only wanted to stop him, not kill him. Not yet. So, she gave him a break.

He practically purred when he spoke to her but the soft voice didn't cover his anger. "I know all the little tricks you have up your sleeve, baby doll. Don't lay there and act like you're giving me a break. I know the defensive moves to all of them."

"I know the moves, too. Including the counter to this." She realized his mockery was a salute to her strength. To coddle her would be the true insult.

"Sounds like SEAL training. You must have been the first lady SEAL. Oh, wait, they don't let pretty li'l baby dolls be big, bad SEALS do they? The poor darlin's might break a nail or muss their hair." He showed her the supreme disrespect of holding both of her hands in one of his and took his time rubbing his hand briskly back and forth on the top of her head, shoving her hair around. Entertaining himself by messing it up. Like it hadn't been a rat's nest to begin with.

She was ready to launch a verbal threat to one of the more treasured parts of his anatomy when she started laughing. She couldn't believe herself. This man had the most unusual effect on her.

He quirked one eyebrow at her. "Is giggling part of some new martial arts method? If it is I'm at your mercy 'cuz I've never heard of it and I don't know the counter."

He leaned down until he was practically nose to nose with her. She noticed he let the pressure off of her injured arm. She noticed he had the clean masculine scent of a physically active male. It was a good smell, musky, elemental.

He said, "You still gonna try and keep me here against my will, baby doll?"

She quit laughing, but she couldn't hold back a grin. "I think, just to save your masculine pride, I'll let you think you won this one."

He let his eyes study the way he had her pinned for a second. "You do have me fooled all right. This is really sneaky of you."

She nodded. "I've captured a thousand men this way."

The look in his eyes was suddenly warmer, more aware of the way they were touching. Nat heard the words she'd said with a slightly different connotation. She started to take them back, but before she could, he silently stood up, moved away from her and stared sightlessly down the last flight of stairs.

She lay for a couple of seconds longer, then she said, "I'm going to break all the rules with you, Case."

He inhaled sharply and turned to her.

She quickly amended what she'd said. "I mean I'm going to tell you where I've been. Everything's on the table. I've already trusted you with my life a couple of times today. That's a couple of times more than I've trusted anybody in a long time."

Case shook his head and blew out a long silent breath. "I still think we're better off apart. If someone wants both of us dead then why not give them two moving targets instead of one?"

A loud metallic bang from the bottom of the stairway jerked Nat to her feet. The alleyway door opened and pounding footsteps from more than one person echoed in the dirty stairwell.

Case and Nat were both moving up the steps without so much as making eye contact. She had her gun out. She saw he did, too.

Case leaned over the edge of the stairway. He jerked his head back as a bullet caromed off the metal railing on their right. Ten more shots rang out as he said, "Three of them. None of them the guy from the Metro."

They quit fooling around and ran.

The tenement they were in wasn't a tall one, but Nat had come close to bleeding to death that day. They were on the fourth floor to start so the next four floors ate up most of her newly regained energy.

Shards of concrete scraped against her face occasionally when a lucky shot would ricochet into the wall near them.

Near the halfway point on the seventh flight of steps, Case grabbed her hand and started dragging her and she realized she was slowing down. They reached the top and Case slammed his way through the door onto the roof. He didn't quit moving as he ran across the flat surface of the old building, dodging dozens of air ducts and chimneys. He reached the edge along the alley where they'd come in and leaped up onto the two-foot-high barrier. He didn't let go of her and he didn't ask her if it was okay. He jumped.

The roof across was about a half a story lower than the one they were on, that's the only reason they jumped far enough. He landed like a cat on all fours. She could do that, too, but not today. Today she barreled into him like an ox wearing high heels. They both rolled and before she could tell which end was up he was on his feet and pulling her along again. He hesitated in front of a little room on top of the building that undoubtedly housed a stairwell similar to the one they'd just run up. Someone started emptying what sounded to Nat's experienced ears like a .38 caliber revolver.

Nat started to disengage her gun hand from Case to return fire. Case must have seen something he liked better than a gun fight because he darted around the little room, yanking her with him. He headed straight for a circular opening on the edge of the building. He paused when he got to it and turned to her.

"Remember these? It's an old fire escape that's like a slide." He pushed her ahead of him.

Nat didn't know if ladies first was gracious in this instance. "Didn't they quit making these in the fifties because of the death toll at the bottom of the high-speed descent?"

"They not only quit making them in the fifties..." he shoved her to a sitting position and jumped into the funnel behind her clamping his legs on the outside of hers and wrapping both arms tightly around her waist, holding her arms inside his, sheltering her stitched up wound, "...they quit repairing them back then, too. Anyway, the death toll at the bottom won't matter if the thing has holes rusted through on the fifth floor."

As he pushed them off, he said, "Either way we get down fast."

He swung the strap of his duffel bag over his head so he wouldn't lose it. The heavy bag whacked both of them in the side.

They whooshed into complete darkness. The sliding fire escape let them race, then slowed them down as they hit debris. They'd knock something out of the way and pick up speed again. Nat felt something live slap into her face as she zipped past it. She was pretty sure it was a rat but it was gone the same instant she knew it was there.

The funnel coughed them up onto pavement that seemed harder than normal cement. Nat prided herself on her coordination and her quick reaction time. None of that kept her from landing in a heap. Case didn't even pull her to her feet this time. He picked her up and slung her over his shoulder. She'd protest that she was fine just as soon as she could form a coherent sentence. He ran down the alley like she weighed nothing.

They heard a scream as someone plummeted from high up on the fire escape. The scream cut off as someone hit the alley floor with a sickening thud. They'd had their share of run-ins with pavement today. It sounded harder than ever when that body hit it.

Several shots followed them, all coming from the rooftop. Like miners sending a canary into a coal mine to test the air, their assailants had sent one of their own ahead to test the fire escape. The other two learned their lesson the easy way.

Case set Nat on her feet without her ever saying a word, then they dodged down a stairway, found an escalator, sprinted down, and jumped on a train.

The doors slapped shut and Case and Nat slumped into seats in the empty Metro car.

Case breathed hard through his mouth for a few seconds then he turned to her. "How'd they know where we were?"

"They missed." Claudia slammed her hand into the monitor.

The screen wasn't damaged and she didn't complain about her hand. But Sloan knew she liked pain. She liked causing it and she liked receiving it. Sloan grimly watched the blip on the screen pick up speed. "They made the Metro," he said.

"And they're headed into a crowded part of town. We don't want a hundred witnesses to this, you fool." Her voice could shatter glass it was so shrill.

Sloan cursed himself for getting in a spot where his life depended on a mad woman. She had it dead right when she called him a fool. He watched the moving lights on the screen.

"Why did it take you all day to get access to the tracking device?" she harangued him. "Normally we can tap into it from my office."

"They routinely change the security code. It always takes me a while to get access to it. It's not my private toy. We had to wait until the place cleared out for the day. I've got the coding on my computer now so you can follow it with the computer in your office again. We know where they are and they don't have any idea we know. We'll pick them up when we find out where they're going to surface from the Metro. They'll try to hide but they won't be able to, then we'll finish this."

"I want them dead!" she shrieked. She hit the monitor again then she pivoted and backhanded him.

The blow was so unexpected he staggered backward into a chair and fell over it. From the floor he watched her eyes change from deranged fury to amusement.

"They'll be dead," he promised, trying to deflect her hysteria. "I've got my men. You've got Prometheus. They can't stay ahead of us much longer. Not when we're watching every move." He touched his lip where she'd hit him and wiped away a trickle of blood.

Her eyes latched on the blood and she wet her lips like she was thirsty. He got to his feet never taking his wary eyes off of her. When she was calmer, he leaned over the desk and watched that blip, two blips they'd been searching for ever since the bugs had been planted over a year ago, slide along the Metro line for a little longer. Claudia had picked the wrong two lab rats this time, but she'd picked them from their fake identities. She had gone after rats and tagged two full grown lobo wolves.

CHAPTER SIX

They got off the Metro at the next stop. Nat said, "We've got to keep moving while I think."

He was tempted to say, 'while we think' just to bug her. He didn't know how she kept moving and she had to be too exhausted to think but, even in a coma, she'd find a way to defy him if he gave her an order, so he kept quiet.

She'd let him drag her around a little there for a while. So, he let her get some of her psychological power back by following her lead. He was finding out he liked her best when she was at full strength.

"We've got to keep moving, but we've got to stop and rest and have time to think. How can we do both?" he asked, actually hoping she'd come up with the same solution he had. So far, they were proving to think almost exactly alike.

"We jack a car and take turns driving and sleeping?" She had started out of the Metro at a good clip but her pace was already slowing.

"If we have to, we'll boost a car. But I am an officer of the court. I'd just as soon not steal one if we don't have to."

He heard her mutter, "Boy Scout," and couldn't stop himself from grinning.

"They know where we are. You said it. But how? Even if one of us was ratting the other one out, we haven't been apart since this started."

"Not true. You went into the pawn shop." She offered it without any venom.

He realized she trusted him and was just arguing for the sake of accuracy and because arguing was the basis for their whole relationship.

"Yeah, but I tried to get you onto the Metro then remember? My theory was to put some space between us and the hit man. The hospital was your idea." He really had wanted to put some serious miles under them. And he hadn't known how weak she was.

"I was asleep for over two hours in the hospital."

"So, why didn't I have them come there for us?" He grinned at her and waited for whatever she said next, to bat it back in her face.

She shrugged. "And why didn't you shoot me yourself? Forget your pathetic effort to defend yourself, I trust you. How can I help it? You won't even steal a car. How about we find something moving and stow away on it."

"The space shuttle sounds good." Stowing away was what he wanted to do so he was careful not to agree too quickly.

"NASA is too far from D.C. Pick something else." They strode quickly along the unpopulated streets.

A truck rumbled to a stop behind a warehouse a hundred feet in front of them. A burly man jumped out of the cab and hustled around to the back.

Case pulled Nat close to the building until the warehouse door opened. He noticed she didn't move to hide herself. He had done it instinctively. She should have, too. He was afraid she was near collapse.

In the still night air, they could clearly hear the delivery man's friendly voice in the vast warehouse. "Last delivery of the night. I want to be halfway to Chicago by sunup."

A skid loader hummed out of the building. Case held Nat close to him while they waited, hoping they had the time for this delay. They watched the truck being emptied for the next fifteen minutes.

The last time the skid loader came out it carried a load that must be returned merchandise. The men dumped their load and went inside. Case and Nat were settled behind a stack of slightly dented microwave ovens before the driver returned.

He locked them in. The rumbling engine of the idling diesel truck dropped into gear and they were on their way to Chicago.

"Okay," she said getting down to business, "how did they find us?"

"We weren't tailed. Not even by a master." He'd checked constantly and he knew all the tricks.

"Agreed." She hunkered down on the floor, leaning against the front end of the semi with the boxes between her and the truck's back end.

He sat beside her.

She pulled both knees up to her chest and wrapped her arms around them, ignoring her wound.

Case sat with his legs sprawled out in a vee, hands rested on his thighs. He tilted his head against the vibrating cargo trailer.

"A bug?" What else could it be?

He looked at her clenched fists and tight jaw. "If it is, then we're still carrying them. Whoever is after us could be right outside this truck."

"It could be anywhere. I've seen bugs so small they can pass for stitching in a pair of jeans." He studied his jeans unhappily.

"So, we get rid of our clothes," she said matter-of-factly.

"Only the ones we started the day with." Case was glad of that. "I have no desire to sit around naked on the cold metal floor of a semi."

Nat started yanking off her leather hiking boots.

He pulled off his Nike's.

"Socks, underwear, everything. Including your billfold and everything in it," she ordered.

"How about the cash? We need it."

She tilted her head, considering as she scooted around so her back was to him. She shed the blue, long sleeved denim shirt and the white T-shirt and pulled her blood stained sports bra off over her head and tossed it into the pile with her shoes.

He was human after all, so he quit undressing himself and paid attention to the sleek, taut skin on her back for the few seconds until it vanished as she jerked her shirt on.

He didn't think it hurt to mention the obvious. "You're in great shape."

"I'm a workout freak," she said, then she added a little more sternly, "Quit looking at me."

"What's the point of getting into this kind of shape if you don't let people see? I've got a real fitness jones, too. That's why I bought those weights. I get crazy if I can't work off some of my energy. It worked well with my cover. I spent a lot of time in remote, rugged areas, lots of hiking and rock climbing."

She looked over her shoulder at him. "Rock climbing, yeah I love that. I got a few chances to do it where I was on assignment."

"Where was that?" he said it just to test her.

She hesitated then said shortly, "Afghanistan."

Then she went back to the original subject. "I've gotten to be an addict. Lifting weights burns off a lot of tension. I get edgy if I don't do it."

"I think it's just our age," he said returning to the business of pulling off his socks. "We're in the prime of our lives."

She laughed, "I like that better than what I call it. I think of myself as an adrenaline junkie. If I don't have bullets to dodge then I go to the gym to get my fix."

He had a nice vivid memory of how her muscles ripple under her evenly tanned skin and his hands itched to touch her back and feel her move under his palms. "Well, whatever you're doing, it's working. You look great."

"Thanks, but I think my back looks like I've survived a wolf attack." She looked away from him.

He'd noticed the scars. Most looked like knife wounds. There'd been several small burns that his gut told him were intentionally inflicted by someone who wanted information from her. She had a couple of long, thin silvery scars that stretched the whole length of her back slashing from shoulder to waist that could have come from a whip. And there were two bullet wounds. One that looked like an exit wound low on her left side and another that looked like she'd been shot from the side. There was an entrance wound by her right shoulder blade inches from her spine and an exist wound that came out the top of her shoulder.

She was battle scarred but she was still a beautiful woman. She moved like a dancer and, even when she was issuing orders, she had a voice as sweet as a siren's song. But she was a soldier. A Viking warrior. Her body told a story of victory and agony and above all, strength.

"They've got bugs now that used to be science fiction. Metallic threads can be programmed to raise a red flag in a specific computer. That's not the same as sending out a homing signal but I suppose, in theory, a computer could track those threads somehow. It would be cutting edge. I've never worked with it."

Case was only minimally conscious of his hand reaching toward Nat's ravaged back. He lay one finger on her shirt right where he'd seen the thin white lash marks.

Nat flinched away from him when he touched her. "Back off."

Pulling his hand back, he said, "Tell me about them."

"They're ancient history, Case." She sounded tired all of a sudden.

"So, give me a history lesson. What's the higher bullet wound?"

"It's funny you picked that one, except it's the ugliest. I suppose it's the obvious one."

Nothing about Nat was ugly but he didn't say anything, afraid she'd clam up and start saying 'need to know' again.

"That is the one that started it all. It is courtesy of a drug runner I befriended in Mexico. It was one of my first deep cover assignments."

"Some friend."

"Actually, that bullet saved my life. It happened while I was trying to make a drug buy from one of the top aides to a Colombian drug lord. The little worm who was working with me decided he didn't want to split the payroll so he shot me. My cover wasn't broken, I was just the victim of greed.

"The Colombian dealer saw the whole thing. He killed my betraying little friend and decided I'd be after some revenge. In his mind, me getting shot made me completely legit as a courier. He took me into his inner circle. They were trying to move into new territory, territory I represented. My shoulder blade was broken but he had access to excellent doctors. They patched me together and I let them convince me to sell out my old partner." Nat exhaled sharply, quickly though her nose. Her shoulders lifted again and the corners of her mouth curled up and down in one brief instant. It was a grim parody of a laugh.

"By the time I was done, a six-week undercover assignment turned into two years. I was living in Colombia in a military compound run by one of the biggest drug cartels."

"You were in their compound for two years?" Case asked quietly. Everyone in the intelligence world knew about the deadly drug runners.

"I ran communication. Money flowed through that place like the Amazon River in the rainy season. There was nothing we couldn't buy. The communication center could tap into spy satellites. Pick up and descramble U.S. military micro burst transmissions. Track competitors from all over the world. They had access to high tech weaponry. Stinger missiles, grenade launchers, guns, every size, every style. And they had the names of all the weapon suppliers.

"They had informants everywhere. In every nation in the world. I uncovered the names of CIA agents, FBI agents, Scotland Yard officers, KGB agents, politicians everywhere. I kept track and I kept my head down until I had enough information to bring the whole place down. Then I didn't trust the Colombians to do it or the U.S. to agree to intervene with the force necessary. The cartel was too well connected.

"The one vulnerable thing about the compound was that they believed they were completely safe from an all-out military assault. They had paid off everyone in the Colombian government to such an extent that they were safe from a frontal assault. They didn't have antiaircraft guns or Scud missile launchers because they knew they'd never need them. They had tons of perimeter defenses like armed guards, land mines, snares. But no big fixed weapons. So, when the time came, I used their own communication system and contacted someone I'd learned had been harassing them. Someone they couldn't buy off or kill. Then I disabled the early warning systems and the perimeter defenses in certain prearranged areas."

She breathed that same cynical, silent laugh. "Then I made sure a few of the guards weren't in a position to fight. And I marched into the leader's bedroom, a man I'd seen order death with no more emotion than I'd order a pizza, and I killed him in his sleep."

"First time?" Case asked when she went silent.

She didn't answer for so long he thought the story was going to end there. Finally, she said, "First time in cold blood. I hated him. I hated everything he stood for. I knew by killing him I'd save thousands of lives. I knew if I woke him up I'd die. I knew if I took him into custody he'd bribe his way out. I also knew someone would step into his shoes the next day and be just as ruthless. So, maybe I didn't save any lives at all."

"You never forget their face, do you?" Case asked quietly.

Nat had been lost in her story. Facing away from him. His question brought her head around.

"You think you've been there?" she was furious.

"I know I've been there," Case said softly.

She turned away without challenging him. Like it didn't matter. Like he didn't matter. "Then I made sure as many of the power wielders in that compound died as possible."

Nat glanced back at him, "Ever hear of Samson?"

"As in Samson and Delilah?"

Nat nodded. "There's a Bible verse that says Samson wrote a song. The words are, 'With the jawbone of a donkey I killed a thousand men; With the jawbone of a donkey I piled them up in piles'. I heard that verse years after that night, but I always think of it when I remember the compound."

She turned away again and lowered her face into her hands, then as if impatient with weakness, she ran her hands into her hair and caught her finger on her rubber band. She pulled it out, shoved her fingers through her hair a few times and slapped the band back in her hair.

"I stayed there, doing my best to leave a vacuum of leadership, until the last minute. It's funny, that first face haunts me. I see him in my nightmares. But I don't remember much about the others. I did all the damage I had time to do, then I ran out through one of my rabbit holes. I was a hundred yards into the rain forest when the Air Force bombers came."

"Bombers? U.S. military bombers? We've never bombed Colombia."

"Not on the record we haven't, but sometimes things happen that don't make the news."

There was an extended silence, then Nat said, "I came back to America, mostly on foot."

"You walked back from Colombia?" Case asked astonished. "No one came for you?"

"The weird thing was, I was dead. I didn't even know it. As far as the company was concerned I'd died in that shooting in Mexico two years earlier. I tried to come in from the cold but before I could get anyone's attention, the person I contacted about Colombia stopped me. He wanted me to stay dead and work for black ops." She gave that ugly little laugh again that almost sounded like, 'hmmph,' "I've been dead ever since."

Case had heard her laugh. It was wonderful. It changed her whole face. Lightning flashed through her golden eyes when she laughed for real. Now her eyes were flat, menacing. Remembering cross and double cross. And how she'd triple crossed them all.

And how she'd killed a man who needed killing. And killed something inside herself while she was at it. Then found out her death was even more real than she'd imagined.

He rested a hand on her shoulder. "You're not dead, Nat. Your skin is warm."

He slid his hand along the side of her throat and pressed against her throbbing pulse. She tilted her head slightly but she didn't pull away.

"Your heart is beating."

He raised his finger to her lips. "You're breathing."

Her lips move slightly against his fingers, then she leaned forward, separating herself from his touch. "It's not going to happen, Case. We're stuck together for a while, but this is work. There is probably a contracted hit man closing in on us. We don't have time to do any of this."

He dropped his hand. "I agree with everything you said, except 'it's not going to happen.' I'm not convinced of that."

Nat scooted farther from him. She started slipping out of her jeans and Case dragged his eyes away from her before he did something that, considering who he was dealing with, could very possibly get him killed.

They ended up with the packing crate between them and shed the clothes they'd started the day with. They inspected their own clothes and each other's. Nothing they saw led them to believe there was a bug planted anywhere. Case tossed the stuff out of the truck through a little vent door that opened in the back.

"It could be in a gun or a holster," Nat said. "But I'm not parting with them."

Case pulled out his Glock. "My gun is the one thing I would have been sure to carry." He turned it over in his hands, touching all the surfaces, trying to think where a tracking device could be hidden.

Next, he took off his over shirt and slung his holster off his shoulders. He checked all the metal fastenings and inside the pocket that held the gun. "This is definitely the same holster I've had for years. I don't see any new stitching, any metal that doesn't look right."

He finally said, "We probably should replace them but no way am I going unarmed right now."

Nat was inspecting her knife scabbard. "We'll get out of this truck the first time it stops and move at a ninety-degree angle to the direction it's moving. I'm not carrying any credit cards and the only cash I have is two twenties I got in change for a fifty when I bought myself some breakfast. The cash should be clean, but we need to throw it all away."

Case pulled his billfold out of his hip pocket. "I'll go along with everything except the cash. It might be bugged but we're putting ourselves in a precarious position to be completely penniless."

"Agree," she said, like they were negotiating a business deal. "Don't forget your watch and anything you have in your pockets."

The truck started downshifting and Nat looked around the sides of the truck. "I'll see where we are." She headed for a front corner where rungs stuck out of the wall. She climbed swiftly to the top and slid a trap door out of her way.

Case saw her head disappear into the opening at the same second he heard a dull metallic thud on the side of the truck.

Nat dropped ten feet to the floor, landing in a crouch with her gun already drawn. "He's out there!"

In that second the restful cocoon they'd been riding in became a death trap.

"He'll force the driver off the road." Case had scanned the interior of the semi-trailer as soon as he'd gotten in. There were a series of hatches on the sides and the roof. He went for the one on the front of the trailer.

The hatch opened from the inside about two feet over Case's head. He reached the latch. Wind blew the small square door open. Case turned to yell at Nat to follow him.

She was already behind him tucking her gun in its holster and snapping it down. Case stepped back and boosted her up. She took hold of the opening and hoisted herself up, twisting her body to put her feet through first. She paused, sitting on the door frame for a split second. "He won't bother to force him off the road." She fought for balance against the buffeting wind and yelled back to Case. "He'll just kill the driver and let the truck crash. Then he'll hang around to pick up the pieces."

She reached for the cab in front of her and disappeared. Case grabbed the opening and swung himself through. Nat was clinging to a row of lights on the cab roof. She went toward the driver's side.

Case needed Nat's handhold. The wind pummeled his body, roaring in a dozen directions between the two halves of the big rig. Nat had one hand fastened onto the railing on top of the truck. She swung herself around to grab hold of the driver's door. She held for a second then a volley of gun fire blasted sparks off the driver's side of the cab. She fell back, dangling for one heart stopping moment by one hand with her back banging against the cab. Her eyes met his for an instant, the screaming of eighteen wheels within inches of her swaying feet.

The trucker reacted to the shots by sharply reducing his speed. The car, driving at full speed, pulled alongside them and roared past. They had just a few seconds before they were pulled to a halt and picked off their perch by gunfire.

Case reached out and grabbed a fist full of Nat's shirt front. He held her steady until she gathered her strength. She nodded when her grip on top of the truck was firm. He released her and watched as she found an almost supernatural depth in the straining muscles of her right arm. She turned her body to face the cab and tried again to find a handhold on the driver's door. She caught and braced herself, her body wrapped around the corner.

Case waited until he was sure her hold was solid then he jumped across the hitch that held the trailer to the cab, dodging the coiled power cords. He had a momentary vision of the highway rushing underneath him. His balance wavered as he steadied himself between the movement of the cab and the trailer, the wires and the streaming asphalt. The roar of the monstrous diesel engine deafened him. The vertigo passed and he headed for the passenger's side. He swung around the corner, climbing the length of the sleeping compartment of the cab by picking out handholds and toeholds in the truck. He got to the window and his stomach twisted in horror to be face to face with a little girl.

There hadn't been a child on this truck when they'd climbed aboard at the warehouse. Case hesitated, uncertain what to do. He looked through the cab and saw Nat's gun come crashing through the window of the opposite door. He saw a late model Taurus slow down, dropping back for another shot. Traffic in the oncoming lane kept the Taurus in front of them. The assassin slowed down further and the driver started applying the brake. The truck's headlights lit up the whole inside of the car. Case looked into the dead eyes of the man who'd tried to kill him and Nat in the Metro. The gunman held his steering wheel in one hand and reached straight behind him aiming his gun at the cab.

There wasn't time to reason with a frightened child. Case took a firm hold on the roof of the truck with his left hand, flipped the tie-down loose on his shoulder holster and pulled the gun, ramming it through the window as far in front of the child as he could.

Nat came through her window feet first, kicking the terrified man aside. She grabbed the wheel as the rig veered toward the ditch. She straightened them out and shoved her foot down hard on the accelerator, slamming into the trunk of the car in front of them. The back end of the hit man's car fishtailed, almost turning the car sideways. Another car raced toward them in the oncoming lane. With sickening skill the shooter controlled his car and straightened it out, missing the traffic by inches. They hadn't stopped him but they'd bought a few seconds before he could start shooting again.

Case didn't bother to open the door. He kept a grip on his gun and levered his body through the glass with one hand, breaking a hole large enough for himself as he went. The little girl scrambled onto her father's lap in the center of the long bench seat.

The trucker man yelled at his daughter, "Get in the back. Stay there." He boosted the girl over his shoulder.

"Take what you want. Take the truck. Just don't hurt..."

Case started to reassure him when the windshield exploded in their faces. Case shoved the man's head down and ducked low covering the trucker's body with his own.

Nat yelled in a fierce growling voice no person on earth would ever disobey, "If you want to live through this get in the back with your family."

Family? Case turned. Another child's head, not the one he'd seen before, poked out from the curtains behind them. A terrified woman who had to be the driver's wife, pulled the child back. Case had stowed away in a freaking apartment building.

Case didn't wait for the shocked man to obey Nat. He boosted their unwilling host into the back. Pushing everybody back. He kneeled on the seat long enough to shout, "Get down and stay down. Pull that mattress up in front of you. Someone's shooting at us."

Case whirled back around, sickened to know they held the lives of four innocents in their hands.

"Quit fooling around and shoot back." Nat bellowed. "Or take over and drive so I can do something."

Bullets, illuminated by a blazing row of sparks, ricocheted off the front hood of the truck. Case shoved his head all the way though the front windshield and lay on his stomach on the hood, spraying the car in front of them with his Glock.

An opening in the left lane appeared. The Taurus dropped into it. Nat grabbed onto the back of Case's jeans and hollered over the blasting wind, "Get in here."

He hesitated, annoyed at her for urging caution at this point. She jerked hard enough on his waistband to drag him back inside. He sprawled half on the floor and half on the seat. Nat swerved the semi sharply into the left hand lane crushing in the side of the Taurus. The Taurus went into a spin from the impact, the back end of it sliding into the semi, spinning it hard into a tree in the ditch. The impact reverberated inside the truck. The Taurus hit hard, but Case knew it wasn't hard enough. Unless they were very lucky, the assassin survived.

Nat shoved the brake down to the floor. The truck started to jackknife as she stopped it too fast.

Case grabbed her leg and pulled it off the brake. "Keep going! Leave him!"

She gripped two of his restraining fingers and put an excruciating judo hold on them. He knew she could break them with just a little more pressure.

She said with fiery determination, "I'm not running. We finish this now. We should have taken him out the first time he opened up on us."

She straightened the truck and jammed her foot back on the brake. Several heads popped out of the curtain behind them.

Case didn't fight her. He leaned two inches from her face and with vicious sarcasm, asked softly, "And what about them?" He jerked his head toward their unwilling passengers. "What body count is acceptable? Are they just a little collateral damage? Is your goal to save half of them? Can you live with that death toll? Is that the way you operate?"

Nat threw him a murderous look. He saw her glance in the rearview mirror and knew she was seeing the family that had gotten in the middle of a gunfight through no fault of their own.

Some of her rage had dissipated. "Let me out. I'll go back on my own."

Case knew the gunman could be clear of the car by now, ready to shoot them from cover.

She was driving. She could stop if she wanted to. He'd go with her. Case remained silent. Waiting for her decision.

She looked at the family again and with a furious scowl hit the accelerator again. "Why should we go back for him?" she asked bitterly. "He'll be right behind us as soon as he gets another car anyway."

She pushed the rig up to eighty-five miles an hour. He didn't know what to say to their passengers, so he ignored them. Ten miles down the rode they came to the outskirts of Pittsburgh. They pulled to a stop and climbed out.

As they stepped down from the truck Nat turned to the driver. "You got a pen?"

The man gave it to her like he was afraid she'd kill him if he didn't.

Nat grabbed a piece of paper out of the man's breast pocket and wrote a phone number on it. "Call this number. They'll fix your truck, no questions asked. Tell them Nat Brewster caused the damage."

"Keep your number, lady." The trucker tossed the paper back at Nat and started to swing the door shut.

Case grabbed the door to hold it open. "They're after us, not you. You'll be safe now that we're away from you. But I'd put miles between you and that man for a few more hours."

The man nodded and pulled the truck away from the truck stop quickly. Case thought the man would probably drive nonstop all the way to Chicago.

Nat turned to Case, "What do we have left?"

"Maybe he locked onto the truck somehow before we got rid of things."

Nat pointed at the truck stop. "Let's change our money in there."

"It's going to be tricky."

Nat looked at the innocuous little truck stop. "Why?"

Case pointed to the ground. "Because we're barefoot. No shoes, no shirt, no service. It's the law of the land these days." Then he pulled his gun from his holster and studied it. "You up for a little breaking and entering?"

"The Boy Scout is gonna knock over a truck stop?"

Case smiled. "I'm thinking we'll find a gun shop and make a trade."

Nat patted him on the back, "I like your style. You break the law more honestly than anyone I've ever known."

"There's a phone book right over there." Case headed for it, flinching when he stepped on a piece of sharp crushed rock.

Nat caught up with him and passed him as he brushed the imbedded stone from his foot. "Need a piggy back ride, Sweetie?"

Case lifted his head from his feet, raising one eyebrow at the exasperating woman. He tried hard to remind himself that she had almost bled to death today. He needed to give her a little space to be an overbearing hag since she was in a weakened condition. Once she was back to full strength, then he'd kill her.

He remembered the way she'd nearly broken his fingers without any effort and raged about going after the assassin by herself. He couldn't help but like Nat Brewster.

Then he remembered the scars on her back and how warm her skin was and how alone she'd sounded when she'd talked about finding out she was legally dead. He wanted to see her scars again. He wanted to see all of her.

CHAPTER SEVEN

She opened a battered phone book and started looking for arms dealers—legal ones for once in her life.

Case went into the truck stop hoping to find something for their feet and came up empty. He didn't like the surveillance cameras all around the place.

She cross-referenced the businesses against their current position and a Pittsburgh street map. There was one about two miles away. That was the best they were going to do. It was all she needed, a two mile hike, barefoot, with at least two different sets of assassins breathing down her neck.

"Let's get moving. They're coming." Case didn't say, 'maybe or might be'. Neither of them had any doubt.

Nat wordlessly headed for the highway and jogged across. Case tagged along. They moved through the dimly lit business district that bordered the busy highway, keeping back from the street as much as possible.

Nat had lived on the run before but she'd never had such a feeling of being hunted. She felt like a wolf pack had caught her scent. And she was weakened, ready to be thinned from the herd. She put her mind on automatic. Ignoring her exhaustion and her throbbing arm. She was on full alert, registering every bush waving in the breeze for manmade motion, scanning every oncoming car for danger. She took note of each sound and whether it belonged in the mix of nighttime sounds of the city. She was acutely aware of Case beside her, keeping the same vigil, his hands relaxed, swinging free, ready to grab his gun, ready to fight for her life and his own.

She couldn't remember ever walking beside someone and trusting him this way. She held men in contempt for the most part. Oh, who was she kidding, she held everyone in contempt, including herself most of the time. But she hung around with killers and drug dealers for a living so she might judge the rest of humanity a little harshly. No doubt about it, she was a cynic.

What she wasn't right now, was alone. It was a unique experience. One she hadn't had maybe since she was in her teens. She liked it. She liked him. But she knew better than to depend on anyone. It was a good way to end up dead.

Their ground eating walk worked off the two miles in fifteen minutes. They moved around the side of the gun shop, checking the security system.

"Any store that sells guns and ammo is going to have good security," Case said, studying the building for surveillance cameras.

Nat said softly, "Keep your voice down."

She pointed to an electrical box high on the side of the single-story building and murmured, "Oh, please, do not tell me it's this easy."

"He could have an independent power source." Case eyed the obvious electric line coming out of the building and going straight to the box.

"Wanna bet?" Nat shook her head, disappointed in the pathetic attempt at security. "If we kill that, we'll shut down the whole system."

"Okay," Case pulled out his Glock and took aim.

Nat rested her hand on the barrel and whispered to him irately. "Why don't you just take out an ad on TV telling people we're here."

Case rolled his eyeballs, "Always the slow way with you."

"Lift me up there."

Case groaned, then he crouched down directly under the electrical box. Nat planted one bare foot on his bent knee. Case gripped her calf, helping her balance. She put her other foot on his shoulder. He held that leg steady. She balanced herself with one hand on his head and one on the building, then with a soft oomph she stood on his shoulders facing the opposite direction he was.

She hissed down at him, "Let's go."

Case stood.

She was face to face with the box. A quick slit with her knife killed the whole system. "Done."

Case grabbed her around her ankles and heaved her into the air. She bit back a tiny shriek of surprise. She thought they were working pretty well together until then. She had a different dismount planned.

She landed in his arms and said, "What are we, a circus act now?"

He grinned, set her on the bricked alley and jimmied the lock on the back door of the shop. They picked the locks on the gun cabinets.

Case whispered, "If you're taking ammo, take a cheaper gun than the one you're leaving. And remember yours is used."

Nat smiled agreeable then took a Glock just like the one she was carrying, three hundred rounds of ammo, a new hunting knife and scabbard, a holster for the gun and broke into the cash register to exchange her money for different bills. She virtuously took the same amount. It wasn't hard to be virtuous, the till was mostly empty.

Case exchanged his cash, too, although he looked annoyed at the broken cash register. Nat was headed out the door when she spotted a rack of hunting clothes. She pointed and Case shrugged.

"We'll pay them back," he grabbed a pair of socks and some Red Wing boots in his size.

Then he went to the counter by the cash register. He found a pen and a piece of paper and jotted a note.

Nat looked over his shoulder. The note said:

'Get an independent power source for your security system. We are undercover federal agents. We have left our guns in trade for the ones we were carrying because we were concerned some of our possessions were bugged. Do not keep these weapons on the premises, it could be dangerous for you. Give them and everything we've left behind, including the cash, to the police. Our guns will not be traceable but we are licensed to carry them. As soon as we are able we will pay for the things we took. I am sorry.'

Nat muttered, "Boy Scout." And headed for the back door. She knew what he was going to do but she didn't have to witness it.

Case went to the phone and punched three buttons. He didn't wait for anyone to answer, he just left the phone off the hook and exited the building behind her.

"Did you call home to tell your mommy you loved her?" Nat asked sarcastically.

"I do love my mom and I should call her. But no, I called 911. Cops on the way, let's go."

He grabbed her hand and the two of them, newly armed and shod ran down the alley. They were five blocks away when they heard the sound of sirens.

Nat sneered, "Great response time."

"We couldn't leave a gun store with no security overnight."

Nat stopped abruptly and turned to Case. "How'd you like to put some serious distance between us and the little trouble of the last few hours?"

"I'm listening."

Nat pointed and Case laughed, then they crouched low and ran toward a ten-foot-high fence. They scaled the chain links and dropped onto the grass. They waited until no one was looking then sprinted across the tarmac. Not that hard. Apparently stowing away on a UPS cargo airplane wasn't a common event. They hid among the products Americans ordered by the planeload until the plane took off.

"That's it." Nat checked her gun and slid her new knife in and out of her holster a few times to loosen the leather.

Case nodded as he loaded the clip in his new Glock. His was the next caliber lower than the one he'd left behind. It didn't matter. He could do some damage with this one. "We've got nothing left. We're in the clear. When we land we should be scot-free."

Nat browsed through the cargo for a while. "Why am I having so much trouble believing that?"

"Because nothing in your life has made you an optimist. Because you're suspicious by nature. Because you've never been much of a one to run and hide and it grates on you that we just did exactly that. Don't worry, Nat. There's nothing left. There's no way they can track us."

"Good, because when this plane lands, we start figuring out what's going on." Nat found the softest cardboard box available and lay down, letting the day catch up with her. "Case?"

"Yeah?"

"Whoever is after us is good. Really good. They're going to be waiting for us when this plane lands."

"That's okay, I'm in the mood for a little payback."

Nat said, "You got any idea where the plane is going?"

"No idea in the world. Get some rest. We're probably going to need it." Case lay down and they both fell asleep.

An hour or so later, Nat woke up shivering. A warm blanket pressed itself against her back. When the blanket proved to have an arm and that arm came around her waist she started to say something, but she recognized Case from his muscular chest and the iron bands of his arm and his clean male scent. She kept her mouth shut and spooned her back against his front.

"Cargo planes must not be heated," Nat murmured.

Case wrapped his arm tighter until she was snuggled up close against him. "Whatever you say, baby doll, now go to sleep."

For a woman who would probably face death five times before she had breakfast, she felt wonderfully safe.

She slept.

Another man would have spent at least the night in the hospital. Prometheus climbed out of the smoking wreck of his car, and was undercover before the tires quit spinning. No one came back for him. He made a call on the burner phone he'd toss away a few miles from here. He hiked away from the wreckage, confident there was nothing in the vehicle that could be tied to him.

As he walked, he wiped the blood from his face. He had several loose teeth. He'd broken his nose again. A gash high on his forehead didn't want to stop bleeding.

His vision blurred from time to time. From the feel of it, he'd cracked a couple of ribs. And his knees had hammered into the dash, both of them were bleeding through his torn gray slacks and swollen to double their normal size.

Nothing serious. He did his best to get rid of the blood to avoid attracting attention but beyond that, he ignored it. He was picked up within thirty minutes.

The man driving didn't look at him. He'd been carefully instructed. Prometheus climbed in the back of the late model dark blue sedan. An opaque Plexiglas shield slid into place between him and the driver turning the back seat into a private, soundproof room. The car contained a change of clothes and a laptop computer programmed to track his prey. He changed, checked the tracker for a location, found nothing and dialed.

"Where did the pigeons land this time?"

Sloan said, "They made it to Pittsburgh, wandered around town a while. I tied them to a robbery at a gun shop. I haven't gotten a complete copy of the police report but assume they've restocked ammo and weapons, then they vanished."

Prometheus spoke minimally into the cell phone. "Assume they're airborne." His was a secure line but he still didn't say anything he didn't need to.

Sloan spoke more freely and Prometheus decided, not for the first time, that the man was a fool. "We traced Brewster and Garrison to an airport. The signal disappears at ten thousand feet. We tracked the plane that was at the altitude where we lost the signal. It's a UPS cargo flight. It has a single destination, Denver. We have people heading for the airport."

"They're my job. Tell your boys to back off."

"They can be there twenty-four hours before you."

"This is personal now between me and them. Nobody does this job for me. Time doesn't matter. I'll get them."

"Time does matter. They could stumble on to the truth."

"They're mine, Sloan. You don't want to make it personal between us."

"All right, fine, we'll do it your way."

He heard the fear in Sloan's voice and relished it at the same time he had contempt for it. "I'll head out immediately and pick them up there." Prometheus hung up. The first time they came to civilization, his driver got out and Prometheus drove away, leaving the driver standing by the side of the road.

It was two a.m. He planned to be in Denver before nightfall the next day.

CHAPTER EIGHT

The plane seemed to land before Nat had gotten to sleep.

She shoved herself reluctantly away from Case's warm arms and went to the tiny windows in the cargo plane. It was still the middle of the night. Great, they'd been heading away from the rising sun. At this rate it would be dark forever.

She worked the stiffness out of her arm, careful not to dislodge the stitches while she studied the airport, what she could see of it. She knew every major airport in the world. This one wasn't hard.

Case came up behind her and glanced out the window. "We're in Denver."

The way he leaned close to her reminded her of the brief time they'd slept so close. The way he knew an airport at a glance garnered her respect. She looked at him. He had his gun out and was checking the clip with the smooth efficiency of an expert. The whole package thawed something in her that made her think of global warming.

If her personal polar ice cap was melting, well, ice and snow weren't popular. A warmer world sounded good. But she knew a disaster when she saw one. She didn't dare to thaw. Keeping cool kept her alive. So, the man knew his airports, big deal.

The plane taxied to a stop and a crew immediately approached with a mobile staircase.

"Let's don't foul this up. I don't trust anyone, and I don't want any more innocents involved." Nat looked around the interior of the plane for a hiding place. Not easy when everything was going to be unloaded.

"I know people near Denver and I agree with you. I don't want any of them anywhere near this." Case said, "They've abandoned the cockpit. Let's sit up there while they unload the back, then get out of here."

"Simple," Nat said. "But we're giving someone a lot of time to catch up with us."

"Let 'em come." Case headed for the separate and mercifully well heated cockpit of the airplane.

Nat couldn't think of any alternative so she followed. The huge plane was unloaded in thirty minutes. One after another, dark brown UPS vans pulled up and were loaded. Nat thought the UPS team deserved a commendation for efficiency. Then the whole crew cleared out. They even left the mobile staircase behind. Nat and Case walked away from the plane as if they were paying customers.

Case found a shuttle bus headed for downtown Denver. In an uncharacteristic move, he actually paid their fare.

They rode into the center of Denver, climbed off the bus and stood on a busy street corner, alert to everything around them.

Case said, "We need to regroup. We need to eat."

"And shower," Nat supplied.

"And figure out who's trying to kill us. I know a guy..."

"No. I told you. No 'guys'. We're not going anywhere we'd normally go." Nat was adamant.

"I'd have never thought of going here if we weren't in Denver. I promise you this is no where I'd normally go. Bannock's name will not be in my file."

Nat looked at him narrowly. "Any contact we make endangers someone else. I don't want to risk civilians."

"This guy can handle trouble if it comes his way. As long as it doesn't interfere with him combing his horses."

Nat dropped her head back to stare at the sky. Why did she always get the weird ones? She wasn't sure if she meant Bannock or Case.

"Tell me about your 'guy'."

"Well, for one thing, I don't know if he's really here. I assume he is though."

"You know what they say about when you assume something?" Nat said darkly.

"No, what?"

"It makes a corpse of U and ME."

Case nodded. "Bannock spent one stint as a marine. He hated the military and he only ever wanted one thing."

"Which is?"

"To go home to his mommy and daddy."

Nat rolled her eyes. "This is the tough guy? The one who can take care of himself?"

"Oh, yeah. He hated the military but that didn't mean he wasn't good at it. The only reason I know him is because I faced him four times running in the inter-base martial arts competition. He won the Marines competition and I won Navy four times then we'd get together with the nearest Army and Air Force winners and fight it out."

"You soldier boys don't have anything better to do than play games?"

"We have a couple of other things to do. But once a year we take a break from killing people and blowing stuff up to see who is toughest."

Nat shook her head.

"Anyway, Bannock just wanted to go home. I swear that man was the biggest wimp who ever wore the uniform of the United States Marines. He reminded me a lot of my little brother Brett."

"This wimp was in the finals of the base martial arts competition every year?"

"I'll admit that was one little non-wimpy thing about him—that and the sharp shooting and the high security clearance for his military intelligence work."

"Is there a point to this walk down memory lane?"

"All I ever knew about him was that he'd come in from brushing the Marine parade horses, stomp me into the dirt. Apologize like crazy for hurting me, offer to bandage my wounds, collect his little trophy and go back to the barn."

"He beat you, huh?"

"Made me look like a kindergarten girl. He'd pound me. He did it quick, like it was unpleasant for him, offer my bleeding corpse a hand up off the ground and dust me off like he really cared."

"You're making me all misty. This guy sounds like a couple hundred pounds of marshmallow to me. Just because he could mop the floor with you big, bad SEALs, doesn't mean he's got a killer instinct and he might need it if we bring all this trouble down on his head."

Case waved a dismissive hand at her. "The point is, I only remembered him because of the way he talked, the few times I was around him, about going home to his home town, a little town in the mountains outside of Denver. He'd decided he wanted to be a vet—just like my brother did. That's probably why I remember. Bannock spent every waking moment studying for it, training himself for it. It was a passion for him, and I'd bet anything he's up there, in Grizzly Bluff, Colorado, tending horses and dogs. He's the most honest man I've ever met, and probably the nicest. But he's a man who would be able to protect himself if trouble came his way. He'd help us.

With his military intelligence connections, he can contact someone and figure out what's going on without that connection leading back to me."

Case went on, "The mountain is a good idea, anyway. It'll get us away from civilians. I'm good in the wilderness."

"You know," Nat said, "when I walked back from South America, I lived on capybara and paca rats."

"Paca rats are my favorite. They taste a lot like chicken."

"Tasted like rat to me." Nat shrugged. "I ate fruit and nuts and some of the time, bark and leaves. I hiked through the Andes until I was as competent as a mountain goat and smelled about as good."

"Been there." Case grinned.

"I walked out of an assignment that went FUBAR in Afghanistan, too. The mountains in Afghanistan seemed almost human part of the time. Human in the sense that the mountains made a premeditated attempt to kill me several times a day."

"Which is your way of saying, you're good in the wilderness, too?" Case asked.

"Oh, yeah. The mountains are a good idea, even if the wimp with the black belt isn't there. Are we walking to this mountain? 'Cuz if we are, let's get started."

"We'll have to walk it." Case turned to face the mountains to the west. "I don't want to stow away again. I hated endangering that family."

"How far?" Nat knew that the Rockies seemed to loom right overhead but getting to the slopes would take miles of strenuous hiking. She had no idea where Grizzly Bluff was, but everything in the mountains was farther away than it seemed.

"If I remember Bannock right, it was only about fifty miles west of Denver." Case sounded like he wasn't thrilled with the idea.

"We could make that in three days." Nat started walking east. "If we're lucky."

"Three days? If we push it we could be there by nightfall. I can do fifty miles in a day, except we're not going straight there. I'm not going near another civilian until we figure out how they're tracking us."

"Agreed." Nat looked at the sun just beginning to lighten the sky over the top of the highest peak. "I once walked a stretch of the Himalayas that was so rugged, one day I only made three hundred yards. Miles don't mean much up there."

"We'll be on a highway most of the time. Don't get all nervous on me, baby doll. I'd hate to see you start biting those pretty fingernails."

"I didn't say I couldn't do it. I just wanted you to know what you were getting into. Three days could turn into a week."

"It is mostly uphill," Case acknowledged as he fell in beside her.

Nat looked at the huge mountain range in front of them and muttered. "Thank you, Master-Of-The-Obvious. We'll stop and rest anytime you get tired."

"And we're not going straight to Bannock's either. We're going to find out how they're tracking us first. While we walk we can solve our little dilemma. We can figure out who our mutual enemies are or where you and I crossed paths in our life. You start. Start naming all the people on this planet who want to kill you." Case snapped his fingers as if he'd been inspired. "To save time maybe you should just name the ones who don't want to kill you."

Nat laughed. She shook her head. Amazed at the sound coming from her very own lips. Nobody made her laugh.

Nat made her voice sound like a little child asking for a playground favor. "Okay, now national security you know. You can't tell anyone."

"Cross my heart and hope to not die." Case drew an exaggerated X on his chest with his finger.Case started laughing and Nat couldn't help but join in. They walked swiftly out of town at a ground eating pace, putting miles behind them. The feeling of being safe that Nat had reveled in during the night returned.

They walked for two hours, swapping highly embellished accounts of their exploits with enough truth thrown in to find out if they'd been in on the same case without knowing it.

"The arms dealer you busted in Ireland said he had a connection in South America." Case jammed his hands in his pockets as he strode along.

"And you were in Bolivia that same year pursuing a fleeing felon. I can't see how he had contact with the terrorist cell I brought down in Chile."

"It's a stretch, I know, but let's pursue it for awhile."

"It's a waste of time." Nat kicked a chunk of gravel on the side of the two-lane highway they walked along.

"Yeah, but I want to talk about it because it was really cool how I tricked this loser into turning himself in. I dressed up like a hooker and stood just outside this lonely fortress he'd holed up in, with my skirt pulled up to my..."

Nat spent most of the morning laughing.

They finally started to feel safe enough that they hitched a ride. Afraid to stay in any car too long in case trouble caught up with them, they road the first time as far as Coalville. The folks there stopped at a fast food place with plans to head north. Case and Natalie stocked up on food, and set out to eat while they walked on west. By the time the food was gone they got a second ride. A young couple planning to spend their honeymoon hiking in the Sawatch National Forest. Case and Nat were careful not to mention their destination.

The couple offered them a Coke. Nat would have traded the sweet liquid for water in a second but she knew better than to pass up calories in any form.

The young couple got to the base of Grizzly Bluff Mountain and offered to go off-roading in their Chevy Blazer and take them as near the summit as they could.

Nat thought it was a great idea. Case, without consulting Nat, assured the couple he and Nat were dying to start climbing. The Blazer disappeared down the road and Nat stared at the daunting peak in front of them.

"Why didn't you let them take us? We could have trimmed another five miles off this hike? You told me it was fifty miles but we've come that far already. It's another fifty miles straight up. And then we have to wander around looking for Bannock."

"We're within spitting distance of the town of Grizzly Bluff already. Instead of three days it took us an hour and a half. No one's shooting at us. We didn't even miss lunch."

"It might not be lunch time but we've missed dinner last night and breakfast this morning, plus a night's sleep."

"You must be wimping out because you got shot." Case patted her on the back with mock sympathy. "Or maybe you're just a hot house posy. Don't worry, baby doll, I'll take care of you."

Nat shook off his hand. "So, which way to Bannock's house? Let me guess, he doesn't have a street number."

"The way?" Case looked around. "Let's try up, whatta ya say? After we find Grizzly Bluff, we'll get into the hills and figure what the connection is that makes us targets. And we'll stay away from everyone until we do."

"We talked for a long time this morning and came up with nothing."

"It's got to be there. We have to dig deeper."

Nat nodded for a second and started walking. It actually felt good, she'd been idle too long. "I need to work the kinks out of my legs. I've been hiking and climbing nonstop for the last couple of years. Especially the eighteen months I was in Afghanistan. I spent every weekend hiking in the mountains around the city pretending to love them but really watching weapons dealers buy and sell to the highest bidder."

Case strode along easily.

Nat remembered he'd been shot, too. He'd never so much as mentioned it. Of course, his was a scratch.

"I split my time between the U.S., Mexico, and Canada, and I hiked the Rockies a good part of the time. The Rockies make the Alps look like a molehill."

"Molehill?" Nat snorted inelegantly, which was really the only possible way to snort. "So, how exactly are you planning to find one little man on a one-million-acre, heavily wooded mountain top?"

"We'll just sit up at night and listen for the sound of his heart bleeding." Case smiled broadly at her.

"As long as you've got a plan," Nat said dryly and kept heading up.

"Where are you? They have a huge head start."

Prometheus refused to answer Sloan's whining. "I've locked onto them."

"They're in the mountains. The tracking device isn't dependable out there. Our signal won't be able to pinpoint them if they get in a low valley or canyon or get too high."

Prometheus promised himself he'd retire after this. "That's only the reading from the satellite. I can pick them up if I get within two miles of them. If you lose them, I'll find them." Sloan had e-mailed a more complete dossier on Case Garrison. Rage washed over Prometheus every time he thought about first Claudia's stupidity and now Sloan's.

They'd sent Prometheus after a full grown, alpha male, he-wolf. And Prometheus' instincts told him the woman was worse. Sloan's info about her was so sketchy Prometheus actually had a little thrill of fear to think how hard edged an agent she might be. Agents that deep got used to doing whatever it took to survive. And they were used to doing it with no backup. Prometheus had no doubt she'd be as formidable as Garrison.

Prometheus hungered for the challenge.

The fury, even the fear, made him feel alive. And when he killed them he'd be God again. Sloan told him they were heading west from Denver, into a national forest.

Going to ground. That made them weak and afraid. He'd brought them low. He'd harried and herded until they were hiding like wounded birds. Prometheus had a rush of power so strong he wanted a woman. Not any woman. A woman who would like it when he demonstrated the entire force of his Godlike power. A woman who liked it when she hurt.

Claudia.

CHAPTER NINE

They crossed a long open valley that surrounded the highway and walked into the woods. There was no trail. They had to climb over dead timber and push past waist deep brush.

Their only goal? Up.

Case noticed Nat working the stiffness out of her wounded arm and regretted suggesting the mountains. The climb was slow and hard. And they hadn't had to go up a rock face yet. Nat wouldn't die, she was too pigheaded. But she'd been badly injured yesterday. They'd eaten, but she needed rest and good food for a week to rebuild her blood and let that wound close. Even worse, it was going to be freezing when they reached higher altitudes.

He should have come up with a better plan. A least he could have stolen a coat from the gun shop last night.

Nat never flagged. She had reserves of strength that seemed endless. Once she walked over to a tree, slashed the pine needles off and ate them. She offered him some. He'd lived off the land before but this particular type of tree was new to him—as lunch.

He took the clump of pine needles and looked at it doubtfully.

Nat said, "Many parts are edible."

"I'll just watch you eat for a while, then, when you don't die, I'll eat mine." He walked along and finally ate the needles. They tasted awful.

He said, between bites of pine, "So, you were in America for long stretches before this last assignment. Mostly on the east coast."

"Yeah, after that I searched for white slavers. I was undercover as a helpless little lamb."

"I'd like to see that," Case laughed.

Nat said darkly, "I deserved an academy award. They sold me to some creep from Egypt of all places."

"Why of all places? There are dirt bags everywhere."

"Don't I know it?"

"So why not Egypt?"

"It just seemed like having a white wife in your harem would be noticed, you know? But this guy lived way out in the Sahara. On his own private oasis. He was a law unto himself."

"Were you a good little slave girl?"

Nat laughed, then caught herself and shook her head in a little back and forth motion. Case had seen her make that same movement nearly every time she laughed, like she'd done something that surprised her.

"I sucked at it. I suspect I was the worst slave in the history of the world. When I say he was a law unto himself I meant it. He was untouchable. We broke up the slavery ring but I couldn't bring the sheik to justice inside the system. I handled the problem myself."

Nat drew her knife out of her boot and examined the razor-sharp edge. "In the end, changes were made to my *master* that made him, shall we say... uninterested...in women. Permanently. That wasn't part of my job. I threw it in as a bonus."

Case laughed again and wondered if he might be falling in love. "And was the 'end' long in coming?"

"The end came right at the beginning. I brought six women out of that place with me. Two from America, two from England, one each from France and Switzerland. And ten children the six of them had given birth to. That only left him fifteen wives. The women I saved wanted to stay. Can you imagine? Considering the anatomical alterations I made, fifteen should be more than enough."

Case couldn't stop himself from laying his arm across her shoulders. He smiled at her and said, "You are my kind of woman."

Nat laughed, then shook her head. "I am no one's kind of woman. Trust me."

Case didn't agree. But he didn't say anything. He just leaned over and kissed her on the cheek and let her go. She looked at him for a while but she put her knife away without using it on him. Case took it as high praise.

The sun started dipping low in the sky as they walked and ate trees and compared notes.

They came to the first rocky stretch of the climb. They didn't need rock climbing equipment but the footing was poor and the rocks were all easily dislodged. They spent an hour adding a football field's length to their trek.

They reached a grassy plateau that stretched a mile in front of them. A craggy slope rose out of the plateau. It stretched off to the left and right as far as they could see. Above that the summit raised its massive head forever.

"We're going to have to stop and make some kind of camp and find some real food," Nat announced at around five o'clock. "Night gets cold up this high. I don't want to be caught out in the open. You look for a cave or an overhang in those rocks ahead. Then scout around, see if there's a game trail that goes up there." She pointed at the summit. "If we have to go straight up it'll take a long time to scale that rock face."

Nat kept giving orders. "Find the trail and a place to sleep and get a fire started. Make sure you gather enough wood for the whole night."

"What are you going to do?"

"I'm putting myself on food and water detail." Nat pointed to a place where the trees grew thicker and taller than the rest of the spindly growth on the rocky incline. "I'll look for a spring there and try to snare a rabbit or a grouse."

It took them an hour to reach the rocky outcropping. Nat headed off. "Don't pick a site near a spring, we'll have wild animals to contend with."

"Wait a minute." Case fished around in his duffel bag. "I kept those Coke cans we drank out of. Haul water back in them." Case handed them to Nat.

She walked away and he spent the next hour preparing camp. He found a cave that was just a space between a jumble of rocks. He felt like a badger climbing into the side of the mountain.

The cave was about ten feet wide and it was six feet high at the highest spot. There were enough solid rocks over their heads to keep the rain off, but there were open spaces in the roof near the lower end of the cave near the entrance so he could build his fire inside, out of the wind.

He cut pine boughs to use for blankets, and maybe have for breakfast. He gathered deadwood and, as the sun began to disappear and the air got cooler, he decided to light the fire to preserve the daytime warmth in their little home. He added to his firewood, scared a ptarmigan out of its nest and, with an expert throw of his knife, caught it before it took flight. He killed a rattlesnake and skinned it. Then he started the snake and the bird cooking on a spit over the open fire. He was so hungry it was all he could do not to tear into the bird as soon as the smell of cooking meat started wafting up from it. To keep his protesting stomach in line he got out the weights and worked until his appetite cooled and his muscles relaxed.

He was in a calmer state of mind, tending the supper when Nat returned.

Nat came back with three grouse and a wild turkey. She offered him the

Coke cans. "I drank my fill at the spring. Drink all of this and I'll go back for more."

"Just show me where it is. I could drink ten cans of water."

"A fungus will probably grow inside us because we drank unboiled water," Nat warned.

Case tipped the first can and finished it in four gulps. He hadn't realized how thirsty he was. "It wouldn't be the first time."

Case offered her the rattlesnake, which was the first thing done cooking, while he prepared her contribution. He couldn't help but laugh when she didn't comment on eating snake. The woman was a trooper.

They kept busy cooking and arranging the camp as best they could. Case was stuffed after they'd eaten about half the meat. Nat rearranged the spit to smoke the rest of their catch. Case went for more water. By the time he came back with two filled cans, it was bedtime.

Nat unsnapped her holster from her waist and pulled her gun out. She ejected the clip, checked the gun over, then slapped the clip back in place and lay the gun on the cave floor within inches of her hand.

Case raked part of the fire to the side, away from their turkey jerky and built the fire up, laying some thick chunks of wood on the top that would burn all night. Then he shrugged his shoulder holster off, checked his gun, put it within reach and lay next to Nat. He didn't pull her against him like he wanted to. He was afraid he'd reach out his arm and pull back a bloody stump. He'd wait until later, when she was cold.

Nat rolled up into a sitting position. "I'm never going to get to sleep. Hand me your weights."

"Nat, you're exhausted."

Nat made a sound of pure disgust and got onto her hands and knees. She reached across his body to the duffel on the other side of him.

Case sat up when she was stretched across him. "Don't tell me you haven't had enough strenuous exercise for one day." He wrapped one arm around her and pulled her to face him.

She looked past him to the bag, her eyes flitting between him and her goal.

"Nat, I know how you feel. I get itchy if I don't work out, too. But your arm's still not healed and we've climbed a mountain today. Go to sleep."

He thought for a minute she was going to commit bodily injury. Then she shook her head briskly like she was trying to dislodge something from her brain.

She gave the short little exhaled breath through her nose that passed for a laugh most of the time. "I know you're right. It's like they're calling to me from that bag."

Her eyes flickered lower, to his lips, then she pulled away from him and lay down, rolling on her side to face him. "We still haven't gotten anywhere on figuring out what precipitated the attack on us."

Case propped his head up on his elbow and looked down at her. He could see the firelight flickering in her impossibly beautiful eyes. "There's got to be something. We just haven't found the key, yet."

They lay silently. He watched her eyes glitter and sparkle in the dark cave. She let him watch. Finally, almost without making a conscious decision, Case reached his hand out to rest his open palm on her cheek. She didn't move away.

"Nat, your eyes. They're incredible." He touched one of her brows with his fingertip and slid it down her eyelid. She closed her eyes and he caressed the delicate lid, imagining he could feel the heat from those magical glowing eyes.

"You are incredible." He pressed his lips to hers. She returned the pressure for just a second then pulled back.

"We can't do this, Case. I don't think..."

Case drew a line from her eye around the curve of her cheek and touched her lips. She stopped talking.

"I know we can't. Not now. Not yet. We've got a lot to do and I don't want to put us in more danger by clouding our thinking with the distraction of..."

Her eyes blinked open as soon as his finger touched her lips and he was under her spell again. He fell silent. This time she moved first. She lifted her head from the ground. His exploring finger dropped away and she kissed him.

All the fire in her eyes transported itself and blossomed against his lips. He slid his hand around the back of her neck and pulled her mouth firmly against his.

The wilderness and the threat of death, the blood they'd shed and the cave, the firelight and the fire in her eyes coalesced, creating something primitive. Something Case had never known. It wasn't about sex. It was about connection. She wrapped her arms around his waist and pulled hard enough to lower his chest onto her. The feel of her under him was just perfect.

A piece of wood broke in the fire and sent a shower of sparks up through the chimney that nature had created for them. The noise and the color caught his attention and he broke the kiss.

They looked at each other. Lost from the world. Found together. Case leaned down and kissed her again soundly but quickly. His raspy voice was rougher than usual. "I don't know what's happening between us, Nat, but I like it. I want to explore it. Not just until we figure this out, but for however long it takes."

Nat smiled.

Case thought it was the saddest smile he'd ever seen.

"That's not how my life is," she said softly. "I'll clear this up and take my next assignment and I'll never see you again. I'm a woman who doesn't exist. I'm not allowed to lead a normal life. All my life is just...now. I'm not granted the luxury of a past and I don't make plans for the future. I don't let people matter to me."

He kissed her again, hard. When he pulled away he rolled onto his back and pressed her head down on his chest. She stayed right there where he put her. "Don't tell me this doesn't matter to you, Nat. I won't believe it."

He stroked his hand through her hair, pulling the ponytail holder out and tossing it into his open duffel bag. He smoothed her hair until he snagged his fingers in a snarl and couldn't get his hand back.

She pulled his hand away. Then she rubbed her cheek against his chest. "It's been a long time since I've let anyone hold me." She lifted her head up so she could look in his eyes again. "It's not like me to...involve myself with a man."

"I don't believe in scoring and my life doesn't allow relationships, so that leaves me with exactly nothing."

"Maybe it's just...I mean...maybe I look good to you because it's been so..."

He grabbed her chin and purposefully held her mouth shut.

"Don't insult me by saying I'm interested in you because you're female and handy. I'm not using you. It's more than that. I had offers in the last eighteen months. No woman interested me. I don't use women to solve crimes, but that doesn't stop me from wanting them. But for the last year and a half," he shrugged. "I haven't wanted anyone. I must be growing up."

Nat smiled and he let her go. She said lightly, "Maybe that's what we have in common. We like hard physical activity and we're celibate."

Case groaned and lay flat on his back, he pulled her with him so she curled up half on top of him, using him for a pillow. "That's probably why someone is shooting at us. That life sounds so boring I'd want to kill me, too."

Nat laughed. "I'm dying I'm so tired. If you don't let me sleep we may save our Dead Eye Dick assassin buddy the trouble."

"Dead Eye. You saw him then? In the Metro and chasing the semi? Got a good look?"

Case felt her nod against his chest.

"I'll never forget those eyes," Nat said. "It's like his soul has left his body but he's still walking around."

Case thought about that for a minute. "That probably explains it exactly, he sold it to the devil years ago."

"Go to sleep, Case."

As usual Case obeyed her.

Sloan called in his usual team. He falsified the necessary documents to request the use of a military jet and sent his boys to Denver.

The team had grown over the years. Sloan had studied criminal files. He'd reviewed the records of ex-military, particularly men who had washed out of the SEALs. He'd hand picked his underlings.

He'd begun slipping them Break Zone.

With help from Claudia's research and development team, he'd slightly altered the formula to make it highly addictive and before long they were his slaves. He'd used all the considerable power at his fingertips to get them past the security screenings and now they had FBI badges.

The altered formula awakened the most aggressive tendencies in his men. He'd watched them change into soldiers who would obey his orders without question. Who would kill without hesitation. Who would die without caring.

All for Break Zone.

All for the next hit that only he could supply.

All for Jerry Sloan.

He had no intention of waiting for Prometheus to drive to Denver. The inaction made Sloan's skin crawl. Garrison and Brewster had information that could bring him down. They didn't know it and if that fool Claudia hadn't told Prometheus to take that first shot at the pair in the Metro, they could have been left in ignorance for the rest of their lives. But it was started now. And Sloan was going to end it.

He had seven men on the plane. The two that had survived the first attack, the attack Sloan had arranged on the rooftop. Sloan had moved quickly once he'd realized what Claudia had done. Those two members of Sloan's team wanted to exact payment for their comrade's death. The team was tight. All of them would have been on the military transport if Sloan would have allowed it. When Sloan had asked for volunteers all nineteen stepped forward. These were his men. They would kill for him. They would die for him.

Sloan corrected that. He didn't want to delude himself.

They would kill or die for Break Zone.

CHAPTER TEN

Nat rolled sideways in her sleep. Her hand molded around her Glock. She was on her feet, crouched low with her back to the cave entrance before she made a conscious decision. Case was across the narrow crawl space from her. She didn't know what she'd heard but Case had heard it, too. That was enough confirmation for her. He nodded at her and she left her post at the door, holstered her gun and threw loose dirt on the smoldering fire to kill the glow and cut off as much of the smoky smell as possible.

Nat's eyes adjusted to the dark, well enough to see that Case never moved. His attention was riveted on the cave mouth. Nat finished with the fire and, thinking to the future, pulled the smoked meat off its spit. She moved back to the cave entrance and Case took over. He slung his duffel bag over his shoulder and head so it crossed his chest. He quickly took the meat from her and shoving it unwrapped into the bag. He put their Coke cans in. Everything else was already packed, in preparation for rapid escape.

Nat didn't even know what she'd heard. But it was human. It was close. It was hunting.

Case jerked his head. Nat went down on her belly and slithered out.

She moved immediately to the side, scanning every shadow. Defining every sound.

She didn't wait for Case. If he waited for her, he deserved to die. She moved stealthily, taking advantage of every inch of the pitch black night. She headed straight up the rock face. She tested every foothold, mindful of scattering rocks. She chose the path of darkness, used every possible inch of cover.

Sometimes she slid up stones flat on her stomach. Sometimes she went around boulders taking advantage of the chance to put stone between her and whoever was out there. She moved silently, never making a noise, not even fabric against stone. Ready, every moment, for a bullet to slam into her back.

Case saw the tip of Nat's boot disappear into the inky night. She headed left. He went right. He didn't make a sound. He didn't hear Nat moving. He would have been disappointed if he had. He sidled along the base of the cliff for a few yards hoping two moving targets, some distance apart, would divide the hunters. He knew Nat would think the same thing.

The night before, he had studied the craggy rocks that sheltered them. He found the huge, rounded boulder that had marked the base of a gentler slope and started up. He eased himself, step by step. Going only by touch. He felt himself leave the safety of the level ground behind. The slope got steeper and, without seeing, he knew he now dangled far above the meadow they'd crossed the afternoon before.

A twig snapped ten inches above his left ear. He didn't think, he reacted. He grabbed at the sound and closed his hand over a booted ankle. A hard tug and a man slid down on top of him. Case pulled the man, hand over hand, downward. The man turned to face him and Case felt the keen edge of a knife slice across his chest. Case fumbled for the slashing hand. Fastening first on an elbow, diverting a second thrust. Then he found a wrist. In desperate silence the two battled. Neither was trained to call for help. Neither wanted to reveal his position. Case jammed his forearm into the man's throat. With a sudden twist he slammed the knife back and down.

Case's attacker stiffened. Case felt the man's throat work against his arm, struggling for air. With sudden decisive intent, Case released the pressure on his adversary's neck and a harsh, broken scream escaped. Case caught the front of his shirt and tried in the dark to see the man's face. A black ski mask.

Case yanked off the mask and looked into the eyes of someone he'd never seen before. Case memorized the rigid features, then the coiled muscles of his attacker relaxed and Case heaved him away from the cliff.

Case didn't wait to hear him land. Case moved sideways, away from the people he'd summoned to the spot by allowing the scream. Away, but not far. Case had never been much of a one to run and hide.

Case found a crevice in the rock face. He pushed his body into the cleft and waited for the men he heard above and below him to merge at the spot of the scream. After a few moments he realized they weren't doing it. But someone seemed to be moving sideways up the slope directly toward him. Either they were very smart or they were tracking him. Case knew the latter wasn't possible but he'd tangled with the whipcord muscles of the man he'd fought. The man had been coming toward him. Unerringly finding him in the starless night. They had to still be bugged somehow. Which meant right now, they were also headed straight for Nat.

Case resisted the urge to go to her. Protect her. Instead he prepared for the next attack. He realized he still clutched the black face mask in his hands. He envied their assailants the black clothing. He also saw a glistening darkened patch on his blue plaid shirt and remembered he'd been cut. He didn't have time to see how deep the gash was. He took the ski mask and shoved it up inside his T-shirt. He tucked his T-shirt in tight and clamped his forearm down hard on the cut, to stem the flow of blood, or at least prevent him from leaving a trail of blood that someone could follow tomorrow. Assuming there was a tomorrow.

Nat heard a choked scream slightly below her and off to her right. She'd known Case three days. He was not a man who would scream. He'd found one of them and he'd reduced the odds. He'd also given away his position.

She didn't go help. In the dark it would be easy to mistake him for the enemy. But that's not why she stayed away. It would be insulting to rescue him. She refused to demean him like that. She continued her ascent.

She knew where Case was. The scream came from twenty feet to her right. Case would be long gone. He'd be moving up and away from her. She heard a buckle rattle two steps above her. A buckle like the harness of an automatic rifle sliding off someone's shoulder. To repay Case the favor of giving away his position, she plunged straight up, mindless of the steep rocks. Mindless of noise. She fastened her hand on someone's belt. Before she threw him down the mountain, she made sure he'd stay down. She caught his rifle as he plummeted. She slung his gun across her back, not letting the buckle clatter like her pursuer had, and climbed on. Two down. How many to go?

She heard two more directly below her. Following like bloodhounds who had caught a scent. Another one off to the side, not heading for the spot Case had been. One overhead - directly overhead - about two hundred feet. Four of them. All perfectly aligned with Nat and Case's position. They knew exactly where she was. These men had to be tracking them electronically.

A line of rock shattered four feet over her head. Automatic rifle fire! She kept climbing, grimly heading straight for the spot the bullets had hit.

She realized she'd miscounted. There was one standing on the plateau below spreading searching fire along the cliff.

They were very well equipped. She shifted the long gun on her shoulder. It was an M16. A soldier's weapon like the one that had fired at her. But they must not have night vision goggles or she'd have been picked off like a duck with its webbed feet frozen into the lake. Still they had a good bead on her. The gunfire had been close, very close.

Nat climbed and sifted information, trying to gain the shelter of the line of boulders along the top of this rock face. She wanted to turn and pitch her pursuers down beside their friend but that might give her exact position away. Not a good idea when there was an M16 in the mix.

There was another burst of machine gun fire. This one, ten feet above her head. She had the macabre satisfaction of knowing her attackers thought she was climbing faster than she was. It made her mad to realize three of them were after her, counting the one she'd tossed off a mountain, and one below was shooting at her. Finally, a woman given some respect. Great time to start.

When she got done making dog food out of these punks, she was going to make sure Case knew he must have seemed like a weenie because they were trying to take her out first.

She was always cranky after a shoot-out.

She also made sense out of the sound that had awakened her. It had been the sound of a well-muffled helicopter. Which could mean these seven assailants had friends.

Case heard the gunfire. It was right where Nat would be. He didn't care how good she was, an M16 didn't respect anyone.

His reflex was to rush in on a white charger and battle every one who tried to hurt her. He'd throw his body over hers and take the bullets for her.

Case had been controlling his reflexes for a long time.

He carefully controlled his breathing so not a sound escaped his throat. He heard the movements of a man who was good, but not great. He forced himself to wait until the last possible second then he lunged out of his hole straight for the man's throat. A knee caught him in the stomach, close enough to his brand-new knife wound to send numbing pain to his arms.

His grip loosened and a fist slammed into his face with the force of a sledge hammer. Case fell sideways against the cliff and started sliding down. Case lost his hold and plunged out over thin air.

Nat heard the crackle of a walkie-talkie and a barely audible whisper over her head. "You're getting too close to me. Hold the searching fire."

Nat smiled. Whatever tracking device they had on her wasn't exact enough to shoot wildly a hundred yards upward with your assault team near the target. She heard the muted sounds of a scuffle off to her right. Case had found another one.

She doubled her efforts to be silent and scaled steadily upward. The rock face was nearing an end. She saw the rugged gray vanish in the pitch black of the mountain night.

She didn't veer from her course. She wanted them to head for her and divert their attention from Case. The ones down below were good. Only her acute sense of self-preservation made her aware of the stirring in the air ten feet down.

She picked up her pace, hoping to pull the two men following her apart.

She came to the top of the cliff. She knew there was someone waiting there. She eased herself back a few feet, listening to the men coming from below. She picked her position, annoyed that she wasn't wearing something that concealed her better. She had a boulder to her right and a gnarled tree that grew out of the rock face, to her left. Close enough to protect her on three sides, but not close enough to hem her in when she needed to move.

One of the men coming from below had outpaced the other. Then she heard a third assailant coming from the direction she'd heard the scuffle. He was making too much noise for it to be Case. So, Case hadn't won. Her stomach twisted. She felt like she had lost something at the exact moment she'd found it.

For a second, she wondered what she was fighting for. Then she was furious. They'd killed a good man and he wasn't going to die for nothing. She braced herself for the attack. She'd take them with her if she couldn't win. She heard the man coming quickly from the right—eager to be in on the kill. She wanted him the most. He'd killed Case and he wasn't going to live long enough to enjoy it. She pulled her Glock from her waistband. She lifted her knife from her boot.

Case caught the webbing on the gear bag his assailant wore. The only thing between him and a fall to his death, the body of a man who was trying to kill him.

Case swung against the cliff again and rolled across the man. His attacker landed a numbing blow to the base of his neck. Case drove his fist into the ribs of the attacker. The man's position was right so Case's fist came in under his ribcage. It knocked the wind out of him and Case followed up with a knee in his groin and his knife.

The soft grunt of death shot Case's adrenaline off the charts. He'd been running on training and determination. But now the furious blood lust that hit him in the midst of a battle roared through his veins. His chest quit hurting. He ruthlessly stripped the man he'd killed of his weapons. Case shoved two pistols, an M16, a stiletto and a garrote into his duffel bag. He took his assailants walkie-talkie, his webbed utility belt. He pulled the man's black shirt off and put it on. He confiscated everything of value and a few things just to be perverse, then left the man laying where he was. If whoever left them here in a helicopter wanted to come in and do a clean up, he wasn't going to make it easy for them by leaving them all neatly at the bottom of the cliff.

Then he headed for Nat and the four men who were focused on her. His male ego pinched a little that they seemed to think two men could handle him while they sent four after Nat. That mistake was going to be one they didn't live to regret.

He wished he had a white charger.

Nat brought her feet up most of the way to her chest. She braced one foot against the boulder, one against the tree. She didn't want anyone grabbing an ankle until she could reach him.

The man coming from the right was going to be late. Good she'd have him to herself. Then she'd climb up and break the creep on top of the cliff in half and climb down and feed the M16 to that lazy jerk on the plateau. If he wanted a woman who was half way up a mountain, he'd better be prepared to climb.

A head, covered with a ski mask finally became visible beneath her. She shoved against the boulder and tree and brought the full force of both her legs right into his face. He fell backward and was still falling when the second one was on her.

Her legs were extended now. She rammed her knee into his jaw. Her attacker slipped backward a few feet, then caught at her, fastening an iron grip around her calf. She saw the flash of metal and deflected the descending knife with her own. The man parried and blocked her blade. For an endless second they battled, the scrape and clash of steel on steel echoed around them. She thrust and heard fabric rip. She felt the nasty slice of his blade on her arm. She hammered her fist into his face, parried his swirling knife, caught an upper cut to her jaw and saw that blade rocketing toward her heart.

The pressure of his weight on her disappeared. She heard the repellent cracking she recognized as a neck being snapped. She whirled toward the third attacker.

Her wrist froze as it hit an immovable object. Case caught her arm just before she slit his throat.

Nat smiled. She was so happy to see him alive that she threw her arms around his neck and kissed him. Then she said in a voice that didn't carry beyond his ears. "You take the one over head. I'm going to kill the one who's been taking potshots at me down below. He's makin' me mad."

Case said, "I've got a better idea." He handed her a flashlight.

She knew exactly where he'd gotten it.

Case said, "Give them something to aim at."

Nat shook her head, "They'll think its one of their own people."

Case produced a walkie-talkie. "I'll tell him otherwise."

Nat smiled when she heard the wicked menace in his voice. She could feel the vibration of his tense muscles and pounding heart. He was a warrior in battle. She kissed him again. He acted like he was expecting it this time. He wrapped one arm around her waist, lifting her from her feet for a moment. His mouth opened. Hers opened under his. He pulled back and said, "I can picture you as a Viking warrior woman. A Valkyrie."

"In this fantasy do I have to wear horns on my head?"

Case kissed her quick. "You bet."

"Okay," Nat said grudgingly, "But the day anyone says, it must be over, Nat's singing, I'm gonna do some damage."

"Deal," Case whispered.

"Anyway, I've always pictured myself as more of a one-woman Mongol Horde."

Case pushed her away and swatted her butt. "Get going."

She went down about twenty feet. She heard the crackle of the walkie-talkie but she didn't hear what he said. It didn't matter. Case would know just the thing to say to make people want to kill him. She turned the flashlight on and moved quickly away. She had cleared about five feet of space between her and the light when the wuss, Mr. Plateau Sitter opened fire. He missed the flashlight, the moron.

A burst of fire from over head blew the poor defenseless flashlight to pieces. The M16 below her fired with a burst of sparks. He might as well have painted a target on his forehead. She jerked her own newly acquired assault rifle up and took him out with one shot. The gunfire overhead fell silent two seconds later.

Nat started for the top.

Case was there to pull her over the crest.

They tumbled to the ground together.

"I thought they had you." She wrapped her arms around his neck.

He grunted in disgust. "They only sent two guys for me. They sent four after you."

"Five." Nat shed the M16 because she had a trigger digging into her butt. "But let's share the one at the top and you dragged one off of me, plus we share the one at the bottom. That's four for you and five for me."

"You may be able to overpower five armed men but your math sucks. There were only seven of them. You just named nine. Are all the stories you've told me exaggerated like that?" he asked suspiciously.

Nat laughed.

Case made a purely rude snorting sound. "I have my pride you know. That's the only reason I came and helped out. You could have handled it but I wanted to get my share. That's five for you and five for me."

"We're up to ten men now. Man, we're good." Nat remembered that flashing knife. She had seen it coming down. She realized she could see Case now, the slightest graying of the black sky hinted at the approaching dawn.

She quit laughing and whispered, "That guy you pulled off of me, he had me, Case. You saved my life."

She wrapped her arms around him.

He kissed her, then pulled away. "You know you're right. Where is a white charger when I need one?"

"Huh?"

"Never mind." He pushed both of his hands into the rat's nest that passed for her hair, finding an occasional twig or rock. She wrapped her arms around him so hard she knocked him over and they slid over the edge of the cliff.

On the second day Case was missing, Carlos Lorenz put two men on the case. Only two. The only two men he trusted in the whole world now that Case was missing. One was Argus Westport. The other was himself. Carlos wasn't working officially and Argie wasn't even an agent.

Argie threw a fit when Lorenz said Case Garrison was in trouble. He was busy and he thought Case could take care of himself.

Lorenz took great pleasure in telling Argie he was whining like a stinking, wet diapered baby. "We were SEALs together. You're going to stab Case in the back just so your schedule doesn't get messed up?"

"Brotherhood is going to cost Westport E-Systems two point three billion dollars," Argie complained. "That's two point three, jerk. Billion with a 'B'. You ever been in the same state with that much money? How'd you get my number anyway, loser?" Argie slammed the phone down without asking when and where.

Lorenz left the office. He requisitioned an F-22 fighter jet, jockeyed it himself and headed for the meeting place. Case hadn't really stayed close with his old SEAL buddies and most of them were half nuts anyway. But Lorenz and Argie had stayed in touch. Argie had parlayed his computer fixation into a multibillion dollar, multinational dot com company.

They didn't have to decide where to meet. Lorenz and Argie had a system that never failed. Almost.

They met in the next state in the alphabet. They met in the city that *should be* its capital. That meant in Alaska, they'd met in Anchorage, not Juneau. In Alabama, they'd met in Mobile. California had screwed up their system because Argie lived in San Francisco and was adamant that Frisco should be capitol. Of course, Lorenz had gone to L.A. They'd never found each other.

Lorenz reflected that just maybe Argie was a little crazy too.

They were up to Nevada. Lorenz was on his way to Vegas.

Argie was waiting at the farthest north corner of the nicest restaurant in the biggest Hilton Hotel in the city. This was also part of the plan. It still burned Lorenz to think how long he'd sat in the Hilton in Los Angeles waiting for his friend.

Fortunately, that hadn't been about life and death.

"What's going on?" Argus Westport was sitting, smugly sipping some overpriced glass of bottled water—smug because he'd gotten there first.

Lorenz sank into the plush bench, talking before his backside hit the cushions. "Someone took a shot at Case two days ago. He survived the hit, but he's dropped out of sight."

Argie leaned forward. "He hasn't contacted you?"

They both knew what that might mean.

"I don't think he's dead. He left the scene under his own steam. He's got a woman with him, unidentified. I know she's an agent—or at least some kind of cop—from the eye witness reports of the way she handled herself. I have her fingerprints. No match."

"She's CIA."

Lorenz shrugged, then nodded, "Or something like that. Case got himself a spook."

"You're sure she's not part of it?"

Lorenz outlined all he knew. He held nothing back. Argie went beyond national security.

"Sloan's the key." Argie beckoned a waiter.

Lorenz didn't bother to agree. He'd been thinking along those lines exactly. "I need you to do a money trail. If he's dirty you can bet he's hiring his wet work done. Sloan's gutless."

The waiter approached the table and they fell silent as Argie took thirty seconds to order for both of them. He wanted two of whatever was the most expensive thing on the menu in every course. Appetizer. Salad. Entrée. Dessert. Drink. Sometimes he made the restaurant trot out a wine for every course. Not when they were working.

Lorenz got designer water and exotic foamy coffee.

The waiter left. Lorenz said, "I also want that woman if I can get her."

Argie said, "If she's a spook, Quantico won't like it if we push too hard."

"That's exactly why I'm doing it. I don't expect any formal help from them but informally, I want them on the job. I'll push until I'm sure they're paying attention."

Argie nodded. "Testy spies having their cover threatened. This could get interesting."

"Worth two point three billion easy, right?" Lorenz smiled at Argie.

Argie sniffed. "Chump change."

"I taught you everything you know about computers," Lorenz reminded him. "I even gave you the idea for E-Systems."

"Why do you think I'm paying for dinner?"

Lorenz nodded, satisfied. He sipped his cafe mocha latte. It was one hundred and ten percent caffeine. He drank five cups of it while they ate and planned. It was late afternoon and he'd never sleep, but he hadn't slept since Case had gone missing so it didn't matter.

CHAPTER ELEVEN

Nat pulled them both back. "I saved you. Now we're even. We'd better move."

In the approaching dawn, Case easily saw the huge grin on her face. Case thought back to their first meeting two days ago. It had to be two days because he'd slept with her twice now. It seemed like he'd known Nat for years.

"Move," she ordered.

The woman was predictable. And just when he'd started to think something he hadn't predicted might be happening, he almost fell off a cliff.

"We're still bugged." Nat found the man who'd been guarding the top of the cliff. She stripped him of his gear.

He had a light jacket on. She took that. Case took his shirt. "The guy's a bean stalk with clown feet or I'd take his shoes and pants, too."

"Let's take them just so he looks stupid lyng here naked."

Case laughed, then he looked closer at the dead man. "Look at his arms. They're about twice normal size." Case crouched beside the body. He touched the muscles, now relaxed in death.

Nat tipped the head to the left and right. "His neck muscles are so huge his neck is thicker than his head. Look at this guy. He's Mister Universe."

"The one I fought with was strong, too. I didn't think that much about it at the time. But his muscles bulged almost like this. I suppose they're just in really top condition, but I wonder if there is steroid use involved here. Maybe we've stumbled into some drug ring." Case looked thoughtfully at Nat.

She nodded, then shrugged. "I like to stay in shape, too. It's probably just part of their training. Anyway, I didn't notice it on any of the one's I fought. I didn't pay much attention to tell the truth."

She stood up. "We've got to keep moving. The chopper that dropped them off will be back. They're too well financed. I don't believe this is all of them, and we're still bugged somehow."

Nat bent over their assailant, checked the man's pockets and found a twenty dollar bill in one of them.

Case looked at her firm, feminine backside as she picked the man's pocket. His heart grew a couple sizes and heated ten degrees. She was one of a kind.

"Okay, where's the bug?" Nat started jogging quickly across a new plateau—this one maybe two miles across. Case fell in beside her. They'd run most of the distance when the sun finally came over the top of the summit. Case glanced at the watch he'd taken from one of the team. He stopped—frozen to the spot.

Nat noticed and turned. "What?"

"They were fibbies, Nat. Think about it. They moved like a strike force. They have all the standard equipment."

"It's a big, mean world, Case. Anyone can outfit a crew like that. M16s are there if you can afford them."

Case shook his head, still thinking. "They were official. But the FBI doesn't do assassination attempts on agents. They are a rogue squad. Someone has recruited them to work privately."

"Then the one's on the roof, after we left the hospital? Those were agents, too?"

"But not Dead Eye Dick. He's a professional hitman." Case looked at Nat.

"I agree on the hitman. So, what good does it do us to know if the others were bad seed agents?"

"Maybe not agents. Maybe they're washouts."

Nat turned away from Case and looked at the next stretch they needed to climb. She put her hands on her hips, staring at the sheer, rugged mountain in front of them. "What did we want to talk to your friend for?"

Case stared at the daunting rock face.

Nat said, "Hand me some jerky." She turned to Case. Her eyebrows rose nearly to her hairline.

"I didn't know you'd been injured!"

Case looked down. He'd forgotten too.

The black shirt he'd taken made the blood less noticeable.

Nat reached for his T-shirt, lifting the hem. "Have you still got the bandages in your bag?"

Case stayed her hands. "Let's find a secure place to sit before we look at this. I want my back to the wall."

They climbed the craggy rocks in front of them. Hiked across the next plateau until they reached the next rock face and chose a spot at the bottom. Case pulled off the black shirt he'd swiped from his attacker. His gut twisted at the amount of blood on his white T-shirt.

Nat said, "Take your clothes off. I want to get a look at your chest."

Case made his voice deep, husky, wildly lustful. "You don't know how long I've been wanting to hear you say that."

Nat laughed.

Case pulled off his shirt, going easy where the blood had dried the shirt to his wound. It wasn't bad. Five inches long running diagonally just below his left nipple. Not deep. No stitches required. He couldn't believe it, but she looked a little pale at the sight of the mean little gash. She certainly quit laughing.

He looked down at himself reassessing the wound. On closer inspection it was still a paper cut. "It's a scratch. I want to put more space between us and the place the helo set down. We'll slap a Band Aid on it later. Let's get going."

Case noticed her right arm was slashed high up on the back. She didn't seem to care whether her arm fell off or not. He left the white shirt and his blue plaid shirt behind. "We don't need to worry about leaving a trail. They're on us anyway, right?"

"Right," Nat said severely.

They ate half of the jerked meat as they walked along the rock face. They found a little spring gushing out of a fissure in the rocks. Nat insisted on washing. Case called her a prima donna, but he washed too just to neutralize what threatened to become a lifestyle of blood and filth.

They drank deeply to hydrate.

"If we keep losing blood at this rate, we'll be drained by the end of the week," Case said, downing his fourth Coke can of water even though he was bursting with it.

They rested by the spring for a while. Case was dreading the rigorous climb ahead of them but he wasn't about to admit it.

They scaled side by side for about twenty feet when Nat found what had to be a mountain goat trail. It was so narrow and steep that the thought of traversing it was appalling. The only thing more formidable was going straight up. It was over a hundred feet of sheer granite.

They reached the top just as the sun rose to its fullest height. A new plateau, more rugged and not as wide was in front of them. There were more trees here than in the meadow below. Then another craggy outcropping beyond the trees. There were a series of five of these giant steps between them and the summit.

"If we push, we can reach Grizzly Bluff by dark. Bannock may be there, but he always said he wanted a house in the mountains. I'm guessing he's got a vet clinic of some kind outside of town. And he'll be good in the woods. The guys in his unit told me he did a lot of bird watching, brought home injured raccoons, nursed an occasional wolverine back to good health." Case grinned at her. "He should be more than able to help you."

She backhanded his arm, but didn't beat him up, so he counted his blessings.

"I think if we get close to him, he'll find us."

He shifted the heavy duffel and started forward. He didn't know any other way to live.

"While we walk tell me more about your work, Nat. Let's be orderly about this. Let's start from our most recent cases and go back. We can't find any connection between Afghanistan and my terrorists. What did you do before that?"

Nat started talking. Case interrupted her to question any reference she made that might fit with something he'd done. The mountain, slowly, painfully gave up its higher regions to their assent.

They lost track of the time as they sweat, scrambled, and sometimes crawled. As they neared the summit a dip in the mountain revealed a view of the other side and they saw a paved road curving along the far side of the mountain.

"That's the way to town, I'm guessing." Nat studied the meandering road.

"Yeah, but we don't dare go in until we figure out how we're being tracked." Case sank down onto the rugged ground and eased his duffle bag off his shoulder.

"So that means we can't ask directions. We have to find Bannock ourselves."

"It's going to be cold tonight. We'll need shelter but I don't want to be cornered like we were last night." Case said.

"Too bad they don't aim a heat beam on us from one of our spy satellites."

"Heat beam? What, like a laser?" Case had never heard of that.

"No, it's about the weather. In the fifties the government got sick of always talking about the weather and decided to do something about it."

Case switched his bag to his other shoulder. "Another tall tale? Great, let's hear it."

"Telstar was launched in 1962."

"Is this a history lesson or do you have a point?"

"You don't really think forty years of crop failure in the Soviet Union was an accident, do you?"

"The crops failed because the Communist system failed."

Nat said vaguely, "Whatever."

Case shrugged off her ominous response. "We're going to have to start deciding where we want to fight next."

"We just plan on being attacked every morning...what? For the rest of our lives?"

"There's a bright side." Case scanned the area for shelter.

Nat looked all around them. "I can't imagine what it is?"

"Our lives probably won't be that long."

Nat nodded her head slightly with a resigned frown on her face. She pointed toward a clump of white pines. "How about in there. The trunks are so close together it's almost walled. But we can squeeze out anywhere. We'll rig some snares, some early warning alarms. We'll take turns standing watch."

"Sounds good." Case went to work setting up camp. Nat went in search of food.

The night seemed to come even more quickly up this high. As Case worked a thick haze drifted in making everything ghostly. He lit a fire, hesitating over something that would give their position away so easily, then went ahead with it. When it was blazing he listened for Nat, sure she'd find her way back but wishing she'd get on with proving it.

Case had no luck finding food. He didn't lay his snares out. His human snares. He wouldn't set them until Nat returned. She had to know exactly where they were in the likely event they had to hightail it out of here in the middle of the night.

Nat called out, "Hello, the camp," before she came into view.

Case thought that was wise considering the tension level.

She tossed five underage ptarmigans on the ground, already plucked and gutted.

Case said, "I wanted steak. Try again."

She laughed, shook her head and lowered herself to a log Case had dragged near the fire. "I'm tired. Eat the birds or starve."

"Wimp." He cut the meat off in thin strips so they'd cook faster and started them roasting.

Nat said, "Okay, assuming we're going to be attacked again before dawn, we're not going to sleep until we figure out how they're tracking us."

Case propped the meat as close as he dared to the fire, tending them as he considered. "There cannot be someone tailing us, can there? I mean physically tailing us, by air or with a telescope?"

Nat said, "We hopped on a plane at a busy airport, miles from the highway a couple of hours after we got off that truck. I don't know how they did it but somehow, they made that connection to Denver. But how did they make that mountainside? The only explanation that doesn't involve a tracking device is that they guessed you'd come here."

"If they did, then they are tracing every whisper thin lead from my life back twenty years. It doesn't seem possible."

"And you're sure you kept nothing that could have a tracking device in it? No picture of your mama? No locket from your high school sweetheart?"

"I wish I had because it would give us a possibility."

Case shook his head. "Let me take a look at your shoulder."

"It's fine. We need to keep thinking about the bug."

"For once will you just do what I want?" Case said in exasperation. "We can talk while I clean up that cut."

Nat shrugged and turned her back to Case. She pulled one arm out of her shirt.

She had washed the cut well earlier. He put a bandage on the wound. If they were near civilization he might have suggested some stitches, mainly to minimize the scarring. His sewing would probably make it worse. Thinking about scarring made him study her back and see all those mean scars again and it hurt him to look at them. Her jeans rode low on her hips so he saw a few sweet inches of her nicely rounded derriere. Only it wasn't flawless either. She had an odd scar that looked like an X with each leg about an inch long. It was jagged, like she'd been attacked with a serrated knife, but a neat bright red line bisected the scar perfectly. It was right above her hip bone about an inch below the waistline of her jeans.

He had one just like it in exactly the same place.

"Hold on." He pushed her jeans lower. "Let me see this."

She jerked her head around to see him hovering over her. He distantly noticed her movement because what he was looking at was too interesting.

"Back off, Case. I'm too tired for any..."

He cut her off. "I've got this scar."

"Big deal, I've got a dozen scars, some of them are bound to match yours, we make a living in a high-risk business. If you're not going to fix my arm, I'm getting dressed." She shoved her arm back into her shirt and slid away from him.

He wasn't done with her arm but he let her put the shirt on because this was more important than the shoulder wound. "You're not listening to me. I've got this exact scar. Same place, same shape, same size, same fine, red line, like a surgical incision right down the center of it. How did you get it?"

She twisted around to look at her scar, first over her shoulder, then under her arm. "I got it just before I went on my last assignment. It was nothing. Just a fluke. Not like the rest of them. I earned all of them."

"What fluke, tell me?" He turned her around to face him.

She shook off his grasping hands and hiked up her jeans. "It was a car accident. Nothing to do with the job. I fell asleep at the wheel—"

His gasp cut her off. He prompted her, "Go on, you fell asleep..."

"I ran my car into the ditch. The doctors told me a piece of metal snapped off a guard rail and managed to come through the back window and slice through the driver's seat from behind."

Case dropped from his knees until he was sitting. He held her gaze, his mind rabbiting from one scenario to another.

Finally, she said, "You've got this exact scar?"

His heart started pounding hard, so hard it was difficult to breathe. He shook his head in disbelief then, spurred to action, he pivoted, unsnapped his jeans and folded them down on his left side.

He felt her fingers run along the weird scar he'd gotten eighteen months ago. Then he remembered what else she said, "You got it eighteen months ago? Exactly?" He fastened his jeans and turned around to look at her.

She nodded and asked, "That's when you got yours, too?"

"A year and a half ago, two days after Christmas."

"In a car accident?" She asked, but it wasn't really a question.

"I fell asleep at the wheel. I've never fallen asleep driving in my life," he said firmly.

"What is this?" Her hand reaching behind her to touch the scar.

"What it is, is something we have in common."

"You don't suppose..." her voice faded.

It twisted his stomach when he guessed what she was thinking. He didn't want to say it out loud either. But it was there in the air between them.

She found the guts first. "A tracking device?"

Case stood suddenly, his fists clenched. Then he started shaking his head. "We're just guessing. It could be anything. Let's don't go off halfcocked."

"But there has to be a tracking device somewhere. They know exactly where we are. It's happened too many times."

"We've got to do something. We've got to know." Grim determination settled the nausea in his stomach.

The sibilant whoosh of his knife being drawn seemed to fill the mountain night. He held it out to her, turning the handle toward her. "There's only one way."

Millie crouched behind a huge saguaro cactus, one of her favorite photographic studies.

Sometimes a deer stopped in the spring to drink just before dusk. She focused her camera and sat down to wait. The deer were especially precious to her because there used to be more of them. When she'd first moved here there'd been a dozen deer a night. The number had dwindled, probably because of the presence of humans.

The spring had become a beautiful pond because of Matthew's digging for adobe. The sparse desert greenery had flourished around it and for a while the wildlife had flourished, too. But now the wildlife had been scared off and Millie took the responsibility for that. She hoped they came back after she died.

Millie leaned against the rock she'd come to prefer to an easy chair and rested her camera on her knee. Some days she wanted landscapes, today she wanted close-ups. Her zoom lens was on full strength. She visualized the muzzle of a deer, the drops of spring water running down its velvety nose. She wanted it all on film. She looked through the zoom lens again, determined to catch even the bumble bees and scorpions on film. Even the stinging creatures of the desert had their own unique beauty.

She studied the spring, which was unusually low as the long days of summer dragged on. Through the viewfinder she studied a bright red splash of color at the water's edge. At first, she thought it might be a blooming cactus. As she looked she finally realized it was some kind of litter.

Indignant, she wondered who'd thrown it there. It was in the side of the hole Matthew had excavated digging adobe. She hated to pick it up now because she might leave enough scent behind to frighten the wildlife. She'd miss her picture, but more importantly, if she frightened them badly, they might miss their only drink of water for the day. She checked around her, she still had a few minutes before the deer showed up. Disposing of the garbage would only take a second.

She stood and walked briskly over to the pond and plucked at the scrap of paper. It didn't budge. She knelt beside it and saw that it was really a plastic bottle. She worked at the bottle with her fingers. The muddy sand gave way easily and she soon had a cylindrical container in her hand. It was around the same size as a two liter Coke bottle but the top was flat and just as big around as the bottom. And the plastic was much heavier, almost like a Thermos jug. The seams were split in the container and any contents that had been there, were gone. She saw more red in the bottom of the hole she'd dug. She looked at the bottle she held, knowing she didn't have time to dig up the next one before the animals came.

Annoyed at the disrespect someone had shown this beautiful place, she walked back to her hideout. She looked thoughtfully at the container as she waited, then she refocused her camera and snapped a shot of each side of the bottle.

The word Break Zone was blazed in white across the red container. In smaller print Millie saw the words: Contents 100 per cent Brachiiesterone. There was no company name, no clue to what Break Zone was. She suspected it was something to do with cars, Break Zone sounded mechanical. Maybe someone dumped their old oil cans out here years ago.

A prickle of fear made her spine itch just a little. It didn't look like any motor oil she'd ever seen. And the oddly shaped bottle suggested the contents were something unusual. She looked over at the pond, no deer had shown up yet. She'd probably disturbed things too much.

They'd miss a day of water because of her. She gave the can a disgusted look. No, she'd never been one for phony guilt. If she did it, she'd take the blame but these animals would go thirsty today because of Break Zone.

She picked up the container and headed back to her house for a shovel. She was going to get rid of the rest of the bottles, then she was going to get some answers.

CHAPTER TWELVE

Nat took the knife and looked from the blade to Case. Her jaw was so tense it hurt. She could barely force words out between her teeth. "It's not the blood, I can handle that. It's the whole idea that I'll be cutting you open, hunting for something. Maybe I'm shaky because of blood loss, I don't know, but I don't think I can do it. I'd rather you did it to me. I had some medic training when I did my SEAL rotation but I don't want to just start..." she couldn't control a shudder, "...digging around in your body."

Case looked glad for a distraction although he hadn't shrunk from offering her the knife and his back. "Look, I know women aren't SEALs. I was just kidding when I asked you about that."

"I didn't say I was a SEAL. I said I did a SEAL rotation. I had the same training a SEAL does." She hefted the knife. "I passed with flying colors too, even though I'm just a baby doll."

She quoted him and for the first time he looked a little wary as she wielded the knife so comfortably in her hand.

"I was just trying to get your fighting spirit up with that crack."

"We were arguing in a stairway when you first called me that. Why would you want my fighting spirit up?" she challenged him.

"I just had you so totally whipped, with me sitting there on top of you like that. You looked like you were about to wimp out on me at the time.

Start crying and begging. Kinda like now." He arched an eyebrow and waited for her to take the challenge.

She tested the knife with her thumb then took her own out of her boot. "Mine's got a better edge."

She had to swallow hard before she could make the next statement sound appropriately careless. "Lay down on your stomach."

He said lightly, "X marks the spot."

A blaze of anger roared through Nat when he said it. "Like we're some kind of road map."

"Or treasure map," Case suggested as he lay on the ground in front of her. Stretched out like he was, the nasty little crossed scar was below the waistline of his jeans.

"Or branded animals." Nat blew a couple of deep breaths in and out and searched for the detachment she could tap into with a second's notice when she was faced with a crisis.

A vein was doing a tap dance inside her left temple and her stomach seemed to be in permanent barrel roll mode.

Case had his arms folded under his head. His face was turned toward her. Watching.

She saw the utter stillness of his expression. The complete lack of emotion. He would do what he had to do. He would get through this without caring what she did to him. She decided coldly the least she could do was return the favor.

She went on a treasure hunt. She didn't have to hunt long. It was just under the skin. She saw something black the minute she made a slit. It was healed into the muscle, but with the least possible damage to Case, she withdrew a cartridge about the same size around and half as long as a double A battery.

She handed the bloody cylinder to him while she found bandages and patched him up.

"This thing has been inside of me for eighteen months," Case said quietly as he wiped the blood away from the little tube. He turned it around in his hand.

"Is it a tracking device?" Nat reached for it.

He gave it to her without answering. Then he sat up and said with great relish. "Your turn, baby doll."

Maybe he was still working on her fighting spirit but the way he said the insulting endearment warmed her heart. She lay down on her stomach, propping herself up on her elbows and turned the little cartridge over in her hands. He took her gun out of the holster she wore in the small of her back and handed it to her.

"Pretty brave, sweetie, when you're about to stab me in the back."

When he cut her, the vicious little stab of pain suited her mood perfectly.

In under a minute he said, "Done."

She sat up and they looked at the little black things that had been inside them like the larvae of some parasite. Nat knew tracking devices and this was definitely one. But there was more to it than that.

Case twisted the end of his. "It's got a little space inside filled with some kind of liquid. See the mechanism on the end, its similar to an insulin pump. This thing has been dosing us with something."

She took her knife away from Case and wiped the blood off on her jeans. She pried at a little clear plastic cover on the device, at the end away from the liquid. It snapped off and she detached a flat piece of plastic about an eighth of an inch square. "It's a computer chip."

He said, "The kind you find in a bug."

Nat stared at the little traitor she'd carried with her for so long. She was surprised at the waves of bitterness that swamped her.

"I'd like to save the liquid. I want a lab to run a test on it. But we don't need to save this," she dropped the chip on the ground and used the flat base of her knife handle to smash it.

She felt the sharp bite of her rage at being used like this. She hammered at the chip far longer than necessary. Then she gave a swift, satisfied jerk of her chin. She looked up at Case. "I enjoyed that. I recommend you pound on the other one for a while."

He obliged. When his chip was reduced to silicon dust he smiled at her. "Very satisfying. Thanks for giving me a turn."

She looked at him and at the cylinder. "What do you think we've stumbled onto here?"

"Something worth using humans as guinea pigs," Case said casually.

Nat wasn't fooled. The ice in Case's eyes when he was calmly letting his back be sliced open, had been replaced by fire. He was furious.

"Keep the rage in the bank for later, Case. Save it. Let it earn interest."

"I'm compounding as we speak," Case responded.

"Right now, we need clear heads."

He looked at her. "Right now, we need to be logical." The fire was still there and she could see he needed to let it out.

She looked back, a little overheated herself. "Right now, with the bugs disabled, we're safe for a while."

"Someone's been keeping track of me for the last year and a half without my knowledge. I feel like I've escaped from a prison I didn't know I was in. I want to celebrate." He smiled at her.

She smiled back. His eyes narrowed when she smiled and he looked at her eyes like he was lost in them. Her eyes were the bane of her existence. They were stupid, speckled and spooky and always a problem when she was undercover.

"Tiger eyes. Feline. They're stunning." Case spoke as if he was reading her mind and correcting her. He whispered her name and leaned closer, she imagined so he could get a closer look.

As long as he was so close, she kissed him.

She jumped away, shocked at herself. She'd just had a foreign object cut out of her back. This was no time for kissing.

He wasn't looking at her eyes anymore. The way he was looking at her lips made her throat go dry and she couldn't control the tiny, involuntary flick of her tongue over her lips.

She was sure she hadn't meant to issue him an invitation, but he took it as one. He rose up on his knees, buried his fingers deeply into her hair and pulled her head back.

He made a sound deep in his throat that was more animal than human as his lips descended on hers.

The last time she'd surprised herself, but this time she saw it coming. She didn't consider jumping away. She surged forward to meet him. She wrapped her arms around his neck and lost herself in the wonder of his touch.

He held her face with both hands. His thumb slid to her chin and he relentlessly dragged her mouth open. She tasted him and a part of her she'd forgotten in the years of hard, dangerous work and ruthless denial of emotions, caught fire.

She wanted to connect.

"Eighteen months." His grating voice surprised her. He spoke against her lips. Then he turned his head sideways and she kissed his cheek and his jaw and his throat.

He pushed her from him, holding her at arms-length. "Did you hear me?"

"What?" she didn't want to lose all his wonderful heat.

"Eighteen months," he was blatantly furious. All of his passion had turned back to rage. "It's been eighteen months since I've even thought of wanting a woman."

She still didn't get the point.

"The drug, Nat. Did it have anything to do with that? I haven't spent a single night aching for a woman in that time. Not until the minute that thing was cut out of me."

She started tumbling to earth as his words cleared the fog from her brain. "You...you said you'd been working out. Sometimes physical exertion sublimates the sex drive. Maybe that kept you from..."

"That's another thing. Exercise." Case let go of her and sank down to sit on the ground. Staring into space.

She could see his brain adding things together and coming up with a total that didn't include kissing her again. She was amazed how disappointed she was.

He said bitterly, "I've always stayed in shape but the last year and a half especially, it's been like I didn't have a choice."

"Like an exercise junkie." She focused on the evidence.

Case picked the cartridge up from where they'd dropped them. "That's it. I know it is. I can see now the way I've craved physical activity wasn't natural. And forgetting about sex isn't either. If I've thought about it at all, I've just thought I was getting older."

"So, you think taking those things out might be the reason you and I..." Nat didn't finish.

"A drug wouldn't leave your system that fast." He lay his large callused hand along her cheek. "I know you're the most interesting woman I've ever met. I don't want to wonder about anything that passes between us. I don't want to follow my instincts right now and wonder if what I feel is caused by some drug."

"That kiss felt very real to me," she whispered.

He leaned close and brushed his lips across hers. "It is real, Nat. I know it is. But I don't want us to ever doubt it."

She nodded and lay her hand on his, where he touched her face. She pressed his warmth into her face—into her body—into her heart.

Prometheus slammed on the brakes of his navy blue Dodge. The tiny blinking dot of light that had so faithfully led him through the Midwest and into the Rocky Mountains vanished.

He'd been closing the gap. He was in a rugged stretch of tree covered mountains. He pulled over and tried to calculate their last known location.

It was impossible. He sat on the edge of the two-lane blacktop road and fumed. Then he pulled back onto the road and poured his anger into pushing the Dodge as fast as it would go.

After five minutes he got his rage under control and slowed down. He didn't have time right now to kill a ticket-happy state trooper. He cruised on into the night. Planning as he drove.

He shouldn't have taken the bait with the tracking bug anyway. It wasn't his way. It was lazy. Now he'd have to start again. Circling the prey. Keeping all his sources wide awake.

He'd find them the normal way. He'd start by checking known acquaintances in this area. He'd start with Garrison because the woman was still an unknown entity.

They already knew they were being hunted, now they knew they'd been bugged, so they'd be doubly alert. They were professionals just like he was. Something hummed in his chest.

Anticipation. Challenge.

He thought about his burst of high-speed road rage and wondered about himself. He hadn't felt anything for years and he liked it that way. Why now? Why this case? He'd been expecting a sign that told him he needed to get out. Maybe this was it.

Lately he'd noticed people giving him a second look. He knew his eyes were starting to give away his dead emotions. Being average looking was a necessity in his line of work. These days he attracted attention.

His instincts had been warning him for the last year that he was losing his edge. And a man who killed people for a living had to have an edge.

Yes, it was definitely time to put his plan into action. He'd finish Brewster and Garrison and he'd go to his island.

He slammed on the accelerator again just to feel the rush. Was it these two contracts that were riling him? He let the car scream along for a long time. He wished he'd see red and blue lights flashing in his rear-view mirror so he could vent some of this emotion through the barrel of his gun. He savored it, his power over life and death, as he hadn't for a long time. When he'd started, every hit made him feel like God. He held life and death in his hands. Somewhere along the line even being God had gotten boring.

.He remembered how Claudia had enjoyed the pain he'd inflicted on her. He'd gone too far of course. But her screaming didn't bother him. She had wanted to play a high-risk game, he'd played.

She'd threatened and cried and finally begged for mercy, but when it was over she'd made plans to meet again to exchange the money. That could only mean one thing. She wanted to play again. It surprised him that he wanted it, too.

He finally slowed to the speed limit. He couldn't sustain the level of emotion. The ice flowed through his veins again and he picked up the phone to call Denver and start casting his net.

CHAPTER THIRTEEN

They left their campsite at first light. No one came to see them off for a change.

They covered every trace of their camp. Unlike yesterday when they just left their ruined clothes behind, today they had some hope that they could elude pursuit.

Nat thought they ought to start straight down the mountain, put as much distance between themselves and their last known location as possible. Case kept saying he wanted to find Bannock.

Nat didn't know what good he'd be. "He's probably not even here, Case. You're just guessing. We could hike around in these mountains for six months and never find him and you'd be saying…" She dropped her voice to a lower range and talked like a real dumb guy, "Bannock wanted his mommy."

Case replied, "I'm telling you he was obsessed."

"He's obsessed?" Nat rolled her eyeballs. "We're hunting for a man with the single direction 'up' and you say he's obsessed?"

"I want to talk to Bannock even more now, because he's a veterinarian. He'll know something about implanted devices like this. He might even be able to test the liquid and see what it is. When you think about it, if we run it through a lab that works with vets, we might be able to avoid a lot of the rules that apply to doctors in this situation."

Case added, "We still need to know why we had those things inside us. We need to know why someone's trying to kill us. We need some time to think and we need to be where no innocent bystander can get between us and a bullet."

Nat muttered, "Boy Scout." She walked beside him silently for a full minute before saying, "I'll give you one more day then I'm going to kick your butt down the mountain."

"Deal," Case nodded.

Late in the afternoon, they eased themselves down toward Grizzly Bluff and settled in to wait until sunset so they could sneak into town and try to find some evidence of Bannock's whereabouts.

Case studied the little town miles below them. It was so small they could never set foot in town in the daytime without being noticed. That meant going in at night. Breaking into a store that might have a plat map or at least a phone book—and those were getting hard to find. They had to wait. "If we go in there, it's still going to be impossible to find Bannock."

"Let's get the lay of the land." Nat pointed toward a dirt road leading out of town away from the highway. "If Bannock likes the hills, he'd want to get away from traffic. Let's see where that goes."

They hiked, studied the terrain, ate the shrubbery.

Nat gave up first. She moved toward a huge flat rock near the tree Case was walking toward. There was a thick cushion of leaves on the stone. The leaves crackled as she lowered herself.

Case leaned against the tree. She could see how dejected he was. She'd been cut adrift from everyone in the world for so long she was used to it, but Case seemed to need to connect. That must be why he wanted to find his old buddy.

She decided to tell him she was sorry first. Then she'd say 'I told you so'. She turned just as Case flew straight up in the air. She didn't have a split second to react before she was jerked sideways and flipped upside down. She bounced high, her mind scrambled to make sense of the spinning world. She tried to look in all directions at once.

She started falling. The ground rushed to meet her as she hurled head first toward it. She fumbled for her gun but her hands tangled in something that pressed against her back. She didn't crash land. She bounced up again.

She reacted to a movement on her left. Case bobbed down nearly to the ground. Case, wrapped in a net. A net just like the one she'd sat down on.

Nat untangled her fingers as the trap she'd set off by sitting on the rock suddenly made sense. She fought her way to her gun. She had it in front of her, cocked and ready. She reached for the knife in her boot and slashed at the ropes. They didn't cut. She studied the ropes, they were hemp, woven around steel cable.

"Don't cut it!" Case yelled.

Nat, waiting for the men who'd been following them to emerge from the woods and start shooting any second, shouted, "We've got to get out of here."

"Nat."

"We're completely exposed."

"Nat."

"They're probably closing in right now."

"Nat!"

Nat suddenly wanted to be free just so she could break his neck. This was no time for chit chat. "Move, Case. They'll be coming. They've found us."

Case twisted himself around in the net until he seemed to be sitting comfortably upright in it with his knees bent outward, his legs crossed at the ankles. "They haven't found us."

Nat stared at him. He looked like a man who had been caught in a net many times.

Case said cheerfully, "We've found Bannock."

Case focused on something behind her.

Nat turned her head. She tried to bring her gun around but the rope made it difficult.

"Who's there?" A man dressed in a flannel shirt emerged from the woods.

"Watch out you fool. She's gonna shoot you."

"Well, she wouldn't be the first to try."

"If she doesn't shoot you, I will. Let me out of this thing."

The man crossed his arms, not coming any closer. "Do I know you?"

Case snickered. "Now that's humbling, Mike. You kicked my butt four years in a row and now you say you don't remember me?"

Nat watched Bannock narrow his eyes and study both of them. He didn't strike her as being that much of a wimp.

Case said, "Maybe if I was bleeding and laying flat out on the ground, it'd come to you."

"Case Garrison. Are you just passing through or did you come here to see me?" The man straightened away from the tree and started forward, giving Nat's gun a respectful glance.

Nat didn't like to divert her attention from the man who'd trapped her in the tree, but she couldn't help but admire the blue eyes that seemed so kind and wary at the same time.

"I don't remember you being so paranoid, Mike. What's with the traps?" Mike still hadn't let them go, and he wasn't in any great hurry to do it. That's when a slight movement behind Mike drew Nat's attention. A woman stood behind the tree. She had a rifle slung over her shoulder and a .38 police special in her hand. She had none of the kindness in her eyes that shined in Mike's. This was a woman armed for trouble.

"I'm not paranoid. But my wife is a little. We had some trouble up here a couple of years ago." Mike looked behind him. "Come on out, Annie. Case is an old friend."

Annie snorted and stayed where she was.

"Case, meet my wife, Annie."

The perfect manners and the human traps didn't match. Nat didn't take her eyes off the woman. The snort drew Case's attention. Mike might be a wimp, but his woman was a tightly coiled package of trouble.

Mike grinned over his shoulder at his wife and his teeth must have caught the sunlight because his smile was blinding. They gleamed out of his tanned skin. His hair was bleached white as if he spent every spare minute outside and his shoulders were broad and strong the way a man's got who did hard physical labor all day.

"Get us down from here. I respect your net but she's gonna hack it into a hundred pieces she's so mad."

Nat figured she could cut the trap, and take them both out if she half tried. But for right now, she just hung there, bobbing and swaying like an overripe tomato on the vine.

The woman snarled, "Don't you dare cut my net. It takes forever to make those cords." She stepped into full sunlight and Nat reassessed taking them both out. The woman was an Amazon. Her hair was shoulder length and blonde. Her eyes watched every move.

Nat didn't want to beat them up anyway, she'd realized there was no danger. Almost too mad to let that influence her, she growled, "Get me out of this net."

It was a voice no one every disobeyed. Once in the Sudan, she'd made a hungry, wounded lioness back down with that voice. Okay, a few drugged-out, mass murderers had ignored her. But she made sure they lived long enough to really, really regret it.

Mike might have been wary and Annie might have been untrusting, but they weren't stupid. Annie headed for her net first.

"Annie, don't—"

She pulled a single rope near the tree and the net dropped open. Nat saw it coming. Mrs. Bannock's impish plan was to let Nat fall about twelve feet headfirst to the forest floor. The scamp.

Nat wove her fingers into the webbing. She let her feet swing down then, hand over hand, still holding her gun, she lowered herself to within a few feet of the ground and nimbly dropped, landing upright. She gave Annie a quick once over then she returned her gun to its holster.

Case was free by the time she had her gun locked down.

"Long time, Bannock," Case said pleasantly. "I'd like you to meet my friend, Nat."

"Hey, Nat." Bannock sidled over to his wife and Nat couldn't decide if he'd moved close to protect her or to hide behind her skirts—not that she was wearing a skirt.

"Remind me to never throw you a surprise party," Case said to Nat.

"What are you doing up here, Case?" Mike asked.

Nat stepped toward him.

"Did you drop by so I could beat you up again?"

"Something like that."

Nat said, "Nothing like that."

"It's like this," Case said, "We've been running for our lives pretty much full time for the last seventy-two hours. We hopped a plane in Pittsburgh, ended up in Denver. We needed a place to plan some payback and we didn't want to get any citizens hurt while we did it. I figured you could protect yourself in a fight, so I brought it to you."

"I don't want any trouble, Case. I've got a wife and two daughters to protect."

Annie rolled her eyes and exchanged a look with Nat that made Nat like her.

Case began to recount the wild ride they'd been on the last few days.

Bannock interrupted. "This surprises me, Case. I mean, I didn't know you that well back in the day, but you've never struck me as being much of a one to run and hide."

Case said sweetly, "If it was me, I'd have fought 'em. But baby doll here was scared."

Nat narrowed her eyes at him. Bannock laughed out loud.

"Yeah, right." Annie came and stood beside Nat, like she'd decided to team up with her against the men.

Nat appreciated it, but she did remember that little martial arts trophy and suspected Mr. Sunshine could do some damage.

"The traps were yours, weren't they?" she asked Annie.

"Nope. Mike built them. Live traps of course, in case there were any animals accidentally caught."

"Should've built 'em for men." Nat studied Annie. "I've always had trouble catching one the usual way."

Annie grinned and it transformed her face. Up until now, Nat had thought she looked tough and smart, but not friendly. But the smile changed everything. She thought Mike probably had his hands full, but if he could wring a smile out of her once in a while, it'd be worth it.

"I finally did catch one and I have no idea what in the world to do with him."

Mike shook his head. "Not true."

"I think we've shaken the men who were tailing us, Mike, but we could bring trouble down on you."

Mike's shoulders slumped but he didn't tell them to hit the road. "Okay, let's hear it."

Case told Mike and Annie about the men who'd assaulted them on the mountainside the night before, the possibility they were rogue FBI agents of some kind. Case showed Mike the tiny black cartridges they'd found implanted under their skin.

"So, I guess you could say I did run and hide," Case groused as if it hurt him to admit it.

Nat smirked. Thank heavens he hadn't been called upon to ask directions. That would have been the final blow to his manhood.

"But I didn't really make a choice. We spent all our time ducking, then trying to stop the bleeding. Every time we tried to make sense out of the little evidence we had, someone would start shooting at us again. We nearly got a family killed. We found the plane and hitched a ride and ended up in Colorado. We came up here to find a place we could turn and face them without endangering others. I knew you were tough enough to take care of yourself—but that's before I knew about a wife and children."

Case frowned at the little tube. "But the tracking device is neutralized, so we shouldn't bring them down on you. And we don't need to stay here anyway, we should be able to go back to civilization. I shouldn't have brought this trouble to you, Bannock. We'll leave."

"Have you eaten lately? I got the girls down for a nap and started supper, then Annie and I went out for a walk. We could tell there was someone skulking around here, so we set the traps and waited."

"I want to leave the snares up all the time." Annie smiled. "We had a very bad man chasing after us one time and I like to be prepared. But Mike worries about his furry friends."

"What are the chances you'll make another assassin mad enough to want to kill us, honey? A raccoon could set off that trap and be stuck in there for hours before I found him and set him free. Why, he could hurt himself trying to get away."

Nat looked at Case and shook her head. She mouthed the word, 'wimp'.

Case grinned at her.

They followed the Bannocks down the mountainside to a rugged cabin that seemed to be part of the beauty surrounding it. A heavy-set woman hung clothes on a line that stretched between two poles.

"We caught ourselves some varmints, Maud." Annie waved at the lady.

Nat snickered.

After supper, Nat and Case refused to stay in the house with the Bannocks. "I think we're clear, Mike, but I'm not going to chance it when you've got two little girls. We'll camp up in the hills."

Mike insisted on driving them to a spot far from where they'd cut out the tracking devices, which was a good thing because having a belly full of good food nearly put Nat to sleep. They got out, supplied with sleeping bags and a full duffle bag of supplies and three hundred dollars in cash. Mike had also stitched up their various wounds, gave them some antibiotics, and in general treated them like sick dogs. He'd tested the contents of the vial but a quick check hadn't told him much. They'd have to give him a day or two and phone.

Nat settled on the ground against a fallen log. She turned their problems over in her mind for a while as she slouched down until she was almost lying.

She turned to Case to talk to him and was surprised to see him asleep. She blinked her eyes, trying to see him more clearly. The night before they'd had the best night's sleep they'd had since someone had started issuing hunting licenses with their pictures on them.

She was drowsy herself. She'd been drugged before, this didn't feel like that. Nat slid the rest of the way onto the ground and slept.

Nat woke up for a few minutes when the moon was high in the sky. She looked around. Case slept nearby.

She'd been shot before. She'd been hurt worse than anything that wet works team had handed out last night. There was no reason for her to be this tired.

The next time she opened her eyes it was full daylight. Mike Bannock was shaking her. "Better eat something."

Nat jerked upright at the touch. No one sneaked up on her. No one wandered around while she slept unaware. A shot of adrenaline drove her to her feet. Something was wrong. Her muscles ached from the hours of inactivity. "I've got to move."

She left the camp without looking at either of them. She started walking briskly, but something was pressing her faster. She picked up the pace, jogging, then running hard. She didn't keep track of time. She ran until the high altitude made her lightheaded. Then she slowed to a fast walk, picking the most rugged path, climbing an occasional outcropping of rock. She worked out with an imaginary punching bag as she walked. The craving for motion slowly eased. The physical stresses of the last few days caught up with her.

She circled back toward camp. The smell of beef stew led her to the fire.

Case sat alone at the fire. Dropping into a heap beside him, Case spooned up a large serving of the stew and handed it to her. She ate with gusto and fell asleep before she'd even begun to try and decipher the mystery that surrounded them.

The next time she awoke it was late afternoon. She smelled the stew again and her stomach demanded food. Her muscles began humming, urging her to move. Her mind was saying, 'sleep'. She noticed movement off to her side. Case was working with the barbells.

She rested her eyes on him, riveted to the sight of him moving, pumping, sweating. She wanted those barbells and even more, she wanted that man. She swallowed hard to keep from sighing out loud. It hit her that at this moment, after years of relentless control, she was as near to out of control as she'd ever been.

Every sense, every physical need, every emotion clamored to be the first to be satisfied. It was overwhelming. It was frightening.

Overriding them all was Case. She rolled up onto her hands and knees. Ready to follow an instinct so basic she didn't have a choice.

"I've got enough food here to last you for a while."

Nat snapped her head around and scrambled for her gun. She had her Glock drawn, aimed, cocked, the safety snapped off, her finger tensing on the trigger, adrenaline roared through her system pushing her to battle. She did all that in the two seconds it took her to remember Bannock.

She tilted the gun straight up. Gasping for breath. Shocked to the depth of her soul by the fact that she'd almost shot him. Her heart pounded as she returned her gun to the small of her back. She knew herself. She knew her reflexes and her reaction time. She'd come within a heartbeat of blowing him away. It wasn't normal. She never shot blind. In a crisis she turned ice cold. Every moved deliberate, premeditated.

None of this was normal. The uncontrollable focus on everything physical. The deep sleep that disconnected her from her surroundings. The overreaction. The carelessness with her weapon.

Bannock was bent over the fire. Case, always so alert, was fixated to the point of obsession with the weights. Neither man had noticed. The whole thing had taken an instant. She struggled to get her breathing under control.

Bannock looked up from the fire with a plate full of food for her. "I found where the helicopter landed to drop them off and pick them up. The pilot didn't go hunting for them. He sat there a while then took off. I hid your real trail and laid down a false trail heading down the mountain. I stripped the bodies of any useful equipment." Bannock nodded at a huge pile of sophisticated weaponry.

"If those men died near the last known location of your tracker and there's no trail from that point on, then you're in the clear."

"You went all the way down there, did all this work, hauled this gear back up, all while we slept?" Case asked.

"You slept a long time."

Bannock was in good shape but he was no trained agent. Nat was amazed. She shared a look with Case and could tell he was impressed.

Bannock laughed. "I did pretty good for a wimp, didn't I, just like when I used to kick your butt."

"You did great, Bannock. I've been sleeping like the dead for the last twenty-four hours. I don't know why I'm so tired."

"Altitude maybe," Bannock shrugged.

Nat knew that wasn't it. She'd spent the last eighteen months at a high altitude.

Case quit curling the weights and Nat finished eating fast and took them.

Case stopped her. "Let me check the stitches on your arm first."

Nat snatched the weights away and moved across the fire from him. Far enough away that she couldn't act on her desire to touch his body and see if his skin was as damp and warm as it looked. Even with Bannock here as a chaperone she wasn't perfectly sure of her control.

"You've been telling me stories about running for your lives, but you haven't talked much about your girlfriend." Mike flashed that high voltage smile at her. "I've been letting you rest but I'll admit I'm curious."

Case laughed. "She's tough as a whole Delta Force, she's savvy as a Comanche warrior, she's mean as a rabid badger."

Bannock gave Nat a nervous sideways glance.

Nat said coolly, "Don't ever forget it."

Bannock's eyes narrowed then he grinned at her. She laughed. All the aches and longings eased as she became more fully awake. They didn't leave but she had them leashed.

"Did you find anything to identify any of the men?"

"Nothing. They were slick. Not a thing on them." Mike handed Case a tin plate of food.

"You didn't see a scar like the one you sewed up on our backs, did you?"

"No, and I checked because of what you told me." Bannock took Nat's plate and refilled it. She was ravenous. And the weights were begging her to pick them up. She ate quickly.

"Tagged, like someone was doing a wildlife study and they hooked a radio collar on you." Mike dished himself up a serving of stew. "No there was nothing like that."

Case tossed his plate and the fork he was holding down on the ground in disgust. "Just like an animal. Then when it came time to study us they hunted us down. And they've been hunting ever since."

Bannock said, "You've got leads. I'll test what's in that vial. The technology to make it has to be unusual, and that in itself is a clue. You've both seen the hitman. Get a sketch artist to draw him and track down his identity then let the police hunt for him."

Case shook his head. "I'm not ready to involve the police. Those men who were after us were too deadly. I don't want to endanger anyone, and that includes the police." He turned to Nat.

She nodded. "If we're careful we should be able to do this without them finding us. Getting rid of those bugs leveled the playing field."

Nat looked down the endless slopes. "Let's head out. I don't want to wait until morning."

Case stood up. He was furious about that bug. Nat knew he was ready to do some hunting of his own. So was she.

She started packing their minimal gear in Case's duffel and the webbed bag she'd taken from one of their attackers.

Bannock invited them to take any of the gear he'd confiscated. They didn't need much.

Case shook Mike's hand. "Thanks for feeding us and standing guard while we got some rest."

"It was almost worth climbing up and down a mountain."

Bannock said, "Don't you like climbing mountains?"

"Within reason." Nat shifted her pack on her back, her muscles longed for work but she was dreading the long descent.

"I could give you a ride to Denver in my Jeep."

Nat looked at Mike, then exchanged a look with Case. "Do we dare?"

Mike waited. Finally, Case said, "Thanks, we appreciate it."

"None of the simple stuff I know how to do tells me what's in that vial but I know a couple of FBI guys who could test it for you," Mike offered. "I saved their lives so they owe me a favor."

Case said, "I don't want you involved in this, Bannock. If I'd known about your family I'd have never come to you. These men who are after us aren't particular where they aim when they start shooting. I don't want them showing up at your place. I don't want you calling anybody. Those bugs may have been the only thing leading them to us up 'til now, but the bugs are gone and they'll be looking for any other connection."

"We can handle it. Annie is way tougher than I am."

"Just the same, we'll be fine." Nat said. "You'd better give that vial to us and we'll figure out another way to get it tested."

They climbed into the Jeep and headed out.

When they reached the outskirts of Denver, Case said, "This is far enough. I don't want anyone seeing you with us."

Bannock pulled over. "Call me and tell me how it all comes out."

Nat and Case climbed out of the Jeep and waved goodbye.

Case pulled the little plastic canister out of his pocket and studied it for what seemed to Nat like the hundredth time.

He stared at it as if the power of his will would force it to give up its secrets.

The last rays of the setting sun shone over his shoulder and he pulled it closer to his eyes. "There's a weird raised place on this thing. It may just be a seam in the plastic but I think it's..." Case turned the device trying to catch more of the sun.

"I can't make it out." Case looked around him. "We need a magnifying glass."

Nat pointed at a large discount store a few blocks in front of them. "Let's go."

They came out of the store five minutes later. Case held the magnifying glass close to the little container. "It's tiny but it's a word. It says Break Zone."

The Brewsters lived every day to the fullest. They loved to dance. They traveled. They filled their home with exotic works of art.

Peg particularly loved things from the Far East.

Steve particularly loved to indulge his wife.

Steve made veal marsala that was out of this world.

Peg was a militant vegetarian.

They hadn't spent a night apart in ten years.

Once in a while they came across something that made them set aside their fun and games and go save the world.

Everyone needs a hobby.

Steve could translate six Arabic languages. Peg never saw a code she couldn't break or an encrypted computer she couldn't make spill its guts.

When Nat Whoever, their daughter, didn't answer Metal Voice's summons, Peg pouted but she sent her regrets to her Gourmet Club. She'd miss French night—the finest meal of the year—but duty called.

Steve mourned his newest orchid's impending first blossom. Maggie Dawn he'd named it and he expected nothing less than the ocean at sunrise. He'd named it after Peg of course, but he'd named his last fifteen orchid creations after Peg. Coming up with derivatives of her name was getting harder than coming up with the hybrids.

They were packed and at the pickup site before the helicopter from Dulles landed. The pilot didn't speak to them, didn't look at them. They climbed in and he took off.

They came in through a secure entrance. They were never exposed in the hallway. They punched in a code maybe eight people in the world were privy to. They weren't sure who else had it. That information was strictly 'need to know'. They entered a huge war room holding only an oval table and dozens of luxurious armchairs. There was one man sitting, waiting for them. He was the only one they'd ever met. They didn't know his name. Peg assumed he was Metal Voice but he didn't have the synthesizer on so who could be sure?

"Give me everything you know." Steve always took charge.

Peg let him because she loved a masterful man. Steve was masterful in all the ways that really counted. In all the rooms that really counted. Besides, he knew who was really running things. He liked masterful women.

"We've got no picture." The man addressing them had the blackest skin Peg had ever seen out of Africa. He absolutely glowed with intelligence and authority.

"We've got no description beyond brown hair and brown eyes."

"Doesn't she work for you?" Steve was perturbed. Or at least he was pretending to be. They wouldn't have been called in if it had been easy.

"She's deep—very deep for a very long time. No one in this office has ever met her. No one can contact her. We hang possibilities out where she can pick one and we get reports—never delivered to us in the same way twice. And maybe the ruler of a country steps down. Or a terrorist is suddenly standing in plain site and our sniper is standing nearby. Or the remains of an MIA comes home."

"Is she all international?"

"Mainly—but she's In-Country on this."

"You know that for a fact?" Steve said doubtfully.

"We do."

Peg believed him. She spoke for the first time. "How long has she been missing?"

"That's where we can get into this. That's where we have enough to start hunting."

He tossed a folder at them. It slid across the gleaming dark oak of the conference table.

Steve flipped open the folder and Peg caught her breath.

They looked up at their boss. Or were they his boss? Peg had never been sure.

All three of them stared at the picture of the man with dead eyes and said together, "Prometheus."

"He's the hitter?" Steve asked through clenched teeth.

Metal Voice nodded.

"Wow, who brought him in?" Peg asked.

MV wasted two whole seconds smiling at them. "That's your job."

Peg's adrenaline began to pump. "We find him, we find her."

"I hope not." MV responded. "If you find them together she's going to be dead."

Doubtfully Peg asked, "Can't she handle Prometheus?"

"Maybe, but she's got a civilian along."

"Dead weight," Steve said darkly.

"Not completely. His name is Case Garrison. He's FBI—a former SEAL. He's not in her league but she won't have to spend all her time baby-sitting." MV slid them another file, this one thick.

Peg left Garrison's file aside for now. She sorted through the rest of the papers on the assassin. "Prometheus wants them both?"

"Apparently. They were both gunned down but he only winged them." Steve chuckled mirthlessly. "Our favorite enemy is slipping."

"That's what I thought when I heard it," MV said. "It's finally our turn."

"He's not working on this for The Company?" Both men looked at Peg when she used that tone, which was wise of them. "You're clear on that before you send us in?"

"Clear. We checked all the way to the top and right down to the bottom. The company wants Prometheus taken out. He's gone over the edge. We've gotten his picture, undisguised, three times in the last two years."

Peg asked in disgust, "Why haven't you finished it sooner?"

"You know why," MV said.

"The Company uses him," Steve said. "They want him alive."

"Not anymore," Metal Voice reached for the file.

Peg closed it silently. "If we take him out we don't have to find her, she'll just come in once she knows it's safe."

"Nat never comes in. She'll just be free to go back to work."

Peg wondered what it would be like to never, never, never come in from the cold.

"We have reason to believe there is more than one shooter."

Peg's jaw got tense which she hated because it caused tiny wrinkles. "My little girl made somebody very angry. Who else is after her?"

MV smiled again. "We've got a body." He tossed them another file.

"Another hit?" Steve asked centering the file between Peg and himself.

"We're pretty sure it's a victim."

"Of whom?" Peg asked.

"Of Nat and Garrison. The corpse in that file and two others were in pursuit. He fell off a building. We got lucky and found him before they could clean up the mess."

"He's FBI?" Peg asked, surveying the file. "Active?"

"Yeah, and he wasn't working on anything that could explain his death."

Peg tapped the file, considering the ramifications. "Who does he report to?"

"There's no proof that he was acting on orders from his superior," MV said with relish.

"Who?" Steve insisted, closing the file and adding it to the one they already had on Prometheus and Garrison.

"Name's Gerald Sloan. Director in the same division as Case." MV gave them a fourth and final file.

"Sloan and Case knew each other? That's too pat," Steve said.

"And they hated each other." MV stood. "It's all in there. Get moving." The way he said it made Peg think that MV thought he was the boss. He left the room.

The helicopter let them off at a private landing strip just outside Arlington, Virginia. Steve flew the Lear. Peg opened up the onboard computer and started hammering nails in Prometheus' coffin. He was long overdue. She was going to enjoy this one.

CHAPTER FOURTEEN

They needed a research lab. They needed access to the Internet. They needed to figure out what Break Zone was. They needed a moving target they could draw a bead on.

Case insisted they put some space between themselves and the last tracking signal before they got anything they needed. They hiked steadily south out of Denver, debating the wisdom of hitching a ride.

Case was in favor of it he said, to save time. The real reasons were the dark circles under Nat's eyes. But he knew she'd never ask for a break. "It would probably be safe now. No one's tried to kill us in nearly thirty-six hours."

Nat laughed and shook her head.

"Why do you do that?"

"What? Laugh? Because you're funny, I guess."

"No, shake your head after you laugh." Case gave an exaggerated laugh then shook his head in the little motion he'd seen Nat make so many times.

"I do that?"

"Here let me say something hilarious, then you laugh and pay attention to what your head does. Uh...I can't think of anything funny...uh...twenty bucks, same as in town...that was no lady, that was my wife...when I was born I was so ugly the doctor slapped my mother..."

Nat laughed. She shook her head. Case saw the second she caught herself at it.

"I see what you mean."

"So why do you do it?"

"Case, I never laugh. You've probably heard every syllable of laughter I've uttered in fifteen years. But you make me laugh. I know what I was thinking when I shook my head."

"The suspense is killing me."

"It's amazement." Nat shrugged her shoulders and looked over at him. "Every time I hear that laugh I think 'I can't believe I just laughed.' I guess that sounds dumb."

"I'd be disappointed in you if you were a giggler. Your life doesn't sound like a barrel of laughs."

Nat laughed again. This time her head only went one direction before she stopped herself.

"You're getting there. A few more days with me and you'll be thinking about stand-up comedy as a career."

"How about a clown?"

"Excuse me?"

"I'll be a clown. That would combine my masterful ability at disguise with my constant laughter."

"Okay, but no big nose if you ever want to have children."

"What?"

"I can't imagine a more effective birth control device."

"Now you're trying too hard."

Case quit while he was ahead. "Where are we going?"

"I'm thinking maybe LA. We just put Denver behind us. We could have access to a good lab and get lost in the crowd.

"I've got a better idea." Case pointed to an unassuming, one story motel that was nothing more than eight rooms standing side by side.

"You want to rent a room and get some sleep? I am tired but we don't want anyone to recognize us if someone comes around asking questions."

"Not rent a room. Look at that mobile home parked in front of the motel. Let's sleep in there."

"Maybe there are people sleeping in there."

"Then why is it parked in front of a motel?" Case headed for the trailer. It was being pulled by a beige Ranger pickup truck. Case tried the back door. He looked around the parking lot and pulled his knife out of his ankle. He had the door open in five seconds.

He stepped soundlessly inside then poked his head out the door. "Empty."

Nat came in.

He thought she must be too tired to argue.

It took longer to find a place to sleep in the minuscule trailer than it did to break in. The table converted into a single bed—a bed as hard as a table. The couch unfolded to double its size which was still smaller than a regular couch.

Case urged her to go to sleep. He was afraid she was going to collapse. "We'll sneak out in the morning before they get up."

Nat fell asleep instantly. Case settled on the couch to keep watch.

They both woke up when the trailer started moving.

Case's eyes popped open. He rolled onto his side on the miserably small couch and looked at Nat who was still blinking sleep from her eyes.

"I guess we'll ride along for a while," Case said.

Nat laughed, shook her head, settled back against the kitchen table and fell back asleep. Case followed suit.

They woke up from time to time as the day progressed and they began to realize just how safe they were. The senior citizens, despite having their home in tow, stopped at a restaurant for every meal and used public toilets all day. Case thought they'd spent a lot of money for something they were using as a pull toy.

Case threw a fit when Nat took a shower in the two-foot-square bathroom. Then, when she looked so cool and clean, he took one, too.

Case came out of the shower, dressed in the bloodstained black T-shirt he'd been wearing since they'd been attacked on the mountainside. It was the shirt he'd stripped off one of his assailants. Bannock had washed it but the stain was still there.

He'd left his holster and gun on the couch when he'd showered, he didn't put them back on. It was the first time he'd unbent so far. He rubbed his head with a borrowed towel then tossed it onto the kitchen table in front of Nat, disgusted with himself.

"How are we going to get out of here without them noticing this." He paced the five step length of the mobile home for a while.

His eyes kept going to his duffel bag. He finally quit pacing. "I've gotta work off some of this steam."

He pulled his bag close to him and sat on the couch in the microscopic excuse for a living room. He pulled the weights out of his bag and did curls with both arms at once.

Nat was sitting straight across from him on the bench seat of the handkerchief sized kitchen table drawing a comb she'd found in the trailer through her hair. Her knees were facing the aisle that divided the trailer in half.

They were so close their knees would have touched if she'd sat straight across from him.

She tossed the comb aside, leaned forward with her forearms on her knees and turned her head a little sideways to watch him. He knew she wanted a turn.

He was planning to share soon but he couldn't ease off yet. He had to let his muscles burn for a while. He needed the oxygen that started coursing through his blood only when he'd been pumping for a long time.

He noticed the hungry look in her eye and he knew how she felt. She was desperate to push her muscles to the limit. Eager to feel her skin grow damp and take on a sheen from the relentless workout.

"So, do you think the drug makes you crave that?" she asked, her voice sounded like she was wound tight with the need to burn off some energy.

Case didn't answer for a long time. He watched her lips and knew she was counting his reps silently. He passed twenty, then fifty, then seventy-five. She shifted her gaze between his glistening, corded muscles and the bar bell. He liked what he saw in her eyes and he kept moving, wondering whether she was lusting after him or the weights.

Finally, he made one hundred, dropped the hand weights onto the floor and looked up at her. "Wanting to work out eats at me."

He stared at the bar bells for a while. "I smoked for about five years when I was young and trying to be tough."

"You mean you quit when you really got tough?"

He smiled up at her. "I quit because I joined the Navy and they were handing out ten mile runs and twenty mile hikes like they were Christmas presents we should be thankful for. And I had to choose between smoking and breathing."

"You chose breathing. Bright boy."

"Not everyone did. And besides, every time I'd go home I had to give up smoking the whole time I was there. My mom would've scalped me for smoking."

"The big tough Navy SEAL is scared of his mama?"

"Believe it. Hangin' Judge Janet Garrison was no one to mess with."

"That's what you call your mom?" Nat laughed. She shook her head, then stopped herself.

"That's what everyone calls my mom. Anyway, even though giving them up for a week at a time was brutal, and breathing was so desirable, I'm telling you quitting smoking was the hardest thing I've ever done."

"Really, the hardest? I mean, I know it's hard to kick the habit but let's face it, you've been shot."

"It's not hard to get shot, Nat."

She laughed again, grabbed one of his weights and started pumping iron.

"Addict."

She picked up the other one. He grabbed it away from her. "Not the arm I sewed. Not yet."

Nat nodded silently but her left arm cried out for exertion and her eyes kept wandering to the weight Case held out of her reach.

He kept talking, trying to distract her. He became aware that he was curling the weight again.

"The point is, this feels like quitting smoking. It's the same itch that nothing else will scratch."

Nat puffed as she lifted the weight and felt the rhythm of it relax her.

"It's the same mind game a person plays with himself after he's quit for about two days. Like, 'I'll just have one, what could one hurt?' Or 'it's my body. I can do anything I want with my body.'"

Case watched her. She was staring at her pumping arm, entranced with the sight of her muscles flexing under her skin.

"I can feel what you're talking about." She did a few more reps then reluctantly she lowered the weight to the floor.

Still staring at the weight, she asked, "And what about the other?"

"What other?" Case pulled the weight out of her hand and packed both of them into his bag.

She kept looking at the floor. "The other itch I can't scratch. I keep thinking about...you."

He tapped her lightly on the chin and she looked up at him. He smiled.

"You know, Case, you have the gentlest smile I've ever seen. It's completely at odds with the man who draws his gun so smoothly and jumps off buildings onto rickety fire escapes and cuts his traveling companion open without flinching."

Case said, "You did all those things, too."

"If I could just see that smile all the time, I'd be able to control my workout addiction."

"We could just have one. What could one hurt?" he used his cigarette excuse.

"One what?"

"One...whatever."

She smiled back. Heat curled in his stomach.

"It's my body," she said.

Before she could finish, his gravely voice asked, "Are you saying I can do anything I want with your body?"

Case wasn't sure who moved first but they were in each other's arms. They met in the center of the aisle, half sitting, half kneeling on the floor between them.

He was starving for what he tasted on her lips. And that itch, that constant waxing and waning itch she'd talked about. He'd been living with it for days. Kissing her, holding her so close, was making it better at the same time it was making it infinitely worse.

He slid one callused palm up to cradle her face. His other hand slid down her back and she flinched a little when he brushed over the wound in her lower back.

He lifted his head away from her. "I hurt you. I'm sorry."

"But when it's not hurting, it feels so nice. I know you said it's been a long time for you." He heard the longing and the doubt in her voice.

"Shhh." He lay one finger over her lips to silence her then he traced the line of her mouth delicately. He watched her lips. Finally, he looked at her and said softly, "It's not like that. It's not just me grabbing the first woman I see."

"You mean it hasn't been a long time?"

Case surprised himself with a rusty laugh. "A long time, yeah, you could say that."

"So eighteen months, since you started taking the drug?"

With a weary hand, Case rubbed his face vigorously trying to wash the sleep away. Only because he was so sleepy did he let himself admit this. "Nat, I was raised with a mom who drove it home all the time that her boys were to treat women with respect."

"Sounds good to me. What about the eighteen months?"

He was almost annoyed with her for not getting it. He dragged himself onto the seat, then helped her to sit across from him. "I've lived a life for a long time where I didn't dare get involved with a woman. The ones I met who were sweet and decent, didn't deserve to have a man in their lives who might vanish at any time, with no warning, and no ability to be honest about himself."

He let that sink in a few seconds. "And the rest of the women I met, I was either trying to arrest or afraid they might try and kill me."

"So..." she shook her head as if she didn't understand.

"Just think of me as your friendly neighborhood monk."

Nat opened her mouth, then closed it again and kept it closed.

That was probably best.

"The way I've acted...that is, well, I've been so drawn to you, but that's really out of character for me. And that's why I have to make sure this isn't something that is a reaction to that drug. I don't just grab ahold of women I barely know and, well, if something like that were to happen." He was silent a while. Then he said simply, "It's not going to happen. I don't treat women that way."

Nat propped her elbows on her knees and rested her chin in both hands. "And that's because Hangin' Judge Janet raised you to respect women?"

Case jerked one shoulder in a mild shrug. "She raised me to be a Christian."

There was a long silence between them. Finally, Nat asked, "And as a Christian, how did you feel about killing those men?"

Case's eyes met hers. Slowly, thoughtfully, he answered. "I've been too far away from my faith for too long. I think God doesn't condemn us for defending ourselves, but I've picked a life where I have to do it too often. I've gotten callus. It's been happening to me for a long time, way longer than eighteen months. But getting off that drug, I've had time to think and rest for the first time in years. I think when we finish this, I'm getting out. I'm going to get re-acquainted with my family. Find a job that doesn't send me all over the world into life and death situations where I have to kill or be killed. I'm going to recommit to my faith. I've put in twenty years, including my years of military service and that's enough."

"Do you think you can live a normal life?"

She sounded like she wished it was possible. Doubted it.

"I'm going to find out. I think you need to get out, too. And once we stop running for our lives, or vanishing into one criminal underground or another, we can find out if we're just reacting to the drug. I don't think I am. I think it's more. It's so much more."

"Then you think it's real, what we're feeling for each other?"

"I think I really want to find out." The mobile home slowed suddenly then rounded a sharp curve. She tipped forward. She reached for him and he pulled her into his lap.

"If wanting you is just like smoking, then I guess that means we're addicted to each other. That doesn't sound so bad to me." His touch soothed her wounded arm.

She brushed her fingers through the lock of wet hair that had fallen onto his forehead and leaned forward to kiss him.

He held her away, his gaze burning into hers. "Don't. My control isn't that good. This isn't the way I want it to be for us. Not in a crowded little trailer with both of us tender from our wounds. And not with us wondering if what we feel is being caused by withdrawal from a drug."

Nat nodded and they settled for holding each other tightly for a while.

As she relaxed in his arms, Case suddenly felt a wave of exhaustion wash over him.

He couldn't shake the debilitating fatigue. The gun shot had been no more serious than injuries he'd received several times in the past. The knife wound had been a paper cut. Maybe he'd lost more blood than he'd realized but even that didn't account for his acute fatigue.

He didn't realize he'd fallen asleep until Nat fell off of him. He was asleep, lying flat on the couch. From the way she landed, he assumed she'd been stretched out beside him. A beautiful woman lying beside him and he fell asleep. He really was losing it. He tried to reach out and help her up but his arm weighed about a hundred pounds. He'd overdone it with the barbells.

Nat climbed onto the table-bed. The little tin plaque over the Munchkin-sized bathroom boasted that the trailer slept six. Case had to use his imagination. Maybe the microwave folded out into bunk beds.

Nat lay down and dropped into a deep sleep. Case meant to get up but he never made it. He woke up briefly when the RV stopped, ready to abandon ship if their hosts came toward them. The couple rented a motel room again. They even had their suitcases in the pickup with them. Case fell back asleep and slept all night. He awakened briefly when their chauffeurs came out of the motel and started the day's travel.

It crossed his mind that he was starving, but before he could fret about it, he fell back asleep until two-thirty in the afternoon. He was laying there, blaming his lassitude on wounds and remembering how quickly he'd recovered from things like this when he was younger.

He looked at Nat's slumbering form so near him. She was all the way out. He'd watched her sleep while they'd been running for their lives. She slept like he did. Never totally off guard. Now she was out cold. He thought their drivers had probably stopped for lunch and it hadn't even awakened them. He couldn't believe he would sleep through that.

Nat was a different woman when she was asleep. He knew her more by what she was and who she was, than by how she looked. Now he studied her sleek, solid, well defined muscle. Her body was fascinating. He wanted to touch her. He wanted to feel her body move with his.

He liked the way she handled herself. He liked the way she struggled with him to be in charge because that was her nature, and at the same time appreciated his own desire to control every situation.

Case respected strength and there weren't many women who were strong enough for him to respect. His mom, Hangin' Judge Janet, was one. He'd been raised by a tough woman. He thought of how long it'd been since he'd seen his family and realized he'd given them almost no thought for eighteen months. Had the drug done that to him, too? Driven out something so important?

He saw Nat's eyes flicker open. He wiped his hands over his face, glanced at his watch and groaned. "I must be getting old."

She sat up suddenly. "I was just thinking the same thing, Case. It's not old age. How old are you by the way?"

"Thirty-eight. Right now, I feel eighty-three." As he talked he pulled himself into a sitting position with a slow yawn.

"It's this drug." Nat took the little device out of her jeans pocket. "This isn't natural the way we're sleeping. Two years ago, I hiked forty miles through the mountains of Afghanistan carrying a confiscated Stinger missile launcher and five missiles, plus my own AK-47, mountain climbing gear and assorted survival hardware. I lived off tree bark and rodents and slept on the ground. Then I turned around after eight hours of sleep and a hot meal and took an assignment stalking diamond smugglers in Sierra Leone without thinking twice about it. Now here I am acting like a fragile maiden over some scratch and a missing pint or so of blood, most of which I replaced with that IV. It's got to be removing this drug from our systems."

Case ran his hands vigorously over his hair, "So, what is it doing to us to be without it? Are we addicted to whatever it is? I don't feel withdrawal symptoms like I'd expect with a narcotic. But this sleep probably is some kind of withdrawal."

"Let's try to stay awake for a few minutes and talk about this. Can you do it?"

Case looked at her with a humorless smile. "I can do it if you can."

Nat leaned forward with her forearms on her knees. Case sat just like she was, facing her. In the confines of the mobile home they were nose to nose. He looked at her and, although he was looking right into her eyes he wasn't really making eye contact, he was completely absorbed in studying the odd hazel color he saw there. She took longer than she should have to lean back. She rested one elbow on the back of the seats that comprised the kitchen boundary line. She studied the black cylinder.

Then with a show of energy Case thought looked phony, she tossed the cylinder up and caught it. "Let's stop sleeping and come up with a plan."

He closed his eyes for a few seconds. "We need to get the stuff in that vial tested. How do we do that without going to our usual sources?"

"This rig is headed somewhere—although who can tell where since we've slept for most of the trip." She shifted her legs to rest one ankle on her knee. "We talked about a big city. LA maybe, but I can't think of anybody I know in California."

Case grinned at that, "Knowing nobody is just what we need. Except who is going to run the test? This stuff is bound to be something strange.

Your average lab won't be much help and, if they do figure out what it is by contacting someone official, that will be all our hunter needs to locate us."

"Maybe we don't need to worry about avoiding officials. If we find an honest cop and dump this problem in his lap, we'll just head for the hills. We can be ten states away by the time our little potion starts setting off red flags with anyone."

"We could end up getting the cop killed," Case said morosely staring down at his Red Wings.

"We'd better warn him of that going in," Nat said tossing the cylinder again.

Case shook his head unhappily. "A warning isn't enough."

He looked up at her. His eyes followed the ascent and decent of the black tube. She lofted it again. He snatched it out of the air. "They're too slick—too well funded. Whoever did this had access to high tech computer equipment, medical equipment, and a fortune for research and development in both fields. They have access to highly classified security systems. That hit man looked like a pure professional. They spent a fortune experimenting on the two of us."

"Case, that's it," Natalie said uncrossing her legs and sitting forward. She snatched the black device back. "The two of us. Think about it. It can't be just the two of us. It's too big, too complex. No one is spending this kind of money so they can track two people. This isn't about the tracking device. It's about the drug. They implanted it and they're watching its effect." She took her eyes off the device and looked straight at him. "You even said it before. They're using us as lab rats."

"Lab rats," Case muttered and stood to turn his back on her. He paced the trailer, five feet, turn, five feet, turn.

He pointed his finger in her face and said, through his clenched teeth, "That's a real nasty business, Nat."

"I've got an idea how to start tracking them." Nat narrowed her eyes.

"They treat people like rodents, maybe they kill them when they're finished with them like they tried with us. Have any corpses turned up with little X's on their backs?"

Case nodded and quit his useless pacing. "That's right. We figured out what we had in common but, because the attempt on our lives came while we were together, I'd been thinking it was about us. I know how to access police files and coroners' reports. I could do a search with the FBI computers so we could connect with all the police departments in the country using that distinctive mark as a tag. Profilers do it all the time looking for serial killers."

"Can you get us in without giving away our location?" Nat asked cautiously.

"I can make it look like it's a request coming in from a field office. No one will think twice about it."

Nat's chin lifted as she looked at the little black plastic leash she'd been on for the last year. "I think someone's watching this very carefully, Case. When we start asking around about similar MOs and searching for Break Zone, we're going to run into a buzz saw."

Case pulled his own little canister out and stared at it, his thoughts dark. "This time they won't know where we are unless we want them to, Nat. We handled them pretty well when we didn't expect them. I can't wait to show them what happens when I've had time to get ready."

Millie flung the last container into the back end of her Cherokee, furious at what she'd found. Whoever had been using the wilderness area for a dumping ground was going to answer to her. It had taken her two days to dig them all up.

She had to slam the tailgate twice to get it shut. There must be two hundred of these things. All split open, all empty.

Millie Hastings beloved desert land was no garbage dump.

She climbed into the car and tried to figure out how to rat out an illegal dump site. The police? The press? She kept thinking Break Zone, what in the world is it? Who makes it? There was no company named on the label. What she'd like to do is track down whoever dumped it here and throw the canisters on his lawn. With television cameras rolling of course. She smiled at the image. She just might do it.

After some careful consideration she decided her first step was to figure out what the stuff was. She headed for the university, coughing all the way. Someone there would have heard of Break Zone and if they couldn't answer her questions they'd know who could.

As she drove, her body was clamoring with her difficulty breathing and the conflicting need to move, exercise, push her muscles past their comfort zone. It seemed particularly intense today.

She drove straight to the campus and stopped first at the library. Her experience as a photographer had led to many libraries in her life to research a subject or study new picture taking equipment and photography techniques. It was her own observation that the librarians were usually the smartest people on any campus.

She presented her problem along with one of the containers, to the head librarian then logged on to the Internet and typed in brachiiesterone.

Nothing.

She tried Break Zone. She had a few moments of hope when a blank screen appeared and seemed to be loading a web site but the blank screen stayed blank until Millie realized the computer was frozen. She asked the librarian, Opal, for help.

"That's funny," Opal said tapping several different buttons. "I can't even turn it off. It's almost like its deliberately keeping this line open."

Opal waved at the line of open computers. "Go ahead and use a different terminal, I'll have to call in a repairman for this."

Millie moved. She typed in Break Zone and the same thing happened.

Next, she tried looking for brachiiesterone in scientific magazines. She found nothing.

Opal was just a little younger than Millie and the two hit it off. Opal came up with brachii being a root word but unless Millie had stumbled onto a real life Jurassic Park she couldn't figure out what these canisters had to do with a brachiosaur. As the energetic Opal began to share some of Millie's indignation at the illegal dumping, they both poured over medical texts. Studying brachii and anything else they could think of.

"The word Break Zone could mean anything, but the scientific word brachiiesterone has to mean it's a chemical to do with the muscles, that's the brachii part, and hormones. Esterone is the suffix for of all the sex hormones. Like testosterone, you know. Muscles and sex. Hmmm. Sounds like a fun drug."

Millie looked at her overly developed arm and leg muscles and remembered that she and Lee, although they'd always enjoyed a healthy sex life, hadn't been intimate from the moment they'd moved in with Matthew. It hadn't seemed like a big deal to her. Of course, they didn't make love. Their son was dying.

Brachiiesterone. What if the containers hadn't been empty when they were dumped? What if Break Zone was in the water supply at their house? Millie started calling up medical research information.

Opal finally had to return to work. The afternoon passed with Millie chasing one dead end after another.

It was ten o'clock at night. Millie hadn't realized how long she'd been doing research when Opal told her the library was closing. Millie had already decided not to go home without some answers so Opal let her use the phone to make a motel reservation. Opal promised to keep looking and Millie gave Opal the number of her room in a nearby motel.

Millie, stiff from her unusual inactivity and irritable from her failure, found a swimming pool at the motel. It was dark and the pool was deserted. Phoenix in August with its 100 plus degree days wasn't much of a tourist mecca.

Millie hadn't bothered to pack so much as a change of clothes, let alone a swimming suit. Impatient almost to the point of frenzy with the buzzing of her unexercised muscles, and lured by this unusual abundance of water, she stripped down to her underwear. She tossed her clothes under the sign that warned her there was no lifeguard on duty, as if a woman who was dying of lung cancer cared whether she drowned, and dove in head first.

She was just starting to loosen up after a dozen laps across the undersized pool when something caught her ankle.

She twisted in the water onto her back and tried to surface. She couldn't reach air. Just as her lungs were ready to force her to breathe in the water someone jerked her upward by the back of the neck. She managed one clear gasp of air into her painful lungs when a voice so cold goose bumps raised over Millie's flesh spoke into her ear. "You should have left the Break Zone buried."

Her head was forced under again.

She kicked and clawed at her attacker, trying to break his hold, but her panicky motions, slowed by the water, were powerless. She knew she was going to die.

Her last conscious thought was, she wanted to be reunited with Matthew and Lee but it wasn't up to someone else to decide when that would be.

CHAPTER FIFTEEN

The mobile home was like an oasis of solitude in a crowded world. Case and Nat stayed in it and slept. And when they were awake they hefted bar bells. When the trailer stopped at night, they sneaked out and got food. One night they found a second-hand store and bought clothes, then found a Laundromat and washed the ones they were wearing and the towels from the mobile home they'd used. Case was acutely aware of their dwindling funds. They didn't worry about where they were going because they were too tired to do anything if they did get off their rolling home.

By the end of the third day of wild fluctuation between exhaustion and physical exertion, Case thought the overwhelming lethargy seemed to be letting up on him. Their wounds were starting to heal. Nat's stitches were out.

The mobile home got off the highway at Lubbock, Texas and headed into a residential neighborhood. Case was glad to leave the little house trailer behind. Or rather let it leave them behind. He was starting to feel like a leech. It reminded him of the black cylinder that had been riding along inside of him without his knowledge.

Case and Nat made sure they left no trace of themselves. The couple might notice their water supply was gone but Case hoped they'd just think they forgot to refill the tank.

The mobile home stopped at an intersection and Case and Nat stepped out. The couple who'd given them the ride didn't seem to notice.

Case walked alongside Nat, quietly considering their options. "I'm from Texas and my family's name is pretty well known. I think we should get out of the state. The nearest FBI field office outside of Texas is Santa Fe. We'll head for New Mexico."

Now that they had a destination in mind, they couldn't just jump on whatever vehicle presented itself.

"We can look for New Mexico plates. We'll only hitchhike as a last resort."

Case laughed at her.

"What?" she asked, annoyed.

"We just think alike is all." They kept walking through downtown Lubbock.

Case wasn't paying much attention to their surroundings, but he'd been trained for a long time. Be Prepared. In some ways Navy SEALS and the FBI were just Boy Scouts run amok.

They were in the middle of a block with no working street lights when a group of young men, wearing red arm bands and baggy, tattered blue jeans emerged from the alleys and doorways around them and started closing in. Seven of them.

"Eight, three ahead of us, one in the alley across the street." Nat spoke in a voice that barely carried to his ears. "Three behind us. One on that fire escape ledge overhead on the right."

He'd missed the one on the ledge. He couldn't help being proud of her.

Case said in the same toneless whisper, "Knives, I only make knives, no guns."

"I think there's a gun behind us." She looked sideways at him and grinned. "Want to fake an untied shoe lace and check?"

He almost laughed out loud. She was looking forward to it. He knew how she felt. They hadn't been in a fight for days. "I'll take the gun, don't kill any of them. They're young."

"Maybe we can scare them straight." Neither Nat nor Case slowed up. They started putting distance between themselves gradually.

A circle of angry young men tightened around them. Nat walked right up to the one in the center-front like she didn't see him there. Case wanted to watch her work but he thought he'd better at least pretend like there was a loaded gun at his back.

He saw her ram the palm of her hand into a stomach at the same instant that she kicked another one in the face. He did a spin kick that took out two of the punks behind him and tossed a third one into the curb just exactly hard enough to knock him senseless for a while but not do much damage beyond that. A fourth one charged him from the alley. He put a choke hold on him and pulled him between Nat and the vulture waiting to pounce from above. He saw three punks lying motionless at Nat's feet. The whole thing had taken ten seconds.

The kid on the fire escape, all ready to leap into the fray, ran off instead.

Case started to put a sleeper hold on the one he had. Nat stopped him. "Let me talk to him for a minute, Case."

He eased off the pressure. The kid gasped for breath.

Nat leaned in real close to Case's little friend. "You know what all criminals have in common?"

The kid didn't answer, so Case did, "They're stupid?"

"No," Nat shook her head.

"They're ugly?" Case guessed.

That made Nat smile and the kid in Case's hands jerked against the grip that imprisoned him.

She said, "They're poor." Something changed in Nat's expression.

Case saw a compassion that surprised him. He had mainly seen a very tough, self-contained warrior. He'd always seen a very sexy woman. Right now, he saw another facet of her personality—a softer side. Not everyone would feel compassion for a kid who wanted to put a knife in her gut.

Certainly not him. He asked sarcastically. "So, you're saying we should feel sorry for the poor underprivileged kids who are driven to a life of crime by the evils of the uncaring, capitalist system?"

"No, I didn't mean they're poor, therefore they steal." All that soft femininity left her face and something cold replaced it. "I meant that, as a way to make a living, crime sucks."

The chill fit her better than the kindness, and Case wondered if she'd faked the caring.

She said to the kid, "You'd have more money if the eight of you worked flipping burgers for minimum wage. And chances are no one would ever stick a knife in your belly."

Nat's knife appeared in her hand as if by magic. She slit the front of his shirt open with a wicked slash. She didn't put a scratch on him. Then she cut his gang colored armband off and shoved it in his mouth.

That was the moment Case fell in love with her. It probably made him one sick puppy but Nat was the perfect woman for him. He was never letting her go.

He couldn't take his eyes off of her as she relieved the punk of his knife, which he'd never gotten pulled out of the pocket of his oversized jeans, and all the cash in his pockets.

She was robbing him. Case wondered if he could convince her to have his children.

Case let the punk go. He didn't even keep his eye on the boy he'd released. It wasn't necessary, the kid ran. He watched Nat as she stripped the weapons from the other kids.

Nat frisked them for money as well as weapons and pocketed over two hundred dollars.

"Do you really think you should take it, Nat? They're poor after all."

Nat muttered, "Bleeding heart."

He wanted to kiss those mean lips until they were nice to him. Then she pulled up the sleeve on one of their attackers and looked at the needle tracks. She said grimly, but with that strain of kindness showing again, "We might as well have it as the neighborhood dealer."

Case went and put his arm around her shoulder and pulled her close for a long hug. She wrapped her arms around his waist and held on tight.

Finally, he pulled back. "I told you I have family in Texas."

Nat said, "You mean the hangin' judge?"

"Yep, and I haven't seen them for over eighteen months. They're tough, right down the line. Lawmen mostly. One forest ranger. My older sister Avery works for the governor. Brett is a vet who's wimpy but smarter than all of us and he can be tough if he has to. Mom the hanging judge. Dad's a rancher."

"Are you thinking we should contact them? Because that might bring danger right down on their heads. If anyone is searching your background, they'll know about your family."

"I am not even considering contacting them. But when this is over, I'd love you to meet them. You'll fit right in."

No one on the face of the earth knew Case Garrison better than Carlos Lorenz. Carlos had been kicking over rocks and calling in markers like a man possessed ever since Case hadn't returned his call eight days ago.

Every reflex in his cop's brain told him he was racing against death. He didn't think it was too late. The gun shots at the Metro were Case. His instincts told him so and he trusted his instincts. Now he had DNA evidence that proved it.

Argie was tracking the money trail. He'd been at it day and night since they'd met in Vegas. They were sure Sloan was on the take but Sloan knew all the tricks. Whatever he was getting he had buried it deep. Nothing was deep enough to beat Argie, though.

Lorenz worked other angles. Witnesses at the Metro didn't mention the shooter, but Carlos thought a couple of them had seen something. He didn't blame them for being afraid. But Lorenz had a knack for interrogating innocents that seldom failed.

And he knew where to find truth serum if it came to that.

Case hadn't surfaced in any of the usual places. His family hadn't even heard he was back in the country. Case hadn't even left a message that he was alive. Lorenz knew that meant Case either suspected Lorenz or suspected someone who was privy to information Lorenz had. And Case would know that Lorenz would know that Case was suspicious just by the act of not returning his calls.

By not phoning Case was saying in effect, 'Watch your back, Lorenz. Trust no one'.

Unless not phoning meant Case was dead.

Then all Lorenz' speculating was just so much bat guano.

"Where would I go?" Lorenz played a litany of questions over and over. "What would I do?"

He put himself in Case's shoes. "Where would I run?" It was a tough question to answer. Case was never much of a one to run and hide.

Case had a woman along but, by all accounts, the woman had handled herself better than Case. Witnesses talked about her saving him, dragging him, shouting orders at him.

Lorenz had to smile. She'd thrown Case in front of an oncoming train. He wished he'd seen his old friend's face.

There'd been blood. Case had been DNA matched long ago. The blood was his. But it wasn't all his. And a bloody hand print on the far side of the Metro platform had been her fingerprints and, Lorenz assumed, her blood.

It was definitely female. Fingerprints and DNA were a bonanza as far as Lorenz was concerned but he couldn't find a match. Neither her fingerprints nor her DNA. And since she sounded like a player, that meant information about her was restricted and that narrowed the field even more.

He put out some very careful tracers on the woman. He put them where people who were looking for her would notice. He knew it wasn't only good guys who would have access to his inquiry but that was okay. Right now, he'd welcome a fight.

It sounded like Case had run out of the Metro under his own steam. Case Garrison wasn't an easy man to kill. If he was still moving when he left the Metro station, then he'd lived.

At least he'd lived through that particular attack. Lorenz assumed there'd been others. But if Lorenz couldn't find him, then nobody could find him. And that was the only bright spot in this whole mess.

Lorenz leaned back in his chair and put his feet on his desk. He tapped his lips with a pencil eraser and ran his mind over the people Case would trust and chance contacting. It would have to be an old connection, one that wasn't tied in any way to the bureau, because Case would figure phones were tapped, e-mail was monitored, homes were under surveillance. No one had the money to do all of that to every acquaintance Case had, but Case wouldn't know who was bugged and who was clean. And he wouldn't know who was the enemy.

The old SEAL team. That's where he would go, if he went anywhere. Argie hadn't heard from Case—that left six of them still alive from the years Case had served. Two were still on active duty in the Navy. One had gone rogue and made a living in the Far East as the killing machine the US Navy had made him.

One lived in the woods somewhere, in camouflage fatigues, hearing enemies all around him.

Lorenz was the other one.

Lorenz knew Case wouldn't go to any of them if he could help it. But if he couldn't help it, Case would turn to his old team.

Lorenz made a few discreet phone calls from a pay phone ten miles across the city from FBI Headquarters in Washington, D.C. He remembered many times they'd bugged the public phones within a five block radius of a suspect just in case the guy had a suspicious nature and didn't use his own phone.

Without saying much, everyone on the old team got the message. Lorenz didn't get a glimmer of a clue from any of them, whether they'd heard from Case or not. But they were SEALs. They didn't give much away.

Just on principle he called his wife and, assuming his home phone was monitored, he used their agreed upon message to send her and the kids to a safe house. Man, she hated when he did that. She'd feed him his face for breakfast when this was over.

He grinned to think how much he enjoyed calming his wife down. She had been in the business before she'd gone straight and started having babies. She was full of tricks. She'd be safe.

He'd done everything he could think of to make it easy for Case to know how to contact him without exposing himself.

And he'd been digging deep, trying to figure out what had triggered all this.

Case had walked away clean from his last assignment. He'd been out of circulation for a year and a half. If someone had a grudge against Case they could have been waiting all this time for him to surface. That would explain why he'd been hit so soon after he'd come out from undercover.

So, what was Case working on a year and a half ago? Two years ago? Lorenz started making notes in his own indecipherable shorthand—an enemies list for Case Garrison. It was sickening how long it was.

Lorenz remembered the car wreck that Case had just before he took off for the grim world of would-be terrorists. That had always seemed odd.

Lorenz had wondered if someone had tried to kill his buddy back then. Case hadn't made a big deal about it, shrugging off falling asleep at the wheel of his car as if it embarrassed him. A weakness to be swept under the rug, like asking for directions.

Lorenz had seen him a day after it had happened, uninjured except for that weird stab mark in his back.

Lorenz had meant to follow up on the Emergency Room that had treated him. Lorenz prided himself on his knowledge of the city he'd lived in all of his life. He'd never heard of the place. And he'd meant to look over the wreckage of Case's totaled car. He'd even had it towed to the holding yard the FBI had. But before Lorenz could get a good start, Case had dropped out of sight and Lorenz had been distracted by other things. He wondered if the car was still there? This was a bureaucracy, Lorenz bet the car was gathering dust in the impound lot all this time.

Lorenz quit jotting and tapped his lips again. He couldn't imagine what this had to do with Case's current trouble but it was a rock Lorenz should have turned over at the time. It was something he could do for his friend. What had the emergency place been called? He stood up from his chair and started digging through a filing cabinet full of old notebooks. He never threw them away. He was sure he'd written it down somewhere.

CHAPTER SIXTEEN

A s long as we're in the right area code, we don't have to go to the FBI office to route our request through their phone lines. I know an access code that will get me inside." Case started tapping at the computer in front of him and Nat stationed herself at the door of the computer lab they'd broken into at the University of New Mexico's Santa Fe campus.

Case worked silently for a minute, trying to get inside the system in the blessed moments of silence before Nat started ragging him again.

Stowing away in the back end of a farm truck full of crated chickens had been his idea. He still thought it beat the refrigerator truck that she came up with but he admitted it was a choice between two evils.

Nat didn't appear to have a vain bone in her body but she had balked at the smell of chickens until Case thought he'd have to cold-cock her to get her on board. Case didn't want the exposure of checking into a motel and it'd eat up their money fast, but every time she pulled a feather out of some unplucked part of her body she started insisting on a shower again. He'd rarely seen a woman be such a bad sport about anything.

He thought he'd been more than agreeable in general during this cross-country trek. He'd stood his ground on this one. He wanted to set things in motion.

First the FBI modus operandi computer check.

Then the Break Zone search.

Then the shower.

A man had to set priorities.

His computer started spitting information at him almost immediately. "Nat, look at this. It's unbelievable."

She was beside him instantly. "How many matches are there?"

"I don't want to take the time to count them all. The same scar we have. Not all homicides, mostly accidental deaths under circumstances unusual enough to warrant an autopsy." Case pulled a fist full of papers off the printer and thumbed through them. It was just a list of names, hundreds of names. "It's all over the country. And the cause of death in these cases doesn't involve the scar. No police department put it together."

"Did any pathologist find the canister?"

Case shrugged. "So far I've just got names."

"What do you want to bet they didn't find one? I'll bet the rules are; Kill the rats. Dissect them to retrieve the cylinders. Dump the bodies."

"Let me get particulars on each case." Case called up the detailed autopsy files. It would be thousands of pages of information. Case considered packing the papers back up into the mountains near Bannock's. He could spend the next three years going through all of this.

If Nat went with him it might even be fun.

She leaned over his shoulder and he felt her warm breath on his neck. She smelled like chickens.

"We'll be here all night printing this out," she groused.

"I'm sending it to every printer in the room. It will only take a few minutes," Case said.

Then he couldn't help adding, "Relax, baby doll."

He was pretty sure he heard her pull her knife but he didn't turn around. He turned to a new computer and started searching for the word Break Zone. Almost immediately a blank screen came up and froze.

Some days Case hated technology. He hit the usual buttons and a few unusual ones that only experts knew. He hated technology but he was great at it.

"I'll have to change computers," he finally said, disgusted.

"What happened?" Nat came up beside him. She wasn't waving a weapon. He was sure that meant she liked being called baby doll.

"It froze. I can't even get it to turn..." He fell over backward.

She was on her hands and knees under the table with her knife out. She slashed at a metal cord repeatedly until it gave.

"Get what's printed and get out of here." She was on her feet grabbing handfuls of autopsy files out of the printers.

"What's going on?" he asked, but he scrambled to his feet and snatched paper. He'd been around her long enough to know when to debate and when to ask, 'How high?'

"They're coming. That was an electronic echo on that computer."

"Electronic echo?" He waited at one printer for a sheet that was almost done.

"You typed in Break Zone and they were tracing it back to the source. We've been running around hiding like a couple of frightened squirrels and now we've logged into their front office and yelled, 'Come and get us.'" She slapped her fist full of papers angrily on a table, then whirled to check the rest of the printers.

"I've never heard of an electronic echo."

"I have. It's the gun shot on the lower left." She pointed in the general direction of the bullet wound on her back.

"Maybe you got it disconnected in time."

"Maybe." She didn't sound optimistic.

He looked at the busily working printers. "If we leave these records behind, they'll know we're onto them. We know Break Zone. We know about the scar."

"They already know all of that because the tracking devices implanted in us shut down. They know we found it. Besides, they can check the computer for recently contacted web sites. I could erase that but what's the point."

"Let's go." Case looked at the pages still being spit out and headed out the door right behind Nat. She stopped so suddenly he ran into her.

She turned to him and the look in her eyes made an icy chill race down his spine. He hoped after they were married she never looked at him like that.

"It occurs to me that we ought to wait right here."

That icy chill had reached his tailbone and climbed right back up to his neck.

Then he got her point. With an arch of one eyebrow, he said, "I never was much of a one to run and hide."

"If we stay and die we might never get to the bottom of this," she said dispassionately, looking at the papers. "And we have a great lead now."

"And they've killed all these people. If we face them and die they might get away with it." Case rolled his papers into a tube and slapped it against a table top.

"We need more than justice for ourselves. This is bigger than us," Nat said, lifting her gun out of its holster and dropping it back in to make sure it wouldn't get hung up if she needed to get it into action fast.

"Besides, if we stand and fight, we'll only kill errand boys. We'll still have to read through all these papers."

"So, we'd only be staying for vengeance," Nat said.

"Payback," Case added.

"Retribution," Nat caressed the word.

"Offense instead of defense," Case supplied.

"And sure, they treated us like lab rats but that's no reason to be petty."

"Vindictive." Case pulled his gun out of his holster, checked the clip and jacked a shell into the chamber.

"We'd be sinking to their level." Nat looked him in the eye.

"No better than they are." Case returned the look.

"So, where do you want to ambush 'em?" Nat lay her papers aside.

Case leaned over and brushed a kiss across her lips. "If we die I'll never get to make love to you."

Nat inhaled sharply and pulled his head down for a harder kiss. Then she let him go and grabbed up the papers. "You just saved their stinking lives." She sounded disgusted and aroused at the same time—which all boiled down to frustration in various forms.

"Only temporarily."

"Does this mean we get to go to a motel?" Nat asked, running around to fetch the papers that had come in since they'd paused to contemplate revenge. It doubled the stack they were carrying.

"Only if it's a motel in Las Vegas." Case latched onto her arm and towed her relentlessly out of the room.

"What's in Las Vegas?" Nat asked, confused, as they hurried up the steps into the night air of Santa Fe.

"No waiting period. No blood test. We're getting married."

It was the first time she followed one of his orders without a lot of fuss.

He'd thought she was agreeable. He soon learned, she was just stunned.

The 'stunned-into-agreeableness' lasted until he had them tucked into a farm truck hauling several dozen unhappy yearling lambs from a New Mexico sheep ranch to a meat packing plant near Phoenix. It was a giant step in the right direction.

Sheep turned out to be the dumbest animals God ever created. An hour ago, he'd had to listen to Nat swearing it was chickens.

With real swearing.

Sheep looked woolly and gentle. At least from a distance spread across a meadow they did. Close up they just reeked. Case was finding out that was a recurring theme with animals.

It was about then Nat's shock wore off.

"I can't believe you came here right during a work day."

He'd known Claudia was unraveling but this was the end. This was a death sentence for both of them. He'd known from the minute he got in how big the thing was—the wealth to be had, the power to be leashed.

Claudia. Vain, stupid, underachieving Claudia. Sloan shook his head in contempt. She'd thought it was a beauty aid—the fountain of youth. She'd wanted to start fitness centers and make an infomercial.

Sloan wanted to raise a personal army.

He'd needed Claudia as a figure head or he'd have killed her five years ago when the first formula turned so ugly on them. He'd thought it was over then. When fifty out of fifty of your lab rats die of lung cancer within six months of starting a drug, you were out of business. Even if the rats did have the energy of heroine addicts and the strength of a punk on PCP. And all without any signs of addiction or mental impairment, beyond the constant supply of energy and the vanished sex drive and the insatiable hunger for more Break Zone. Then came the side effect they couldn't overlook. Rapid painful death.

Claudia hadn't quit. Without his knowledge she'd continued the experiments.

Now they had their data. The second batch was perfect. They had the human subjects to prove it, but no one could know that. They'd have to play the Food and Drug Administration's game and bide their time. Five years, maybe more. The money should start rolling in about the time he had his thirty years in at the bureau.

He'd been terrified when he learned how she'd been collecting her test data but the string of accidental deaths ended nearly a year ago. No one had raised a single question.

Until last week.

Two of the test subjects had slipped out of Claudia's grasp. She should have let them go. They could have lived with those things in their backs for the rest of their lives. Even if prolonged exposure to the new formula caused lung cancer they'd have never connected the cancer to Break Zone.

But the idea that two people were carrying her cylinders around ate at Claudia like acid. She wanted to know how it had affected them. She wanted the cylinders to be collected and destroyed. She wanted them to die together so no slip-ups could happen to warn her last two guinea pigs.

Mainly, she just wanted to order the death of someone else.

She liked it.

When he'd first found out she was having people killed he'd controlled his instincts telling him to get away. He'd been ready. He'd made arrangements. But he'd thought things could come out all right.

Until he learned one of her subjects was Case Garrison.

Sloan had never known the names of the test subjects. He'd wanted it that way. What piece of rotten luck had conspired to plant the Break Zone in Case? Claudia said they'd picked people like a public opinion poll. They'd crossed all ages, income brackets, races, regions of the country. It was a good way to kill because there was no tie between the victims.

Then Garrison went undercover before he could be harvested.

Then the unthinkable—Prometheus missed.

And now, two hits on the Internet site that covered inquiries into Break Zone. One had been taken care of. A nosy old lady, nothing to taking care of her. But how had she come up with the word Break Zone? The second had to be Garrison. He was on to them. Claudia, who'd gone back to de Nobili headquarters, had flown back to D.C. in a panic.

Prometheus had never failed before. Sloan had never killed anyone in his life. He thought that for someone who needed to die as much as Claudia, he could make an exception. But his office in the middle of a work day wasn't exactly a discreet meeting place. An FBI office—an office full of people who were suspicious for a living.

He thought about those tickets hidden in the false drawer in his office desk at home. He itched to make the necessary phone calls to transfer the money.

It was time to run and hide.

CHAPTER SEVENTEEN

Nat couldn't believe what he'd said. She shook her head every once in a while thinking the words would bounce around into some combination of vowels and consonants that made sense.

They stayed the same. Married.

For a while she thought she was panicking, hyperventilating, maybe even crying.

She wasn't. It was just the sheep. They smelled so bad and crowded so close—she wasn't hyperventilating, she really couldn't breathe and the crying was the sheep wanting their mamas.

Case and Nat were forced to hunker down in opposite corners at the very front of the stalk-rack set on the back of a pickup truck because the driver could see into the back through the cab window. No matter how hard she tried to have a rational conversation with Case she couldn't understand a word he said over the baa-ing of their traveling companions.

She settled for picking wool and chicken feathers off the blue T-shirt she'd purchased during one of their forays out of the mobile home. It said Portland Trailblazers and, since they'd bought it in Texas, the shirt was dirt cheap. The short sleeves didn't cover her bullet wound, but she just had an unobtrusive square gauze pad on it so she didn't think it would matter. The shirt's main attribute was that it was big enough to hang loose over her gun.

It was four o'clock in the morning when they hopped aboard. Sleep wouldn't have broken her heart. One of the sheep seemed to think her hair looked edible—a sad commentary on her physical appearance.

She passed the time pushing Lambchop away and thinking that the only bright spot was that the people who were after them would never find them here. Case was a genius—mentally deficient and sadistic—but a genius nonetheless.

The forty-seventh time the sheep started munching on the luscious looking bush on her head she decided she'd marry Case just to make him miserable.

She wanted to smile but, unless she wanted to French kiss a soggy sheep, she didn't dare open her mouth. So, she suppressed the expression but not the desire. She was pretty sure he meant it. And she knew she was never going to get her mitts on a man she liked more. She was thirty-five for heaven's sake and she'd never even met a man she wanted to stay in the same room with.

She had decided in the trailer that if he'd let her, she'd follow him around for the rest of his life.

It was impossible to find a man with enough strength to stand up to her. Even if she found someone strong, he needed to use his strength honorably when it came to a woman. Because of that, she'd sublimated any interest she had in a romantic relationship long ago. She'd grown used to seeing herself as always alone.

Case thought it was significant that he hadn't wanted a woman since he'd been tagged with that disgusting little cylinder. She didn't bother to tell him she couldn't be drugged into giving up a sex life because she didn't have one. Submitting to a man in that way went against her nature. Most men seemed to be interested in taking pleasure for themselves and most women seemed to think their place was to provide that pleasure. To Nat's way of thinking, the whole deal sucked.

Until Case.

She'd finally met a man who stirred her.

She'd relished honing the muscles in her body. She'd never for a moment considered that it might be anything but a new phase in her life. Her desire to work out had felt real. She stared at him and wanted him and wondered what she could trust. Didn't matter. She was going to grab him before his head cleared. If it was the drug, tough luck. She was a highly accomplished woman. It was well within her abilities to see an escape coming and keep him prisoner for years.

She wondered if he'd let her shower before they got married. She looked over in time to see a sheep treat a delicate part of Case like it was edible. Yes, she was certain he'd want to shower. But he might decide they couldn't afford one. He had their change of clothes in his bag. She'd found chicken feathers in the duffel when she'd gotten the weights out earlier. So, she wouldn't bet those clothes smelled very good.

She wondered if she should get married smelling like a sheep or a chicken. That seemed like a bad omen. She longed for the mobile home. He'd done okay finding a ride that time, but this was beyond lousy. When it came to picking vehicles to stow away on, Case was fired.

The sun rose over the desert. For a while Nat's spirits lifted as the daylight renewed her. Then it started to get hot. It turned out that the only thing that smelled worse than a bunch of tightly packed sheep, was a bunch of tightly packed overheated sheep.

The truck seemed to take the minimum speed limits as a divine edict. So, the temperature climbed past one hundred and the day passed at forty miles an hour. At some point Nat remembered what she was made of and tuned the discomfort out. She tested her bullet creased arm with the hand weight and found out she could handle it. If she wasn't afraid of getting wool in her wound, she'd have taken off the bandage. It was time.

She worked with the weights for close to an hour, working every muscle group in her arms, losing herself in the physical high like she always did. She was startled when Case snatched them away from her.

She looked up, annoyed—frankly she'd forgotten he existed.

"You're still a workout junky. I'm saving you from yourself."

She clamped her jaw shut so she wouldn't say the angry words that came to mind—especially since he was right.

His raspy voice added, "Besides, it's my turn." Then he started lifting, pumping his arms.

She couldn't wait to marry him.

He sat across from her in the sleeveless tank top they'd bought for him, the kind she'd heard called a wife beater. He was smelly and soaked with sweat. She kept the high from her workout soaring just by looking at him. His neck was corded with the strain. His face was rigid from his obsessive concentration.

She forced herself to close her eyes and think of sheep.

When she opened her eyes he was still working the bar bells but instead of watching the motion of his arms he was staring right at her.

"Why do you think I took them away from you? Why do you think I'm keeping both of my hands busy? Why do you think I'm pushing myself until I'm exhausted? Why do you think we're getting married?"

A sheep stuck its nose between Case and the weight in his right hand, getting smacked in the head for its curiosity. Being clubbed with a bar bell only made the sheep friendlier.

Case shoved the sheep away and kept lifting.

"Case do you really want to marry me?"

Nat could see Case's lips moving but she wasn't sure what he said. It sounded like "baa-a-a-a."

A sheep about five sheep away picked that moment to stumble sideways which caused a muttony chain reaction that ended with a sheep sitting on Nat's lap. The sheep, in its amazing stupidity decided it was happy there. Case conked another sheep in the head. Or maybe it was the same one. Sheep didn't seem to have a learning curve.

The sheep on Nat settled in and, in a lot of ways, it reminded Nat of a fluffy woolen blanket. A real, one hundred per cent, lamb's wool blanket cost hundreds of dollars. Nat was getting one for free. Except for the stink and the hundred degree heat, she would have been grateful.F

The stifling heat and the long sleepless night, and probably the residual effects of the drug, caught up with her as her aerobic high wore off. She fell asleep with a lamb's ear batting the flies off of her face.

She slept fairly well, only waking occasionally for a few minutes when a gear shift or sudden pressure on the brakes sent a truck full of sheep tumbling onto her. Case was out cold on the other side of the truck.

She woke when they pulled to a stop. It was full dark but she saw bright lights around a long low building surrounded by pens full of sheep and knew the ride was over.

"Here's where we get off." Case pointed at the driver walking toward an office door and he climbed up the side of the truck and swung over, leaping to the ground.

Nat was right behind him. "From now on I pick the rides."

They hurried to put some space between them and the truck in case anyone saw them.

"Come on, admit it, baby doll. That was fun."

"You know," Nat said dryly, "I hate the name baby doll."

Case slung his arm around her shoulder and smiled. "Oh, you do not."

Nat had to laugh.

Case kissed her on the neck and said, "You smell terrible."

Around sunrise, they found a plain, non-animal bearing pickup heading for Vegas. The driver said they could ride along but he refused to let them up front with him. It was probably the fluffs of fleece that puffed off them when they moved. Although it could be the stench.

They didn't go to Vegas, they got off at the first town across the Nevada border. The whole state had wedding chapels.

Holding her hand, towing her along in his wake, he headed straight for a little white chapel.

"A shower, Case. I'm not getting married looking like this."

He smiled. "Not going to happen. I want to marry you and then we'll shower. Trust me, this is the right order of things."

She wanted to yell at him. She wanted to apply a jujitsu joint lock to his brain.

She wanted to marry him.

She tried, with her years of training in masking her feelings, to keep the wistfulness out of her voice. "Do you really think it's a good idea for us to get married?"

His highly focused efforts to get them inside the building ceased and he turned warm brown eyes on her. Eyes the color of fudge. Hot fudge. Eyes that touched everything cold inside of her and melted her into a sweet puddle.

"Oh yeah."

"Really?" She heard it that time—the wimpy eagerness. She wanted this so bad. But this wasn't her. The woman he'd been with the last few days was someone she didn't know.

And the woman she'd been for the last year and a half was someone created by a drug.

And the woman before that had lived so many lies and spawned so many versions of herself Nat didn't have any idea who she really was. And she'd never know. Not with her life the way it was now—which meant he'd never know. So how could he make a rational decision to marry her?

"Case, you don't know what you're getting into. You don't know about my life. I have a thousand things I'll never be able to tell you about my past. You don't know me."

"Sure I do, baby doll."

"Case, I'm the kind of person who kills people for calling her baby doll. The fact that I kind of like it when you say it just means I'm not myself. But I'm probably going to turn into myself one of these days and then you'll be stuck with me."

"Nat, don't you get it?" He picked up her hand and pulled her grubby fingers to his lips. He kissed her fingertips and she worried about him catching some sheep virus.

"The fact that you're the kind of person who kills people for calling her baby doll is the thing I like best about you."

She shouldn't have laughed. She never laughed. The fact that he made her laugh was the best reason to marry him of all.

He still held her hand near his lips and looked across her hand intently into her eyes. "I want to marry you then hole up somewhere for a while. Every time one of us wants to lift weights, we'll make love instead."

Heat coursed through Nat's body when she thought how often that would be. "Every time?"

"I'm throwing the weights away—cold turkey. It's the best way to kick a habit." He drew her full against him, pulling her hands around his back. His arms slid around her and her heart flipped over.

"We'll study these printouts and figure out what's going on." He hunched his shoulder to indicate his bag and its hundreds of pages of autopsy reports.

Nat said, "We'll find whoever is behind Break Zone and kick their—"

Case kissed her. "And when we're finished with that, we'll either throw in together doing field work for the government or retire. I can see myself ranching. I think I understand animals better than I did a week ago."

Nat laughed again and even though she knew it was hopeless she reached her lips up and kissed him. "We're going to regret this."

"I won't—at least not for a while. You saw how much time I spent on the weights everyday."

She laughed again and wondered if this was what it felt like to be happy. It was a completely new feeling. "You know I haven't spent a lot of time thinking about weddings but I never thought, if the time came, I'd smell this bad."

"What, now you want a long white dress and a veil?"

Nat laughed again. "I want a bath."

"You can have it for a wedding present—after the ceremony. We have that money lifted from those punks. We can find a cheap hotel and have ourselves a honeymoon."

Nat didn't laugh this time. She pulled out of his arms and tugged on his hand. "Let's go." They raced each other to the chapel.

"I've got Prometheus. I can't believe he's getting this sloppy." Steve tossed the surveillance photo to Peg.

Peg looked at it thoughtfully. The chill she couldn't suppress every time she looked into those eyes chased itself up and down her spine. It wasn't just a zip of unease. It went deeper. It was fatalistic. She knew her day was coming to face this man and make those dead eyes come true.

Unless he made it come true for her first.

"A man with a death wish is a dangerous man," she said quietly.

Steve nodded his head and flipped off the auto pilot.

He cruised into Phoenix Sky Harbor International.

A helicopter was waiting for Steve to fly it to Maricopa Medical Center. They landed on the hospital roof. No one met them. No one directed them.

No one passed them in the hall. Millie Hastings' security was air tight—submerged nuclear submarine air tight—Prometheus tight. Peg had made a point of scaring everyone she talked to, until they were all in fear for their lives—as well they should be.

Millie sat up when the beautiful young couple came in the room and started to smile her usual open greeting. Company, at last—she was bored to death.

That last cliché made her cringe. Her smile faded as she studied the couple. Not as young as she first thought but beautiful and full of energy. And since she was suspicious these days, she could see that their eyes missed nothing.

"You're a very lucky woman, Mrs. Hastings," the woman said bluntly. "You are one of three people in the world who have survived an attack from the man who tried to drown you two nights ago."

The man added, "He's one of the most effective hit men in the world."

"The world's best hit man tried to kill me? Why don't I feel lucky?" Millie was lucky though. She knew it. She shoved back the light blanket on her bed and stood up, fully dressed. There was nothing in the world wrong with her. She was just being held in the hospital. As prisons went it was pretty comfortable but when someone says you can't go where you want—you're in prison. She'd about had it with serving her time.

"Mrs. Hastings, we are after him because he's after two of our agents." The woman spoke more gently now.

"The other two people who have survived?" Millie asked pertly.

The man nodded seriously. "I'm agent Brewster."

The woman smiled. "And I'm agent Brewster. Call me Peg and him Steve." She jabbed her thumb at her companion.

"I'll help you, but I've got a problem of my own." There'd been plenty of time to think about this while she was in medical lock-down. "I don't know if it's connected, but I found something at my home in the desert, near Canyon Diego. I think it might be a toxic waste dump. I may have upset someone who wanted their trash to stay buried. Whether it's connected or not I want someone to look into it and find out who dumped it there."

"We've been informed of the canisters, Mrs. Hastings. We're inclined to believe you're right, although we have no idea what Break Zone is or Brachiiesterone. We're definitely checking that angle. We've retrieved the canisters from your car and sent them to a lab for testing. And we'll continue to follow up, even if it turns out not to be related to this crime," Steve assured her.

"Now, we want to know everyone you talked to," Peg said. "You yanked on a tiger's tail somewhere along the line."

"Go to the library at the U. Ask for the head librarian there, her name is Opal. She helped me research Break Zone. She'll tell you what little we did. We never reached anyone or found anything. We never went beyond speculation and hunting around on the Internet looking for anything that said Break Zone. She said she'd keep hunting. They haven't let me contact anyone so maybe she's found something by now."

"One of the reason's we are here, Mrs. Hastings—one of the reasons you've been cut off so completely from outside contact—is that Opal Peintzmeyer is dead," Peg informed her gently.

Millie couldn't respond. She was overwhelmed by the news. She'd walked into an innocent woman's life and gotten her killed.

"Her killer left a calling card," Steve went on. "The man who killed her always signs his work. He leaves burned wooden matches—always three of them—always stacked the same way—always burned to within an eighth of an inch from the bottom. He calls himself Prometheus, the Greek god who gave man fire. We know he killed Mrs. Peintzmeyer."

"But how did you connect it with the attack on me? Did someone notice us working together that day?"

"No," Peg shook her head. "We found matches by your clothing by the side of the pool."

"He left them even though he didn't kill me?"

Peg came farther into the room and sat down beside Millie's bed. "He must have thought you were dead. A janitor found you floating face down in the water. He pulled you out—performed CPR. Prometheus wanted it to look like an accident and I'm guessing he underestimated your strength. Even with the matches, no one would have reported it to the FBI if you hadn't revived and said you'd been attacked. Then the police came in and secured the room. When Opal turned up dead the next morning, apparently from a fall in the bathtub, the matches set off an alarm in the cop who was called to the scene because he'd just come from where you were."

"We need your help, Mrs. Hastings," Peg said. "Despite failing to kill you and our two agents, Prometheus is still one of the most dangerous men alive. We will protect you but you need to know what you're getting into."

Millie shifted her eyes between the two agents. Finally, she remembered Matthew and Lee, and she remembered her failing lungs. They were killing her but they were still good enough that they'd saved her life in the pool. It was a good time in her life to risk everything.

"You know I have a particularly vicious, fast growing type of lung cancer. I've got about two months to live."

Peg nodded solemnly, "We saw that in your file."

Millie shook her head, and with a sad smile said, "There's not much I'm afraid of these days. I'll help you any way I can."

"Thank you, Mrs. Hastings," Steve said somberly, "Opal went home minutes after you did. If this is about the canisters you found, then anything you did to attract Prometheus, you did that day in the library. Tell me about your research."

It was one of the shorter interrogations on record. Millie started her story by saying she typed the word Break Zone into the computer and the computer froze.

Peg had her laptop out and humming within seconds. "I'll bounce it off our safe house."

She typed in the word and her computer screen went gray. A blinking cursor in the bottom left indicated the electronic echo. Peg pointed at the cursor, "It's working. They're picking up the contact."

Steve barely spoke above a whisper. "That little blinking light got a woman killed and another, maybe three others, attacked. What do you suppose they're trying to hide?"

Millie leaned forward from her bedside and looked at the innocuous screen. Her stomach twisted in fear. "If you do that won't the same man come after you?"

Peg looked up from her computer and Millie remembered her first impression of the couple was that they were young. Right now, she was looking into eyes as old as creation.

Those ancient eyes studied her for a second. Then Peg said with soft menace, "Oh, I surely hope so."

CHAPTER EIGHTEEN

C ase loved to watch her work.

"Three days and all we've got is statistics. They're all connected. They're all being tested for Break Zone. We know that. But no canisters found. Just scars." Nat sorted through the stack of papers in front of her. Sifting and analyzing.

She looked away from the paperwork she was grousing about and smiled at Case. "Believe it or not, this is the part of my work I like best."

But even more, he loved to watch her quit work. He decided he'd try to get her to quit work right now. "We've got all we need to prove a crime was committed. That in itself will justify an investigation. We just don't know who to arrest. But the bureau has the resources to track this down."

Case pushed one stack of papers down to the foot of the bed and laid the handful he was studying on the floor beside him. Apparently, the extended exposure to the drug hadn't done any permanent damage—at least none that showed up on these autopsy reports and none he could detect in himself or Nat. He picked up the bar bell from the floor beside the bed and, with an exaggerated grunt, hoisted it over his head.

Nat yelled, "I'll save you!" and threw herself on top of him like he was a live grenade.

He was definitely going to detonate.

"It's time to go back," Nat said much later.

Her voice in the darkness only made him hold her closer. She was tucked up along his side, her head resting on his shoulder.

"I know." He spoke softly, wishing no words could break the spell they'd cast over each other the last three days.

They'd paid a few dollars a day to rent this shabby little room. There was plenty of water. Air conditioning—but they were still overheated and glistening with sweat all the time for reasons that had nothing to do with the temperature. They'd been living on the continental breakfast for free, hauling away enough to last all day when it was laid out in the morning. No one noticed any of it over the bright electronic ringing of the slot machines.

Neither of them wanted to let the world intrude. But they weren't foolish enough to believe that it wouldn't sooner or later. And they wanted to pick the time and place instead of waiting like victims for trouble to come to them.

His hand settled at her waist. "We've got enough to start an investigation rolling. We can make enough noise that even if we're killed nothing will stop the truth from coming out."

"Would you mind not saying that again, Case?"

He knew exactly what she meant. They'd both talked about 'if we die' dispassionately. Case had talked like that for two decades without hesitation. But for the first time he could remember, Case was looking forward to what the future held. He wondered if that didn't make him terribly vulnerable. He was afraid he'd sacrifice national security and innocent human lives and his honor in order to keep Nat safe. He'd never wanted like this before.

She lifted his hand and touched his fingers to her lips. "We'll do what we have to do, but we'll give a little more thought to staying safe ourselves."

He turned to face her, raising himself onto one elbow. He could see her cat's eyes glowing in the dark, like a beacon calling him home. "I just realized something, Nat."

"What?"

"That's what we've been doing all along."

She was silent, waiting.

"When that man came after us in the Metro, all I wanted to do was grab you and get you away. We latched onto each other and we ran. We ran that day when normally I'd have stayed to fight. And we've been running ever since. First, I wanted your arm healed. Then I wanted space between you and the men who were after you. Then I wanted that awful cylinder out of you and the drugs to wear off of you. It's been you from the start."

Nat nodded. Case had excellent night vision, but the starless night, the darkened room, and the unlighted parking lot outside, made it black as pitch in the room. He knew she agreed because her magical eyes moved up and down.

Finally, she said, "We need to hunt the people down who are after us. We need to go on the offense. We've been going about this all wrong."

Case caressed her face until he touched her lips, then he lay a finger gently on them to stop her from speaking. "Not all wrong, just differently. That's not so bad. We're not required to offer up our lives for our country constantly. From now on we'll be a little more careful. We'll make sure we have a backup plan and an escape route."

"I usually don't bother with those," Nat whispered.

"That was before you had someone who wanted to grow old with you," Case murmured.

There was deep regret in her voice when she repeated, "It's time to go back."

He leaned down and found her lips in the dark. He whispered against them, "I know, baby doll. But tomorrow is soon enough. Tonight, we're the only two people in the world."

He memorized her by touch in the dark. He entwined his body with hers until he didn't know where he ended and she began.

He'd never thought about the phrase, 'the two shall become one.' Now he couldn't think about anything else.

Lorenz looked up from the printout in front of him. He gripped the side of his desk to keep from storming out of his office, finding the slimy traitor and shoving him off the top of the building. Lorenz had been controlling his impulses for a long time. Only those years of training kept him seated.

Instead of the satisfaction of feeling Sloan's neck snap under his hands, Lorenz had put plans into motion to slam a jail cell in Sloan's face. After Lorenz imagined that clang he was back in control. Yes, the jail cell was infinitely better. Sloan the toady—Sloan the nepotism king—Sloan, the guy always one step above Lorenz, who had to be kicked upstairs first before Lorenz got handed Sloan's old job and cleaned up his mess.

Lorenz had to give himself ten full seconds to savor the impending payback of Jerry Sloan, the inferior superior. The man Lorenz had been subordinate to all his adult life. It was incredibly sweet. When the ten seconds was up, Lorenz didn't waste another one.

He made some phone calls. All to carefully selected people Lorenz trusted. All to people who hated Sloan as much as Lorenz. There were a lot of people who were going to enjoy this.

After he had his plans laid, Lorenz turned his attention to the file that had him baffled.

Case's car accident.

Lorenz couldn't find any trace of the emergency medical center Case had said treated him. He'd tracked down the address and found a donut shop that had opened six months ago. A trace of the records showed the building had been owned by a real estate leasing company for a long time. A close check showed a renter had moved in days before Case's accident. When no payment had arrived for the second month's rent, a check of the premises showed the building was deserted. The real estate company had first and last month's rent and a substantial damage deposit. They simply put the place up for rent again and dismissed the whole incident.

Lorenz traced the renter to a holding company that had a dozen layers of dummy companies and quickly opened and closed bank accounts. It was hours of work but the company wasn't that good at covering its tracks. Lorenz found dozens of similar rental agreements. All made, all broken. The locations were nationwide. There was no overt reason for any of it.

But covert was what Lorenz did best.

Lorenz kept digging and, without finding any explanations, he did find a name. de Nobili Cosmetics. What could a cosmetics company have to do with Case having a car accident?

Lorenz kept at it. His job only bothered him when he couldn't think of any more questions to ask.

And when his friends were being stalked by hit men.

The phone rang. Sloan had secured a seat on a military jet leaving early in the morning.

The location surprised Lorenz because he'd just been thinking of the same destination. So, what business did Sloan have in Phoenix, Arizona?

Phoenix, corporate headquarters of de Nobili Cosmetics.

CHAPTER NINETEEN

Case strode along the sidewalk at Nat's side.

Nat smiled at her husband of three days. She still couldn't believe she'd married him. Such insanity. "We have almost no money left. We'll have to hitchhike."

"I've got enough bagels and apples to last a while." Case took hold of her hand and picked up the pace until they were almost jogging.

The exercise in the sultry heat was exhausting. Of course, she'd barely slept in three days. "I haven't had the urge to lift weights or swim the English Channel in over twenty-four hours. Do you think we're completely off the drug?"

"You can't say the last few days have qualified as sedentary," Case smiled over at her.

Nat almost dragged him back to their room. She was pretty sure Case would let her.

His smile widened as he read her mind. She decided to get back to business before they gave in to the impulse.

"Ever since the hit, we've been going on the assumption that whoever is after us has a high level of security clearance."

Case nodded. "Absolutely."

"And we've cut ourselves off because we haven't wanted anyone to know where we are."

Case rephrased. "We decided to run and hide."

Nat smiled. "Our lives would be a lot more comfortable if we could have, say—money."

"Money's nice."

"And we're wondering how to travel without any money. We can't, for example, use a cash machine."

"Even though I've got a perfectly good debit card," Case interjected.

"Because if you use it, you'll set off alarms, assuming whoever is after us has feelers out everywhere."

"Go on," Case said placidly as if he knew exactly where she was going.

"So, how about if we march right up to an ATM and get some money."

"And set off those alarms." Case grinned at her.

"Then," Nat said, "I want to buy a computer—"

Case interrupted, "With that same credit card—"

Nat smiled and nodded, "—and then we take that computer and go somewhere there aren't a lot of innocent bystanders and type in the words Break Zone."

"That sounds like a plan. While we're at it, I think I'll call my office and tell them what we've found in those autopsy reports."

Nat looked doubtfully at her husband.

"Do we have a backup plan and an escape route?"

"Carlos Lorenz is my escape route." Case pulled his Glock out of his shoulder holster and checked the clip and made sure there was a round in the chamber. "I've got this and you as my backup plan."

Nat nodded. "I'll be yours if you'll be mine."

"That sounds like a Valentine."

Nat laughed. "I thought it sounded like I wanted to play doctor."

"With us, it's the same thing, baby doll." Case dropped her hand and wrapped his arm around her waist.

Nat didn't even draw her weapon, although she was sure she'd told him she'd kill him if he ever called her that again. Instead she laughed again. Shaking her head, she said, "I must be losing my killer instinct."

Case planted one hard, quick kiss on her lips. "Just your instinct to kill me. Hold on to the rest for a little while longer."

Nat sobered. She didn't think she'd ever lose that. And a killer instinct could overwhelm all the gentler instincts without half trying.

They were going to break Break Zone wide open, if it didn't break them first.

Peg looked at the five men sprawled throughout the house she and Steve had rented in Phoenix. A clean up crew was on the way.

Steve was on the computer and it took him less than a half an hour to know everything about all of them. "They were unbelievably arrogant," Steve said, pointing at his screen. "The IDs were real. They had no fear at all that they'd be found out."

Peg held her .45 automatic easily in her right hand and tapped it on the open palm of her right. "But where's Prometheus. He definitely killed Opal Peintzmeyer and tried to kill Millie Hastings. Why use such a heavyweight last time and such powder puffs this time?"

"Maybe he's busy. Maybe he's after bigger game." Steve looked away from the screen and methodically reloaded his gun. He didn't look at the men they'd killed.

Steve did what he had to do, but Peg knew he never really got used to it. It was one of the things she loved most about him. "Bigger game, like Nat?"

"Our little girl is good. Maybe she's onto all of this. Maybe she's doing some typing of her own." Steve settled his Sig Saur into the holster he wore tight against his waist on his right side. Then he checked the load on the .38 revolver he kept in his ankle holster. He hadn't gotten it out but a professional was mindful of his tools.

He reseated his gun and turned to Peg. "If we want Prometheus, we follow these boys back to their source and see if we can track Prometheus from there."

"They all work for de Nobili Cosmetics?"

Steve turned back to the screen and shook his head in disbelief. "They're on the payroll—listed as personal security for Claudia de Nobili the company's owner. I didn't even have to hack through any encryption to access the company's employee records. Arrogant. How many people have they killed?"

"Maybe not that many. Maybe they're not arrogant. Maybe they're stupid. After all, how many people have had cause to type the word Break Zone onto an Internet search engine?"

Steve shook his head, "Yeah, but why set up something so drastic? They must be trying to cover up something huge."

"They did try to rig the gas line in the house before they came directly at us," Peg noted. "A gas explosion might have passed as an accident."

Steve typed a few more words into his computer and the screen started filling up with words. "The preliminary lab tests are in on those canisters. They contained a super steroid." Steve tapped away for a while. "A drug pulled off of animal testing over five years ago because it caused cancer in lab rats."

Peg looked at the screen and said grimly, "Lung cancer."

"Just like Millie Hastings and her husband and son."

Peg tapped the final line of the monitor. "A drug developed by de Nobili Cosmetics and tested under the name Break Zone."

Steve asked again, "How many people have they killed?"

"Good question. Let's go pay Claudia de Nobili a visit and get some answers."

They left the house before the clean up crew got there.

Case hung up the phone and turned to Nat. "Lorenz is out of the office. He's in Phoenix for some reason."

"They didn't say why?" Nat faced the opposite direction Case looked. Case had never quit scanning the surrounding area. Nat watched his back while he watched her.

"No, but they said he's been looking for me. They told me where he was staying in Phoenix." Case had heightened his awareness since they'd crossed the border. If his withdrawal at the ATM machine didn't do it, then this phone call definitely would. He didn't have to be psychic to predict that someone was heading for this little Vegas town right now—as fast as they could come.

"It's a darn shame we laid all those juicy clues out for someone to follow to Nevada." Nat headed for the car they'd rented.

"Yeah, but we never played the Break Zone card. We'll wait and do that when we get to Phoenix."

Nat opened the door and slid inside. "They're going to be flying all over the country hunting us."

Case tossed her the keys as he settled into the passenger's seat. "If I have anything to say about it, they're not going to have any use for their frequent flyer miles."

CHAPTER TWENTY

Sloan walked through the revolving door of a sleek modern building in the heart of downtown Phoenix. Sloan had good reason to be a wildly paranoid FBI agent. Lorenz had tailed him without a hitch.

He didn't get worried when Sloan disappeared into the building. Sloan was carrying a tracking bug in the platinum card in his wallet and a listening device in the solid gold pen in the breast pocket of his dark suit. He also had a tiny video camera in his Italian leather briefcase.

Lorenz had obtained a search warrant and tagged him with all of them two days ago, deliberately selecting all the overpriced status symbols Sloan surrounded himself with. The electronic leashes were very well hidden, although a competent agent would have found one or more of them immediately.

Lorenz knew the moron didn't do any work so he probably wouldn't open his briefcase, which had a slightly thicker lining on one side than it had before. Or use his pen, which now didn't have any room for ink.

And Lorenz had known Sloan long enough to know beyond a doubt that the arrogant jerk wouldn't ever pay for anything with his own credit card. The man had FBI credit cards that he used for everything with impunity.

When Sloan had called to arrange the seat on the executive military jet at Andrews Air Force Base early this morning, Lorenz had left immediately. He'd been waiting in Phoenix when Sloan landed.

Sloan kept looking around him, obviously up to something secretive. But being incompetent, old Jerry didn't notice anything amiss. He'd headed straight for this building, the one Lorenz expected him to head for. Only Lorenz' *lack* of arrogance kept him from coming directly here and waiting for his prey.

Lorenz gave Sloan a head-start, then took an elevator to the penthouse floor and went to the office marked 'de Nobili Cosmetics' on its white glass window. The lettering had so many flourishes that it was unreadable which struck Lorenz as counterproductive—thus stupid. A second line, equally fussy, read, Claudia de Nobili-Owner/CEO.

It was the same name as the one on the checks that had been flowing into Sloan's Cayman Island bank account for seven years.

Lorenz double checked his monitor. Sloan was on the other side of the door.

Lorenz reached for the knob.

An iron grip stopped him before he could touch it. He looked up into the eyes of one of the few men on the planet who could tail him undetected or sneak up on him.

Case Garrison.

"I've been looking for you, bud." Lorenz noticed the woman behind Case but nothing much about her registered because Case was blocking his field of vision.

"I've been on vacation," Case said, dryly.

The woman spoke from behind Case's back. "What's behind the door?"

Lorenz said, "Sloan."

"You think Sloan's behind the hit on us?" Case's eyebrows arched in surprise. "I knew he hated me, but he hates everybody who is competent.

Why's he picking on me? Why not shoot you if he wants to get rid of someone who bugs him?"

Lorenz stepped away from the door so they could talk. He looked left and right down the plush hallway. The lower floors buzzed with activity from what Lorenz had seen, but no one wanted to talk to Claudia, and who could blame them? She was a psycho.

"Sloan came into my office the day you disappeared, crazy to find you. So crazy I started asking some questions. He's been taking money from Claudia de Nobili for years. He's got enough money socked away in the Caymans for the rest of his life. And he's not going to have to budget carefully."

"What does Sloan being on the take have to do with me?"

"The connection this has to you is, de Nobili Cosmetics is the company that paid the rent on the medical clinic that treated you that time you fell asleep driving your car."

Case turned and grabbed the woman behind him just as she raised her foot to kick in the door. "Not yet, baby doll. Soon."

The woman turned to Lorenz. "We've uncovered a string of murders related to that accident." She spoke in a rapid fire way that said she itched to get to the door. "Murders committed to recover drugs that were implanted in test subjects. We believe the attempts on our lives were delayed because we happened to be unexpectedly out of the country when it was harvest time."

Lorenz shook his head, noticing for the first time the fire in the woman's eyes. He wasn't afraid of much on this earth; his wife, Case when they played one-on-one basketball, but he decided right then he'd never want this lady mad at him.

"Harvest time? What are you talking about?"

Case pulled the device he'd been carrying around with him for the last eighteen months out of his pocket. "Have you ever heard of Break Zone?"

"No, what in the world is Break Zone? And what does that cylinder have to do with any of this."

"That cylinder is the last piece of the puzzle."

Case, Nat and Lorenz whirled around at the sound of a voice behind them. All three pulled their guns as they turned.

Case ran into a tire iron, or maybe a jack hammer, or a freight train. His face hit the floor with a dull thud. The knee in his back cut off the feeling to his legs.

Case hadn't let someone take him down this hard, this fast, since his third week of SEAL training over twenty years ago. Even Bannock took longer than this.

His cheek crushed into the floor so he faced right. He looked straight across the floor into Lorenz' angry eyes. Case saw the knee in Lorenz back. From the way it was positioned he could tell the same person had disarmed and flattened both of them. And it was definitely a woman's knee.

"Let them up."

Case looked straight forward then craned his neck enough to see Nat with her gun in some man's ear. He couldn't breathe well enough to smile but he loved having a wife who could kick butt.

A cool voice over his head said, "Nat Brewster?"

Nat didn't speak. She did cock the gun she was holding.

The voice attached to the knee in his spine said, "Nat, it's me. It's Mama."

Nat shoved the gun against the man's forehead, twisted his arm, and never took her eyes off a space above and centered between Case and Lorenz. "How's Maggie Dawn?"

The man she held said, "She's beautiful but she smells like peanut butter spread on an unwashed mule."

Nat lifted the gun toward the ceiling. Letting go of the man, who wasn't a day over forty-five, she said sweetly, "Hi, Daddy."

The woman let the pressure off Case's back, "Where'd you get the wimp fibbies?"

Nat switched her gun from her right to her left hand and offered it— her right hand not the gun—to her 'mother'. "I've always wanted to meet you."

Case got his first look at the woman who'd knocked him around like a 98-pound-weakling at a sumo wrestling match.

She was gorgeous. About three inches taller than him, she had on a skin tight, turquoise tank dress that hugged all her curves all the way to her hips, then flared out and stopped suddenly. She had a head full of riotous, shoulder length blonde curls. She lifted her skirt when it was so short it had nowhere to lift to, and tucked a .45 into a holster on her thigh. It should have been noticeable but, when she dropped her skirt, it disappeared in the folds so she looked perfectly proper.

"It's Assassin Barbie," Case muttered.

Barbie laughed.

Nat laughed and looked at the woman, "He has that effect on me, too. No one else makes me laugh. So, I keep him around."

"Did I say that out loud?" Case asked.

The woman laughed again and nodded like she understood perfectly. Then she jabbed her thumb at herself. "I'm Peg, he's Ken...er...I mean Steve."

Steve slugged Case on one shoulder and Nat slugged him on the other. He noticed Nat hit him right where he'd been shot.

In a snippy voice, Nat said, "Earth to Case." Then turned up her nose at him.

He wondered how long he'd been staring at his mother-in-law.

"I had her when I was eight," Peg said.

"Five," Steve interjected.

"Sweet talker." Peg smiled and arched her eyebrows at her husband then looked back at Case. "I made all the medical text books."

"What's with, 'How's Maggie Dawn' and 'she smells like peanut butter on a mule." Lorenz asked. "Is that what passes for code words with CIA spooks these days?"

"What'd you expect?" Peg sneered. "'The geese fly south'?"

"The CIA's not part of this." Steve reached out his hand for the cylinder. "Now what about this?"

"Eighteen months ago," Nat said, "I was in a car accident that had been staged by Claudia de Nobili, so I thought I fell asleep driving. When I regained consciousness, I had some bumps and bruises and a small surgical scar they said was the result of an injury from the accident. The scar was made when they implanted this thing," Nat flashed her own cylinder at the group. "...in my lower back. We've uncovered nearly a hundred people who had these scars. All of them have been murdered in the last few years—most of them over a year ago. We have no idea when the canisters were implanted in the murder victims but they had a tracking device in them and no canisters were found in the autopsies we studied."

"Why kill all of them?" the woman asked. "Why not just stage another accident and remove them?"

"Maybe they have," Nat arched an eyebrow. "Maybe there are hundreds more who had the drugs removed without being killed. I assume we're the last because the FBI MO network doesn't show any more deaths for the last year. Maybe the test was over and they wanted the last remaining lab rats exterminated."

"And maybe someone just has a taste for killing." Peg studied the little cylinder she'd taken from Case.

"You had that in you for eighteen months?" Steve tipped his head at the cylinder.

"Yeah," Nat pointed at Case. "Him, too. That's how we ended up in this together. They must have lost us when we went undercover. They probably wanted the cylinders back at a specific time."

Case shook his head. "For some reason they went to a lot of trouble to try and take us down at the same time. That doesn't make any sense to me."

"It does if Claudia de Nobili has gotten jaded from all the killing and decided to get fancy to entertain herself. I think she must have selected you two at random. Nobody would be dumb enough to deliberately get mixed up with government agents. Or maybe you had cover identities that attracted her to you. She probably didn't know who she was dealing with. She went to Sloan, her favorite fixer, for help finding her missing subjects."

"If Sloan had a grudge against Case..." Lorenz pointed at Nat. "...and enough inside information to track you down..."

Case said, "Her name is Nat. She's my wife."

Lorenz looked horrified.

Nat's father smiled.

Nat's mother said, "He's gonna slow you down, girl."

Nat leaned close to Peg and murmured just loud enough for everyone to hear, "I like it slow, Mama."

"Who's Sloan?" Steve asked.

Case saw Lorenz perk up. He knew how the guy felt. He'd been playing catch-up since he hit the floor. And now there was a question he could answer. "Gerald Sloan is my boss at the FBI. I followed him here to Phoenix because he's been taking kickbacks from de Nobili Cosmetics for the last seven years. That alone would have brought me here. But when Case disappeared over a week ago I started turning over all the rocks I could find. I discovered de Nobili Cosmetics was the tenant in the building that housed the emergency clinic where Case had his back tampered with. I followed Sloan to this office and I was just about to walk in there and arrest him and Claudia de Nobili when you all showed up. Now that you've fleshed out my case for me, you're all wasting my time."

"You've got a warrant and everything?" Peg asked in a dumb blonde voice as if she were deeply impressed.

"And everything," Lorenz replied dryly.

"How quaint." Steve smiled.

"He's a fibbie," Nat said. "He's got hoops to jump through."

"Yeah, hoops—the Constitution—the Bill of Rights—due process—the rule of law—illegal search and seizure." Lorenz checked his gun. "Any of this ring a bell, people?"

Peg and Steve looked at each other, then at Nat. All three of them muttered, "Boy Scout."

Lorenz smirked at Case. "I thought about tossing Sloan out the window. But something about him in a jail cell really appealed to me."

Case thought about it a second then grinned, "Very sweet. Need some back up?"

"FYI," Steve said, "We think de Nobili might be a homicidal maniac."

"In the truest sense of the word," Peg warned.

"I'll watch your back," Nat offered.

"If the search warrant cramps your style, Case and I should be able to take down that weenie Sloan and the make-up lady all alone," Lorenz said.

"Not if Prometheus is in there."

Nat, Case and Lorenz all turned to Peg.

"Prometheus is in this?" Lorenz pulled his gun out and double checked it.

Case did the same. Everyone with time in crime prevention had heard of the elusive hit man.

"That's who tried to take us down at the Metro." Case turned to Nat. "de Nobili really went big time when she hired him."

"Prometheus sounds like Sloan's contribution to this mess," Lorenz said with his jaw clenched.

Nat nodded silently. Then she turned to face the door. "I hope he is in there. I've seen too much of his work over the years."

"Do we kick it in or do you want subtle?" Steve asked.

"I can help with that." Lorenz pulled his modified cell phone out of the breast pocket of his suit coat. "Want to hear what they're saying before we go in?"

Case looked at the little electronic case. "You've got him tagged?"

"Sloan's got so many bugs he needs a flea collar." Lorenz hit the video button and the three by three inch screen lit up with a picture of Claudia de Nobili's furious face. Lorenz turned up the sound.

"She is a maniac. Look at her." Case watched the woman rave and throw things. She walked in and out of the camera range but always the voice of a mad woman echoed out of the eavesdropping device.

Every once in a while, Jerry Sloan's whining voice would say something about needing the rest of his money.

"It looks like they're in there alone." Case turned to the door.

"You have to go through an outer office. There'll be a receptionist at a desk in there."

"I'll go in first." Steve laid a hand on Case's arm.

"Why you?"

"Because," Peg said, "He's the only one of us that even begins to look innocent."

Case watched a calm, open expression spread over Steve's face. It transformed him into the picture of eager naiveté.

"It makes him look like a virgin." Peg fanned herself for a few seconds and some of the innocence fled Steve's face as they looked at each other.

"I'll secure the front office." Steve reached for the door, then turned back to Peg. "What about Millie Hastings?"

Peg hesitated. "They need to know."

"Watch out, he hates those words." Nat tipped her head at Case.

"Who's Millie Hastings?" Case tried not to sound testy.

"She's a sixty-year-old woman who's in a Phoenix hospital dying of lung cancer," Peg said. "Cancer she developed—probably because of prolonged exposure to Break Zone."

Dead silence fell between the five of them.

"Extremely high levels dumped near the water source for her home," Peg added. "It's possible Break Zone is responsible for the death of her son and her husband and now she's dying."

"You're saying this stuff causes lung cancer?" Case asked, trying to speak calmly.

"I'm saying possibly."

"Probably." Case remembered exactly what she'd said.

Silence fell again.

Nat straightened her shoulders. "No wonder it was so secret. No wonder they killed their test subjects."

Case pulled the canister out of his pocket. They all stared at it for a second. He clenched his fist over it. "Let's go."

"Give me the count of ten." Steve went in alone.

The office was silent. Ten seconds seemed to last thirty minutes. An elevator at the end of the hall dinged but no one stepped into the exclusive enclave of Claudia de Nobili's penthouse office. Finally Peg pulled her gun out from under her skirt and pushed the door open.

Steve sat bent over behind the desk working on something at his feet. He glanced up at them. "I've disarmed the warning system, including the one in Claudia's office."

"Her office is that door right there." Lorenz pointed at one of five doors that opened off the reception area.

"How do you know that?" Peg asked.

Lorenz gave her a disgusted look, "I studied a blue print of the office before I came in here. Some of us do this for a living you know."

Peg's only response to that was, "Boy Scout."

"I'll hold this office," Steve offered. "It shouldn't be hard. I checked the computer. Turns out none of the security guards showed up for work today."

"Imagine that." Peg's smug smile chilled Case's heart.

A frightened grunt drew their attention to a hog-tied woman on the floor under Steve's feet.

"Just before I gagged her she offered to testify against Claudia for anything we'd care to accuse her of." Steve straightened.

The lady on the floor grunted and nodded her head.

"No love lost there," Steve added.

Then, leaving Steve at the desk, the rest of them positioned themselves on either side of Claudia de Nobili's office door. This close they could hear Claudia's raving even behind the heavy door.

Nat stood next to the door and off to the right, Lorenz behind her. Peg was on the left with Case behind her. They all had their guns drawn. Nat and Peg held their guns, two-handed, aimed straight down. Case and Lorenz held theirs one-handed, head high, pointed at the ceiling. Case laid a hand on Peg's gun arm. "Let me go in first."

"Back off, boy."

Case pulled the cylinder out of his pocket. "This isn't about being macho. I remember whose knee was in whose back. This is about being used as a lab rat. I've got a score to settle here. Let me have first crack at them."

Peg gave him a hard look then turned to Nat. After a second, Nat nodded with one hard jerk of her chin.

Peg stepped back and let Case near the door.

He wasn't even going to finish this job. He'd give Claudia the bad news, watch her scream at him for a few minutes. Make her scream for a few more minutes, then he'd walk.

Claudia might want revenge. Prometheus thought of the ungovernable fits of fury that shook the woman. The destruction—the insanity—she'd probably send a hit man after him.

Prometheus rubbed his fingers across two days growth of beard and thought dispassionately about killing her. He owed her for the mess this job had become. He'd spent three days hunting around Santa Fe when de Nobili Cosmetics got the hit on its Break Zone website. Then he'd gone to Nevada and knew he'd gotten caught on video tape sniffing around a car rental agency and a bank.

He was getting sloppy but it was more than that. These two were good. He knew from what he'd found in the computer lab in Santa Fe that they were on to Break Zone in a big way. And they had figured out about the electronic echo. He was convinced the path to Nevada was a false trail. He knew he'd catch up with them eventually but it wasn't worth it.

Missing on a senior citizen—a defenseless, unsuspecting, unarmed old woman—it was galling. The word would get out, and he wouldn't be in demand anymore anyway.

He thought about the coming collision with Claudia and it almost made him feel something. He considered taking her with him, especially if it was against her will. She'd make retirement more interesting—more of a challenge. She wouldn't last long. He'd have to kill her eventually if she came along. But for a while trying to ride herd on a sadist might be viciously fulfilling.

He toyed with the idea as he used his key to go up in Claudia's private elevator.

CHAPTER TWENTY-ONE

Case braced his shoulder against the right side of the door frame. He looked across at Nat. "We'll go on the count of..."

Nat reached across the door, wrenched it open and stormed in. "*Freeze! FBI! Get down! On the floor! Move!Move!Move!*"

Her voice growled, hammered, ripped apart the confrontation between Claudia de Nobili and Jerry Sloan. She swung her gun, moving, overpowering, dominating. Instantly encompassing the entire room. She went straight for Claudia, vaulted onto the desk and slid across it sitting up. Papers and knickknacks exploded in all directions. Nat grabbed Claudia by the throat, shutting her shrieking, cursing, demented mouth. She slammed her to the floor, enjoying the impact.

Case was a heartbeat behind her. He had a split second to see the recognition on Jerry Sloan's calculating face. Then Case rammed the heel of his hand into Sloan's heart, doubling him over at the waist. Case pushed Sloan face down on the floor. Case twisted Sloan's left arm around roughly making the most out of the chance to manhandle a jerk who had been a thorn in Case's flesh for most of his career.

Nat turned from where she was sitting on Claudia's back. Nat had one hand clamped around the back of Claudia's neck, leaning her other hand on Claudia's face, trying to stop the demented screeching. She was having limited success with that but, despite the noise, Claudia was contained.

Case frisked Sloan for weapons, annoyed to realize the man had none. Case leaned close and let the gravel in his voice deepen. "When you stand on the sidelines and let people get killed. That's the same as doing it yourself. You're under arrest for murder."

Case grabbed a handful of Sloan's perfectly trimmed hair and pulled his head back so he could speak into his ear and be heard over Claudia's raving. "You know what I think, Jere? I think what you do is worse. Claudia is a lunatic. She's got an excuse. But you stand by and watch what has gone on over Break Zone without doing anything to stop it."

With a rough jerk of Sloan's head, Case said, "You're supposed to be sane. You think your hands are clean. They're not. At least Prometheus has the guts to pull the trigger. You've got all the evil of a killer and you're a coward besides."

Nat had Claudia completely immobilized but Claudia wouldn't quit wrestling against the restraint. She started intersplicing wailing cries along with the spew of profanity and the general screaming.

"Case," Lorenz tossed Case a pair of handcuffs. Then Lorenz crouched down beside Sloan. "We all know what they do to cops in prison, Sloan. And you're not going to end up in some honor farm. You're doing life in a federal penitentiary."

"Can somebody shut her up?" Nat growled across the room. "Lorenz give me your tie."

Lorenz shook his head, "Gift from the wife." He pulled his handkerchief out of his back pocket. "Here, use this."

He took it to Nat and offered her a second set of handcuffs.

"That's not gonna be big enough," Nat grumbled.

Peg finally spoke once the noise became muffled enough to be bearable. "Okay, who calls this in?"

"Not me." Nat snapped the cuffs on Claudia.

Peg agreed. "You'd just clog up the paperwork. I'm out and so is Steve. We don't exactly exist. We exist more than her," she tipped her head in Nat's direction. "But just barely. We are definitely out on this. Too many questions we don't want to answer."

Lorenz shook his head. "How deep *are* you people?"

"Eyeball deep, baby." Peg smirked.

"I'll back you up," Case said to Carlos, "but I don't want to be the primary. I'm on my honeymoon."

"This case is going to be huge. It's the collar of the year, maybe of the decade," Lorenz protested.

"Great, you'll get the collar of the decade. You could have handled it yourself, Lorenz. You were here first. You've got everything on tape and on video. You've got the warrants. It's all tied up neatly. We were just horning in. Call the police."

"I'll tell," Sloan whined. "I'll tell them about every one of you. I'll have sketch artists draw your pictures. I'll post them on the Internet. You're cover is blown. Your careers are over."

Peg lifted her skirt and Sloan's eyes dropped to the hemline, along with the eyes of every other man in the room.

"Claudia, they won't believe," Peg said, toying with her skirt. "But Sloan could cause trouble."

"I'll cause so much trouble they'll forget about my part in all of this. People will be screaming 'government paid assassins' and 'black helicopters'. I'll come off as the scapegoat for the United States government testing drugs on the population. Lorenz might have a warrant but he blew it when he brought all of you with him." As Sloan threatened, he gained volume and courage. "I'll get the best lawyer money can buy. I won't do a day in jail."

"He's got us good, guys." Peg's hand lingered near her skirt.

"You let me walk out of here now and I'll disappear. Lay this on Claudia where it belongs," Sloan blustered.

Peg said with a southern belle accent, "Ah just hate a man who hides behind a woman's skirts. Don't you hate that, Nat?"

Nat mimicked the drawl. "Ah hate that above all things, Mama."

"But you're right," Peg admitted to Sloan quietly. "We have a problem. I just see a different way to solve it than letting you go. Sorry, Lorenz. I know you liked that jail idea but I've gotta kill him."

Peg pulled her gun and turned away. "Steve, come in here, honey. You're gonna want ta see this."

Peg said over her shoulder to Sloan. "That man loves to watch me work."

Sloan started making almost as much noise as Claudia had been.

Lorenz caught Peg's wink. "Do what you gotta do." He reached for the phone on Claudia's desk.

Case leaned down to tell Sloan to shut up and tap him on the forehead just a few times.

Claudia gave a wrenching twist and almost unseated Nat.

The private elevator slid silently open and Prometheus took in the scene in a split second. He started spraying bullets from his 9 mm Sig Saur into the crowd in front of him.

Nat hadn't even registered his presence when the first shot blew her off of Claudia.

Peg whirled, her gun out, returning fire as a bullet knocked her leg out from under her.

Case threw himself straight forward, clawing at the Glock he'd returned to his shoulder holster, rolling as he emptied the clip at the elevator, thinking 'head shot, head shot'.

Lorenz dropped behind the desk and raised his gun, returning fire.

Steve hit the room running, two guns blazing.

Prometheus never quit shooting. He lunged forward, grabbed Claudia by the collar of her crimson business suit and used her as a shield, dragging her with him into the car. Claudia, riddled with bullets, slipped out of his grasp. Bullets slammed Prometheus against the back of the elevator car. The death in his eyes blazed out at all of them. He sunk to the floor, still shooting, leaving a smear of blood on the wall behind him. The door slid shut on the repeated clicks of a gun still firing from an empty chamber. He was still trying to kill even after he was dead.

Case tried to stand but his leg wouldn't work. He scrambled, crablike to Nat. Her right side was covered in blood. The right side of her head was already dripping red.

Lorenz hollered, "Officer down, shots fired," into the telephone.

Steve had his shirt off. He ripped it in half to tie part of it around the wound in Peg's thigh and press the rest of it against a bullet hole high on her chest.

Case pressed hard with his bare hands, trying to reduce the sickening spate of blood from too many bullet wounds.

Lorenz came to his side, yelling at Steve, "How bad is she hit?"

"I think she's okay. Bad, but nothing vital."

Peg, sounding very cool, said, "It feels vital from here, pal." She started coughing up blood on the last word which ruined the effect.

"Punctured lung, broken ribs. Broken femur. She'll be fine." Steve yelled at Case, "How's Nat?"

Case was beyond talking. Nat had been closest to the elevator. She'd taken the most direct hits and in the most critical places.

Lorenz had his suit coat off. He pulled a knife from a scabbard in his ankle. He ripped the finely-honed edge through his sleeve and moved Case's hand away from the ugly oozing wound above Nat's ear, so he could put pressure on it. "Head wound. Stomach wound from the side with an exit wound."

Case's stomach dived.

"With a 9 mm at that range?" Steve yelled.

Case couldn't look away from Nat. He saw Lorenz' fingers fumbling at Nat's throat for a pulse. His hands, already smeared with blood, marked Nat's neck.

Case didn't breathe while he waited.

"She's got a pulse," Lorenz said. "It's thread-y, weak. There's some arrhythmia. She's terrible—critical."

Lorenz fell silent as if he'd lost the ability to speak. Then he said, "Case, you're hit. You're bleeding."

Case didn't take his eyes off his hands. He was trying to literally hold Nat's life inside her body.

Lorenz looked around the room to make a further assessment.

"Sloan is dead."

"Prometheus?" Steve snarled. "Was he dead?"

"I'm stable," Peg shouted. "Go call that elevator back."

Steve hit the button then returned immediately to Peg's side with his gun drawn. "If he's dead he'll be in it. Claudia took several direct hits. Both of them are dead."

Case pressed with all his weight on the entrance and exit wound on Nat's abdomen, he couldn't spare a hand for a gun.

Lorenz held the compress to Nat's head with one hand and pulled his gun with the other. He aimed it steadily at the closed door. The elevator slid open. Claudia lay crumpled in the corner. Her legs bent awkwardly, one shoulder tipped up by the corner. Her perfect makeup, hair and suit destroyed along with her madness. Her demented eyes were open, frozen in insanity for all time. The back wall several feet from where she lay was soaked in blood—too much blood for anyone to lose and walk away. But Prometheus was gone.

Lorenz surged to his feet. "I know I had at least one kill shot."

"Nat needs you now, Lorenz," Steve said so calmly it was barely audible. "Prometheus can't get far."

The paramedics arrived with the police two feet behind them.

"Let the medics at her, Case." Carlos said, gripping Case's shoulders.

"I'm stopping the bleeding. I have to help her."

"This'll help her more, buddy. Move over, now."

Case let himself be pushed aside, then he tried to follow. Carlos restrained him and, when he fought off his friend, the cops at the scene had to be called in to help strap him to his own gurney.

CHAPTER TWENTY-TWO

They had to sedate him. Not because he was hurt—but because he wasn't hurt bad enough. Case couldn't stand being fussed over when Nat might be dying. Lorenz never left his side. It wasn't devotion, it took two cops, three paramedics and Lorenz to strap him down.

Case had almost made it out of bed when that traitor Lorenz came to his room and called for assistance to keep Case in bed. That was after the first sedative.

"I'm shooting you with an elephant dart next," the doctor warned, loosening his tie so he could breathe after Case used the tie to try and strangle him. The medicine was making his brain muddy and Case's helplessness felt like he was dying.

"His wife was terribly injured. He's crazed to know how she's doing. If you could find out, Doctor, it would go a long way toward calming him."

Case lay immobile in the bed, his fists opening and closing in the restrains. His eyes narrow as he fought to stay awake. He was as calm as a tanker truck of barbiturates could make him.

The doctor was disgruntled and not inclined to be helpful. Case helped by growling threats at him, which Carlos kept apologizing for. When charm didn't work Lorenz pulled his FBI credentials and finally pried some cooperation out of Case's latest victim.

The doctor left in a huff and came back carrying a clipboard. "There were three gunshot victims from the scene. Two deceased, a Gerald Sloan and Claudia de Nobili. That's a shame. My wife goes to the de Nobili fitness club. She wears their makeup and takes their vitamins. She swears by the whole de Nobili philosophy. She's going to be so upset by this."

It made Case sick to listen to the man go on and on about Claudia, but the sedative seemed to be taking effect so he couldn't speak his mind. Lorenz didn't give anything away as he listened.

Carlos waited until the doctor ran out of steam, then said, "You've accounted for three people. Him," Lorenz pointed at his nearly sleeping friend, "and the two DOA's. But there were five. One woman shot in the leg and chest, another woman, his wife, with several wounds, including a head wound and an abdominal wound. What happened to them?"

The doctor looked at a clipboard in his hand. He flipped a page over then flipped it back. "One ambulance came in carrying him. The coroner went for the other two."

"Three ambulances came to the building. I watched them load all three people before I rode here with Case. Is it possible they were taken to a different hospital? They were more seriously injured than him. Is there a better hospital they might have been taken to?"

The doctor seemed to grow five inches taller from pure indignation. "There is no finer hospital in this city than the one you're standing in, sir."

Lorenz cut through his pride. "If they didn't come here, where are they?"

"I'm sure I have no idea. You've been through a shock. Perhaps in the excitement you overestimated the number of people who were hurt."

Case noticed that Lorenz didn't go for the doctor's throat. But that was only because Lorenz had lived with self-discipline his entire adult life.

Case forced his lips to move. "Could you check? There will be a record of the three ambulances. Is there a way to find out where they went?"

The doctor's effrontery deepened at Case's anger. "That is not my job. The police would be the best place to go for that information. Now, if this interrogation is over, I do have other patients."

Lorenz let him go and turned to Case. Case forced his eyes to stay open. "Go find her, Carlos. She has to be somewhere."

With a long worried look at Case, Carlos finally nodded. "I'll get some answers, buddy. Just let the doctors patch you up so you can help."

Case had no intention of obeying him and he planned to get out of here the second Carlos left. His eyes fell shut as he planned how he'd wriggle out of the restraints.

"She's got to be somewhere. Dead or alive she's got to be somewhere." Case grabbed the arm rests of the chair in Lorenz' office to keep himself from tearing the room apart.

"I'm telling you Case, they've slammed the lid so hard on this I can't tell you if she's dead or alive. There is no record that Natalie Brewster ever existed. There's no Peg or Steve Brewster. I've had Argie doing some things on his computer that could end with our necks in a noose."

"How about Prometheus?" Case sank low into the leather chair in the undersized D.C. office. Lorenz would be moving into a bigger one within the week. He didn't just get Sloan's job, he got kicked upstairs about four levels past where he had been. Case was happy for his friend, but that didn't stop him from wanting to beat him to death with a dull shovel.

"Nothing. The Phoenix cops never found a trace of him. There was a trail of blood for a few dozen feet in the hallway of the building coming out of the elevator, then nothing—like he flew away. I'm sorry, Case. I've got pictures of him up in every FBI office, every police station, every post office. Between us and Argie we've spread those drawings of Nat and the Brewsters halfway around the world just to force the CIA to deal with us. We'll keep trying, but we're making some very important people very angry."

"I don't care if they're angry." Case slammed his fists into the arms of his chair.

"And you think I do?" Lorenz exploded. "I'm doing everything I can. We're stepping on the toes of people who think they walk on air. We're getting away with it because I brought Sloan in and you're still golden because you brought those terrorists in, but there's a limit to what these CIA hacks will stand."

Case slumped forward and rested his face on all ten of his fingertips, trying to keep his brain from exploding. He rested his elbows on his splayed knees trying to think of someplace else to look. His knee protested when he bent it, still stiff from three months in a cast. But he was mended, almost good as new. He'd been sent home from Phoenix within two weeks of being shot and he'd stayed at his parents' ranch. His whole family had gathered, though not all at once.

He'd been in constant contact with Lorenz while he stayed there. And the only reason he stayed was because he had no idea where to start hunting.

As soon as he could move, he'd come back to DC. Waiting for answers had almost killed him. Dead or alive—the words haunted him. He couldn't get over the site of Nat lying there in a pool of her own blood. He still washed his hands ten times a day because he felt the red stickiness of Nat's blood escaping from her through his fingers.

Lorenz spoke more gently, "I'm working on the Brewster angle right now. For some reason asking about them seems to upset people the worst. My theory is; it's because they aren't as deep as Nat. If they can be found,

I'll find them. You know how good Argie is. He's gotta be careful because he's outside, but he's really been burning up the wires. He told me he's anonymously dropped a bug in someone's ear that there'll be a picture of Peg Brewster on the network news before the end of the month if she doesn't come out and talk to us. You and I have been hammering them from the inside."

Case lifted his head and nodded wordlessly.

"Case, we're going to keep pushing. One of these days we'll come close enough that they'll tell us what happened to her just to keep us from opening up a can of worms. We're not giving up."

"She doesn't exist. She said that to me. What if she died and they just buried her somewhere in secret? Natalie Brewster, she never lived so how could she die?" Case saw the look of pity in Carlos' eyes. He stood up to leave, he was sick of disgracing himself by harassing his friend. He had to get it together.

"Don't give up. You've got the rest of your life to grieve. What harm can it do to hope for a little longer?" Lorenz gave his pathetic excuse for advice, and Case proved their long friendship by not killing him for it.

"I only knew her for a couple of weeks. We got married but even at the time I knew it wasn't her legal name. It's probably not even a legal marriage. I wanted her so much. Everything she did, every tough, mean, domineering thing she did thrilled me." Case laughed, but it was a weak, painful travesty of a laugh.

"But I never told her I loved her. The words just didn't seem to have that much to do with how totally she seemed like a part of me. And now, alive or dead, she's gone. I'll probably never see her again. I think I could accept it if I'd just said the words, 'I love you' to her once. As it is, I'm always going to regret not telling her. It's something I'm going to have to carry with me for the rest of my life. Which reminds me, how is Millie doing?"

Lorenz paused. "Millie Hastings died in her sleep last night."

"Dead from lung cancer. I should have been there. I liked the old lady." Case had visited, but he'd been obsessed with finding Nat and kept leaving to explore leads…which were more like wild notions that popped into his head. He hadn't been there when Millie died after her courage had helped to blow the case wide open.

"I liked her, too. The noise she made brought Nat's people in on this. We'd have both died in that room if Prometheus had only had three targets instead of five."

Case knew that. If only being alive didn't feel like failure. "And I thanked her by neglecting her."

"She wanted to be alone, Case. She already had one foot in the next world. She was happy at the end."

"Letting those ghouls at the hospital experiment on her to try and understand the exact type of cancer Break Zone caused was so brave. She didn't have to agree to that. She wanted to go home and die in the home her son built. I should have helped her do that."

"She wouldn't ask for anyone's pity," Lorenz said quietly. "All your tests came out fine, Case. Your chest X-rays were clean and the Break Zone dumped on her property had a different chemical makeup than what was in the vial implanted in you. All the lab results we found at the de Nobili R&D facility indicate you're in the clear."

"The doctor still wants to test me every six months for the next five years. No one knows what long term exposure will do. That's just one more little going away gift from Sloan."

"It's him that went away, not you. Remember that."

"They're doing a clean up of the dump site. A wildlife study has found an almost universal rate of lung cancer in the animals that lived near that site. It's an ecological disaster in such a fragile area." Case added, "I've tracked down all the members of Sloan's private army."

"Not much of an army after you and Nat and Peg and Steve thinned them out."

"Well, Sloan wasn't much of a general, so that fits. They've been taking the same type of Break Zone I had, and for longer. They look like they're in the clear so far."

"The prison doctors will be able to keep tabs on them. In the end they were just guinea pigs, too."

"And we tracked down Sloan's money. He had a fortune tucked away in the Caymans. Claudia wasn't the only one paying him. We've uncovered most of his contacts. He's been tipping people off we were about to bust for years. And the legal department is settling his and Claudia's millions on the heirs of all those people buried with little x's on their backs. de Nobili Cosmetics should be bankrupt when they're done."

Lorenz stood from his desk. "There's nothing more you can do, Case. You needed a vacation when this started. Take some time. I've got everyone I can muster working on this. We'll find the Brewsters, then they'll tell us about Nat. Go home."

Lorenz never did find the Brewsters.

Case woke up in the middle of the night, in his apartment in DC, three months out from the shooting and lurched along on his still fragile leg to get a drink.

A blow to the back of his shoulders sent him crashing to the floor. It reminded him of meeting Nat and he twisted his head around, hopeful.

Case groaned. "The doorbell would just kill you wouldn't it, Peg?"

"Shut up. You and your friend are making the wrong people pay attention to us. We want it stopped."

"You only took me down because I'm still recovering from being shot."

"Peg just got a cast off her leg, come up with a better excuse," Steve said smoothly from the end of the darkened hallway.

"I want Nat. I want to know what happened to her. If she's alive I want to see her. If she's dead I want to visit her grave."

"Natalie Brewster is buried in an unmarked grave in Phoenix, Arizona," Peg said quietly.

Case quit struggling against Peg's relentless grip and rested his forehead face down on his carpeted floor. Tears burned in his eyes. He hadn't cried since he was seven-years-old.

"But since I never lived—"

Case's head snapped up at the familiar voice.

"—I really can't be dead, now can I?" Nat stepped out of the darkness beside Steve.

The weight was off his back and he was on his feet, pulling her into his arms.

"Nat," he ran his hands over her. "It's really you." Touching every inch of her, caressing her side and feeling the rough line of a new scar. Brushing back her hair he found a scar where her skull had been cut by the bullet.

"Are you all right? Let me look at you?" Case swept her into his arms and carried her into his bedroom. He slammed the door and locked it, as if that would keep Peg and Steve out if they weren't willing to make themselves scarce.

He laid Nat on his bed, as gently as he would a delicate piece of crystal. He snapped on his bedside lamp and looked until he began to believe. Her hair was a short, choppy style, light brown with honey blonde streaks that brought out the fire in her eyes.

"Is that your real hair color?"

Nat ruffled her hair. "Who knows. I'm hoping to find out what color it really is."

His worry must have shown because she quit tousling her own hair and brushed her hand over the hair that fell across his forehead.

"I'm not breakable," she whispered.

"We've proved that's not true."

Nat laughed. Then she sat up suddenly with her usual graceful strength and wrapped her arms around his neck. She did an excellent variation of a judo toss and landed him flat on his back on the bed beside her and rolled on top of him.

"I mean," she said softly, "there's nothing you can do to me that will hurt me. I've been healing. Then I had some work to do on the leak that let Sloan locate me. That's all taken care of, and now it's safe for me to come out of cover. I'm sorry I couldn't tell you. I was out cold for most of the first week. The head wound wasn't serious, just a crease."

"It was more than a crease," Case protested, continuing his tactile survey of her body. "I've seen a crease."

"Well, I had a fractured skull," she admitted. "But the bullet didn't tap dance around inside my brain. The gut shot was the worst. Spleen, one kidney, part of my liver, a few missing inches of my intestines."

Case groaned and pulled her close. "Nat, I'm so sorry. I let my guard down in that room. I'd have taken those bullets for you."

"I know," Nat comforted him.

"I wanted to be with you. They wouldn't tell me anything."

"You made enough noise that they knew they were going to have to do something." Nat leaned down and kissed him soundly.

"So, they let you come to me?"

"Sort of. Peg wasn't kidding when she said they buried Natalie Brewster in Phoenix. The company made sure it was very covert but not quite covert enough, if you know what I mean. In the intelligence community, to the few who knew she existed, Natalie Brewster is dead."

Case glanced over his shoulder. "Will Peg and Steve stay out of here?"

"They're long gone."

Case forgot about them again. "So, you start over with a different name?" Case tasted her neck and her chin and her ear lobes.

"No, I'm busted. I'm out of black ops. Lorenz put my picture on the Internet, that rat. They had to kill me off. Fortunately, it was a terrible picture. But it was enough to blow my cover. I'm going legit. They're putting me on the record. My real name is now Natalie..."

"Your real name is Natalie Garrison," he said firmly.

She smiled. "That's just what I was going to say. They're giving me a job as a data analyst, which I love. I'm assigned to the D.C. office of the CIA."

She was going to have to transfer to Texas because he'd taken his twenty and retired from the FBI. He'd tell her about taking the job as a small town cop in a little while. "And what about Prometheus? We never found any trace of him."

"Dead. Steve found him at the end of the hallway a hundred feet from the elevator. He had five fatal wounds. Two in the heart, one in the head."

"That was mine." Case nodded with satisfaction. "I remembered that Kevlar vest in the Metro. Can you imagine the strength of will it took for him to make it out of that elevator? The world is a better place without him in it."

Case paused to kiss her senseless. "Steve cleaned that up and took you...where, Nat?"

"The Maricopa County Hospital, next door to Millie Hastings."

"What a tough old lady. I was in her room. And I was making a stink demanding to know where you were. You were really that close?"

"It's just the way the CIA operates. I wasn't awake to pull any strings and make them let you in."

Case kissed her as if he wanted to eat her up. "It's real. You're here. You're going to stay?"

"I'm staying."

"And are we married? If we're not, I want to do it right. If you want to change your name once a week, I'll just marry you again every time if that's what it takes to keep you."

"We're married. I had someone make sure the Nevada license had all the i's dotted and the t's crossed and was filed under my legal name." Nat laughed and shook her head.

Case suspected it wouldn't be good enough for his mom, the hangin' judge.

Case caught her chin. "Aren't you used to laughing yet?"

"I haven't been doing much of it the last few months."

"We'll work on it." Case kissed her.

Nat pulled away from him an inch. "Here's the best part."

Case smiled. "The best part?" He slid his hands down her back. "I already know what the best part is."

"The best part is...I'm going to be your boss, sweetie."

Case's eyes narrowed for a few seconds while he digested that little piece of news. And it still wasn't the right time to tell her he retired. "Are you all right? Not fragile at all?"

"I can toss you around this room just the same as I always could. I'll do it if you need proof."

Case pulled her hard into his arms.

Nat let him.

"If you're my boss, then I've got to get to work." Case pushed away from her.

Nat grabbed him and pulled him right back down. "You're not going anywhere. You're my prisoner."

"I wasn't leaving to fight crime, baby doll."

"Where were you going then?"

"Let's just say, I'm planning to curry favor with the boss in ways that will make your head spin."

"What is this plan?"

"I'll show you. I'm going to be employee of the month every month for the rest of our lives. I'm going to..." Case quit talking.

Like any good boss, Nat knew just how to manage the staff.

EPILOGUE

The wedding vows didn't satisfy Hangin' Judge Janet.

"Mom, you're a born skeptic." Case sounded tough but he was standing here wearing a tuxedo, wasn't he?

Nat stood at his side, her arm linked through his, smiling in a white dress. She'd made peace with being transferred to Texas. Case wanted her at home. She'd do her data analysis while working remotely from home.

"I love your mother." Nat let him go to clasp Mom's hand.

"All the paperwork in the world doesn't convince me that wedding was legal. Not if you didn't use your real name." Mom sounded calm and why not? She was getting her way as usual. "I don't doubt it would hold up in court but that only means it's a good forgery."

"Mom, when a wedding license is signed and filed by the United States Government, that's not really a forgery anymore. It's all in order."

Mom smiled and Case decided to be a gracious loser...since the wedding was already over. If they hadn't been married before, they sure enough were now.

While he stood there, feeling not all that bad being married twice to his wife, an old friend came up to shake his hand.

"Grey, you made it to the wedding. It's been a long time."

"That's because you've got a job where you vanish into the night. How am I suppose to see you?"

"No more vanishing. I'm moving to Gull Cove after the honeymoon." Case was planning a long honeymoon. The job in peaceful little Gull Cove would wait. The retiring lawman there wasn't in any hurry to quit.

"Case," Grey hesitated, "things aren't right at the Devil's Nest."

Nat flinched. "How could anything ever be right in the Devil's Nest?"

Case chuckled, "Good point, Grey."

Rolling his eyes, Grey said, "Yep, very good point." He looked at Nat. "The Devil's Nest is the name of my home."

"It's not your home, Grey," Case broke in. "You haven't lived there, not ever really. You spent more time at our ranch when you had school breaks, than you ever did at that big ugly ancestral home of yours."

"True, but I own it. I support the people who live there. I have to deal with the financial mess they've made."

"I like going over finances," Nat said. "Analysis in any form really interests me."

That got Grey's rapt attention. "Really? You'd be willing to look at the mess I've found? I'm pretty sure my cousin is embezzling from the company and has been for a long time. He might be laundering money he's making…I don't know, running drugs, maybe. He's a low-life."

"But he's never been a low-life who involved your money."

"Nope, this is new."

"I'll be in Gull Cove after the honeymoon. I'm town cop there now. I'll help you clear things up."

"You're not talking shop I hope."

Case's baby brother the veterinarian came up, grinning. "Hey, Brett. Only for a minute."

Brett pulled Case into a real hug, not a manly, one-armed, back-slapping hug, but the real deal.

Case couldn't believe how nice it was to be home. "But no more. I'm going to enjoy my wedding day."

"We enjoyed the last one quite a bit," Nat murmured.

With a smile, he let go of Brett and slung an arm around his wife's shoulders and pulled her close. "We did at that, baby doll."

Brett's wife, Jacie, who was nowhere near as scary as Nat but still a woman to be reckoned with, shook her head. "You let him call you that?"

Nat smiled at Jacie, the two of them had really hit it off. Lucky for everyone there'd be no actual hitting. "Once they know you can beat them up, a nickname doesn't really matter."

Brett pulled Jacie close. "But then you've never known that for sure, have you, Jacie?"

Jacie shrugged one shoulder. "I'll never underestimate you, Brett. I learned that lesson well."

Case saw his brother Ben, with his sweet, mild-mannered, turn-the-other-cheek wife coming next. Trudy didn't fit in the family at all, but Ben was gaga over her. She'd toughened up a little, or so the story went, and Ben had calmed down a lot. Case could see they were perfect for each other.

He saw his dad and his brother Jim at the grill, they'd smoked a whole hog and a half of beef—and invited every neighbor for a hundred miles, all mom's work friends, Dad's rancher friends and rumor was, Avery, his sister, had a big old surprise, the governor was coming. Breaking open all those murder cases, even if he didn't get official credit for it, had made Case a superstar in the law enforcement world.

He'd left a lot of people staggering when he'd retired. But not his family. They were all thrilled.

Except Dad said any more weddings and he'd have to restock the herd. But he said it with a big grin on his face.

Beth and Tate joined the family crowd and little Beth, one of the toughest lawmen in Texas, gave Case the best hug so far.

"We were so worried about you. I'm so glad you're back and you're settling down." She turned to Grey. "And he's working near the island where you've got that mausoleum, isn't he?"

Grey smiled and nodded. "But no more shop talk. I've been warned."

The band struck up God Bless the Broken Road. Nat said, "We've gotta go. This is our song."

"Ours, too." Jacie tugged Brett toward the barn with the wooden floor, perfect for dancing. The rest of the family came along.

Case glanced behind him wondering if Grey would ever find himself a woman. He'd had a weird life and it showed no signs of easing up. Maybe he'd help his old friend evict every one of those spooky relatives, then help him make a bonfire out of the Devil's Nest. That'd be appropriate.

Then no more shop talk, not even in his head, as Nat pulled him close and he wrapped his arms around a whole new life.

Mary Connealy writes romantic comedy with cowboys. She is also independently publishing a series called Garrison's Law. Book one, *Loving the Texas Lawman,* is live on Amazon. Her new historical series, High Sierra Sweethearts, begins with *The Accidental Guardian.* She is also the author of these series: Kincaid Brides, Trouble in Texas, Wild at Heart, Cimarron Legacy and many more.

She is a two-time Carol Award winner and has been a finalist for the Rita and Christy Awards. She's a lifelong Nebraskan and lives with her very own romantic cowboy hero. She's got four grown daughters and four spectacular grandchildren.

FIND MARY AT

SEEKERVILLE
www.seekerville.blogspot.com

PETTICOATS & PISTOLS
www.PetticoatsAndPistols.com

MY BLOG
www.mconnealy.blogspot.com

MY WEBSITE
www.maryconnealy.com

MY NEWSLETTER
www.maryconnealy.com/newsletter.html

FACEBOOK
www.facebook.com/maryconnealy

TWITTER
http://twitter.com/maryconnealy

More Books by Mary Connealy

Garrison's Law

Loving the Texas Lawman

Loving Her Texas Protector

Loving the Texas Negotiator

Loving the Texas Stranger

Sierra Nevada Sweethearts

The Accidental Guardian

The Reluctant Warrior

The Unexpected Champion – April 2019

Cimarron Legacy Series

No Way Up

Long Time Gone

Too Far Down

Wild at Heart Series

Tried and True

Now and Forever

Fire and Ice

Trouble in Texas Series

Swept Away

Fired Up

Stuck Together

Kincaid Brides Series

Out of Control

In Too Deep

Too Far Down

LASSOED IN TEXAS SERIES

Petticoat Ranch

Calico Canyon

Gingham Mountain

MONTANA MARRIAGES SERIES

Montana Rose

The Husband Tree

Wildflower Bride

SOPHIE'S DAUGHTER SERIES

Doctor in Petticoats

Wrangler in Petticoats

Sharpshooter in Petticoats

WILD WEST WEDDINGS SERIES

Cowboy Christmas

Deep Trouble

ROMANTIC THRILLER

Ten Plagues